# THE

# WITCH

# IN

# THE

# WELL

# THE
# WITCH
# IN
# THE
# WELL

camilla bruce

**TOR**

A TOM DOHERTY ASSOCIATES BOOK
NEW YORK

This is a work of fiction. All of the characters, organizations, and events portrayed in this novel are either products of the author's imagination or are used fictitiously.

THE WITCH IN THE WELL

Copyright © 2022 by Camilla Bruce

A Tor Book
Published by Tom Doherty Associates
120 Broadway
New York, NY 10271

www.tor-forge.com

Tor® is a registered trademark of Macmillan Publishing Group, LLC.

Library of Congress Cataloging-in-Publication Data

Names: Bruce, Camilla, author.
Title: The witch in the well / Camilla Bruce.
Description: First Edition. | New York : Tor, 2022. | "A Tom Doherty
    Associates Book." |
Identifiers: LCCN 2022019925 (print) | LCCN 2022019926 (ebook) |
    ISBN 9781250302090 (hardcover) | ISBN 9781250302083 (ebook)
Subjects: LCGFT: Novels.
Classification: LCC PR9144.9.B78 W58 2022  (print) | LCC PR9144.9.B78
    (ebook) | DDC 823/.914—dc23
LC record available at https://lccn.loc.gov/2022019925
LC ebook record available at https://lccn.loc.gov/2022019926

Our books may be purchased in bulk for promotional, educational, or business use.
Please contact your local bookseller or the Macmillan Corporate and Premium Sales
Department at 1-800-221-7945, extension 5442, or by email at
MacmillanSpecialMarkets@macmillan.com.

First Edition: 2022

Printed in the United States of America

0  9  8  7  6  5  4  3  2  1

# THE

# WITCH

# IN

# THE

# WELL

# Prologue

I remember it all so vividly, as if it were only yesterday. I just have to close my eyes and I'm there again, watching it all happen.

We have come out to the well at dusk; the bleak light, filtered through the treetops, paints branches on Cathy's skin. It makes her look unfamiliar all of a sudden, like an alien creature—a wild thing.

"I promise you want to see this. Just be patient, Elena." She looks back at me with her face half-draped in shadows.

"*Cathy.*" I know that I whine but I can't help it. I would rather be back at the castle, writing in our diaries, or even playing stupid board games with Erica. What I absolutely *don't* want is to be out in the woods as the sun sets, draping everything in twilight colors. We are both wearing shorts, and the air is turning chilly. I have two mosquito bites on my calf that itch, and my fingers smell sickly sweet from raspberry lemonade. I ought to take a shower. It's been a musty day.

Cathy turns back to me so abruptly that her long, dark braid dances down her back. "Well, it's you who always complains that everything is boring," she says. "But this is not! Trust me!"

I roll my eyes when her gaze is turned back on the well. I'm not sure if what Cathy considers exciting is the same thing that I consider exciting, which is why it's usually my games we play, even if Cathy is the one who actually lives in these woods. She's just not usually very inventive. When she stops by the well, an ancient-looking ring of stone, and grabs my hand in hers, I shudder. I look around at the dimly lit woods, and wonder what I'm supposed to see.

"There's nothing here, Cathy," I say. Her hand is as sticky as mine is. "What am I even looking for?"

She gives me a look brimming with disappointment, begging me to give her a chance. "I told you, we have to be quiet," she half whispers and squeezes my hand. "We just have to look at the trees on the other side of the well. Just there, between the spruces. You can't take your eyes away from that spot; just stare at it until it happens."

"*What* happens?" I try to take a step forth, to examine the trees, but Cathy holds me back.

"You have to look across the well or it won't work." She sounds impatient.

"What won't work?" I can't help but smirk.

"Oh, will you just wait?" She gives me another scolding look. "I went to the lake with you even if I didn't want to, and I had a great time. You will too if you just do as I say. Don't you want to see something wonderful?"

"Sure," I indulge her and roll my eyes again. Cathy's stories are rarely fantastic, but this one was—enough so that I wanted to come, but now that we are at the well, I'm not sure if I'm supposed to see something that's actually there, or something we just make up. I'm unsure what kind of game this is. I stare at the darkness between the heavy spruces until my eyes water, and the rank smell of the well makes me twitch my nose. I want to ask Cathy why we have to look across the well, but she has narrowed her eyes and is breathing slow and deep, much like Mom does when she's doing her meditation. I try to copy her, if only to have this done with. Then suddenly, Cathy squeezes my hand so hard that it hurts.

"Look," her voice is a quiet hissing. "Look, Elena. I told you so!"

I focus my gaze and then I see it; there's something solid between the trunks. It looks like a large heap of stones, covered by moss and lichen. At first I think it's mist that swirls around it in fine, pale gray tendrils, but then I can tell that it's smoke, oozing out from the stone pile's top. I can't smell it, though; there's no scent of burning.

Then I see the door.

It is small and rectangular, made of wood that looks old and water damaged. Dark stains bleed from the bottom up. The boards are held together by twine, and the handle is made from wood as well. Around it grows some peculiar plants from between the stones; some are light and curly, others long and stringy. It looks like hair pushed into the cracks. On the ground before the door, something glows white in the poor light. At first, I think it is mushrooms. Then I think it is bones.

"Oh fuck," I finally curse. "Oh fuck, Cathy. We have to get out of here!"

"No, no." She grabs a hold of my arm to keep me there with her. "It's not real, Elena. Don't you see? If you squint your eyes, it's gone again."

I look across the well, but the small stone cabin is still there. The smoke still curls into the air. "Looks pretty real to me!" I try to wrestle my arm free but Cathy won't let go. Her short fingernails dig into my skin and it hurts.

"Wait!" she begs. "Wait! Just wait until she comes out." Her eyes are large and pleading, but I won't have it.

"Cathy, we have to *go*!" I can't believe that she's just standing there, looking at that ugly little cabin as if unable to resist.

"Don't you want to know who lives there?" She gives me a weird smile and looks all excited.

"No, I fucking don't! Let me go!" Just as I am about to kick her in one of her bad legs, I finally manage to wrestle my arm free.

"Look," Cathy says again, sounding breathless. "She comes out now."

I dare a glance in the cabin's direction, and keep my gaze there just long enough to see that the door is indeed being opened from the inside, scraping along the ground.

Then I bolt.

"Elena!" Cathy is hot on my heels, pleading and unhappy. "It's not dangerous!" she promises behind me. "She won't hurt us!"

I'm in no mind to stick around and find out, though, and rush down the path toward the castle, with my heart pounding in my chest and my mouth flooding with a metallic taste—like well water.

"Fuck you, Cathy!" I yell, but only because I'm scared.

"Wait for me!" she calls, far behind me now. She can't move very fast on the uneven ground. "I thought you'd like it." She wails. "I thought it was the sort of thing you liked."

"Fuck you!" I cry again, loudly toward the sky, and it does help a little to curse at the moon. I come to a halt, panting and sweating, and angrily wipe tears from my eyes. I wait for Cathy to catch up, but mostly because I don't want to be alone in these woods in the dark—not after what I've just seen.

She keeps rambling beside me as we continue down the path. "It's not really there, you know, so it can't hurt us—"

"Shut up," I mutter. "Shut up!" I keep my gaze glued to the dark ground before me, just so I won't have to look at her. My arm still hurts where her fingernails bore into my skin.

"Please, Elena, don't be angry," she pleads, but of course I'm utterly furious, and remain so until the brilliant glow from the castle windows penetrates the dark night before us.

Perhaps it never truly subsides.

When I ask Cathy about it later, she says that it never happened.

# Woman Found Drowned in Witch's Well

*Police do not yet rule suicide*

Local police confirmed last night that a woman had been found in the "Witch's Well" in the woods just south of F—. The deceased has been described as a grown woman with known identity, but the police are reluctant to give a name as next of kin has yet to be notified. The police will neither confirm nor deny that the woman ended up in the well of her own free will.

When asked about cause of death, Officer Rogers with the F— Police Department said,

—She was found in a well, so drowning seems likely.

## A Sordid History

The "Witch's Well" has long been a cause of divide among the people of F—, with one faction eager to have the site recognized as a historical landmark, and the other just as eager to have the well filled in and its tragic history forgotten. The latter group claims that the well is a safety hazard, which this latest development seems to confirm. The woman who was brought out of the well last night is sadly not the first to meet a horrid ending at the bottom of the 18th-century construct. Previously a source of clean water for the habitants of Nicksby, the largest farm in the county in its time, the well has since fallen into disrepair. According to the town council, the water is no longer safe to drink.

The well is best known as the site of the dramatic events of 1862, when Ilsbeth Clark met her unfortunate end in its cold embrace. Those most eager to have the well filled in have earlier pointed out how the site's melancholy aura seems to attract individuals who aim to end their own lives. If the woman who was lifted out of the well last night belongs to that dark statistic or not, it is too early to tell.

—We have no indication of that, Officer Rogers replied when asked for a comment.—It had been raining and the ground was slippery. She might just have taken a tumble.

# Fall

Part I

# 1

*An open letter to the people of F—*

I will openly state for the record that I had absolutely nothing to do with the death of Elena Clover. Despite our differences, no one could be more shocked by what happened to her than me. I had known Elena since we were girls, and though we later grew apart, she always kept a very special place in my heart.

I honestly think it is completely unfair that I'm being accused of this, as I have never been anything but an asset to this town, giving freely of my time and energy, especially in regards to the town archive and my extensive historical research. To have this taint to my name is a disgrace, and you should all know better! Don't think that I don't hear your whispers, or feel your eyes upon me as I venture the streets of F—. I know what you are saying. I hear it like a snake in the grass, a quiet slithering, barely there, but lethal all the same. You should all be careful. We have a sorry history when it comes to gossip and rumors in this town, and we should all have learned our lesson by now: not a single wagging tongue is innocent when the witch goes down the well.

In the spirit of full disclosure, and in the hopes of stopping the rumor mill, I have opted to write this letter with the aim of sharing all that I know about Elena's return to F—, and what happened between us over the summer. I swear I won't hold anything back, and feel confident that you too will be convinced by the end of it that the villain of this piece (if one there must be) is Elena herself, and not me. Even if things got a little heated and a smidge out of hand between us, that hardly leaves me with any responsibility for what happened to her later. I will tell you what I know, and then I hope the accusations will be firmly put to rest.

The story is a long one, so I will post it in installments here on my Facebook page and on www.ilsbethclark.com. I'm also in discussions with the editor at the *F— Daily,* in the hopes of having a shorter version of the account printed there. As I said, I have nothing to hide, and it is truly *heinous* that I'm even forced to take these steps, but no one is safe when the rumors spread— just look at poor Ilsbeth Clark! It is a shame that it has come to this, but I see no other way of quenching this unpleasantness. It is unfair to Elena's memory too, as she's no longer here to have her say, but I'll do my very best to be fair in my recounts, and tell everything just the way that it happened. I will prove to you all that my hands are clean and that Elena's death has nothing to do with me.

If you would like to read more about the terrible consequences of rumormongering, I suggest you read my novel, *Ilsbeth in the Twilight,* available from the bookstore on Main Street, at the town library, or from my website: www.ilsbethclark.com.

Signed copies are available on request.

# 2

As I mentioned in the first installment, I had known Elena Clover for years. The first time we met, I was a girl of ten, and Elena was one year younger. It was the same year that her uncle, John, bought the summerhouse that's situated on the grounds where Nicksby once sprawled with its many acres of land.

I know the summerhouse is much admired in town, some of you call it "the castle," but I assure you, it is not. It is an architectural anomaly with its multitude of widows of various shapes and garish tints, its gross tower and tasteless spire. How John decided upon that ghastly shade of arsenic green for its outer walls is anyone's guess, I suppose.

Elena always claimed that her uncle was an artist, but I never saw him do anything remotely artistic. Mostly he spent his days by the lake with his fishing rod or in the kitchen with his old radios, tinkering with their innards, hoping to bring one to life. Elena's paternal grandfather came from money and was a judge before he retired, so I guess "Uncle John" could spend his time thus without having to worry too much about the bills.

That first summer, Elena had arrived with her mother and brother to help John get the house in shape. It had stood empty for a time by then, and the walls were rotted through in some places. The paint (a simple white at the time) was flaking, and the plumbing left much to be desired. I remember they had to pee outside for the first three weeks of their stay.

As most of you already know, my father's farm was located just a five-minute walk from the summerhouse, with the properties separated only by an old wooden fence that grew a multitude of lichen. While Nicksby still existed, cattle had been crazing on the land between us, but since it burned, the woods have taken over, and there's a stretch of dense forest there now, rife with pine trees, oaks, and firs.

And the well, of course. The well is there too, badly neglected and almost forgotten, a silent witness to history.

It didn't take many days from the summer guests' arrival before the sounds of other children playing had me venture through those woods to investigate. I was at that time a lonely child. As most of you are aware, both my legs needed surgery after a car accident when I was eight. This required me to stay in the hospital for long stretches of time, and move around on crutches. I didn't spend much time in school and didn't see many children, besides my older sisters. The only other girl my age who lived in our neck of the woods had sadly disappeared the same year, likely kidnapped by her biological father. I had not been very close to Flora, but felt her absence all the same. That summer was also the first time since the accident when I had neither casts nor steel screws spiking out of my legs, having just recovered from the last procedure. Though I did not walk *well* yet, I managed to move around.

I remember being restless, and eager to experience *something else*. Something that was not the farm with its squat little house and a barn filled with lowing cows, the endless wheat fields, or the reek of manure. I wanted to see people who were not my mother with her tired face and drab clothes, my father with his dour expression, or my tittering sisters, already halfway through puberty by then, with glossy lips and ridiculous clothes, not at all concerned with a little thing like me. People who were not doctors, nurses, or physiotherapists with insistent and hard, kneading hands.

I think I was hungry for joy.

Elena had *that* in abundance. Back then, she was a coltish

girl with golden skin and a freckled face. Her hair looked like wheat that had ripened in the sun, and every time she washed it, her mom helped her braid it so it later fell down her back as a crimped sheet of gold. The first time I saw her, she and her younger sister, Erica, were out on the unkempt lawn drinking raspberry lemonade from straws. They had brought out a set of wrought iron furniture that had once been white but had since turned a shade of pale yellow. The chairs and table rested on some flagstones under a gnarled old cherry tree, and the girls sat on seats of iron leaves with the pitcher of lemonade between them on the table. The sun was very bright that day, blazing from a pure, blue sky. Elena wore denim shorts over a red swimsuit, while her sister had donned a blue T-shirt and jeans. Erica had a purple bucket hat perched upon her head, hiding most of her chestnut curls from view.

I remember that I thought the two of them looked glorious, as cut from a Botticelli painting, for no other reason but that their *newness* gave them a special shine. These were city kids for sure; I could sense it just from the way they sat, or the way that they laughed, all loud and carefree in the wildflower-studded grass.

I didn't dare to approach them. I was scared stiff by the worldliness of those two. When Erica whipped out a handheld game console, I thought that I should die. My parents could never afford such luxuries. I stood among the blackberry brambles that edged the garden and just drank in the sight of them until their mom, tall, slim, and freckled like Elena, came out and called them back inside, tempting their bellies with spaghetti. Then I limped back home again.

I never told Elena I was there that day.

That same night, I remember staring at myself in the cracked mirror over the bathroom sink for a good long while. I wondered why my hair looked so drab and lanky while hers was such a halo, why my skin was pale and not blessed with any freckles but just some unflattering splotches of red. I remembered her long, lean legs under the shorts, and thought of my own: weak and marred by angry scars. I don't think I felt jealousy, per se; it was more of a reflection on how unjust the world could be. I didn't think badly of Elena because of it, rather I was powerfully drawn to her, and the next day I went back to the summerhouse. I wasn't merely curious anymore, but it seemed vitally important to connect with this girl. I'm not sure why I felt that way, but I did.

Perhaps I wanted to see if some of her dripping beauty would transfer onto myself, as if just by being near her, the golden sheen would coat me, too.

I found the sisters working that day, or pretending to, anyway. Erica pushed the lawnmower around. It was an ancient thing with no engine; rust bled through the green paint. Elena stood by the table, emptying dead greenery from old flowerpots into a black plastic bag. She had tied a kerchief with a strawberry print over her hair to keep the draft from playing with it and blowing it into her eyes. She wore a pink T-shirt over the denim shorts that day, it was a nice one with puffed sleeves and heart-shaped buttons running down the chest. I immediately wanted one, and tried to picture what it would look like on myself.

The weather was cooler that day, though still warm, and the sky was a pale shade of gray, yet Elena still seemed to shine before me, and I remember thinking how unfair it was from my spot among the brambles.

It was then that she saw me, standing there in my blue plaid dress among the monstrous growth of blackberry, and to my own utter delight, she didn't squint her eyes with disapproval or put up a cold face, but rose her hand in greeting, while a lovely smile appeared on her lips.

"Hi," she called out. "What's your name?"

"Cathy!" I called back, while my heart beat fast with excitement.

"I'm Elena!" answered Elena. "Come over here!"

I thought that I should die then, from happiness, but worry too, for what if this wonderful girl didn't like me? I still did it, though. I went to her, slowly made my way across the lawn, barely even noticing the discomfort in my legs.

When I arrived at the table, she offered me a chair.

"I just have to finish this," she motioned to the row of metal flowerpots bursting with things long dead that stood waiting by her feet. "Then we can play if you like."

I most certainly did want that, and we were friends ever since. Every morning that summer, shortly after breakfast, I laboriously climbed the rotting fence and trekked across the stretch of woods to be with Elena. Sometimes I even had dinner there, grilled cheese sandwiches or chicken salads hastily thrown together by Elena's mother or uncle. Sometimes I slept over too, sharing the queen-sized bed in Elena's spacious room up on the second floor. It looked as if an old woman had lived there before, with a crocheted white bedspread and a flower-patterned wingback chair.

Everything in the summerhouse smelled like fresh paint that first summer, as John and Elena's mom, Susan, were at it in every neglected room, bringing new color and life to "the castle." Even if I lived close by, it was as if I woke up to a whole other world when I was there. The light that came pouring in through the widow every morning was brighter, and the air felt somehow cleaner. The grown-ups were attentive and laughed a lot. Elena told me early on that her father had died from cancer, but that it was a long time ago so I didn't have to feel sorry for her. That was a relief to me, because I would have had some problems feeling that way about her. To me, she did not seem pitiful at all.

It was as if bad things couldn't touch her.

Though *my* legs were in poor condition, *Elena's* were in excellent shape, and she ran more than she walked. She was rarely ever at peace but sprinted across the lawn while chasing a ball or some such, or to the lake when we went swimming. Elena was the one who taught me how to do that. I had found that it was easier to move my legs under water, and so she decided the time was right for some lessons. By the end of that first summer, I could do breaststrokes and float on my back. To me that was a breathtaking victory after all the damage, and I had my new friend to thank for all of it.

So you see, I truly did love Elena.

I don't think her shine ever truly transferred to me, though. I looked much the same every night in the mirror, but it *felt* like it did. It was as if when I was with her, I could do *anything;* I was stronger, faster, and more daring than I had ever been. If we were playing outside below the cherry tree, draping the furniture in sheets to make tents, exploring the hot attic crammed with old furniture, or roaming the woods surrounding the lake, I felt a sense of freedom that was new to me. Elena never pitied me or asked about my legs, she only accepted things as they were and slowed down her pace so I could keep up.

It truly was pleasant back then.

Too bad it had to come to an end.

# Spring

Spring

# 3

*Elena Clover's journal*

## April 28

I really hate being back here. I know I shouldn't feel this way, but I do. I'm disappointed, too, that this is how I feel, as I had been hoping that being here among Uncle John's things, in a place that he loved so much, would be soothing somehow, but it's not. Instead, it only reopens the wound. I just miss him, a lot, and there isn't a place in the castle that doesn't hold memories of him. I even catch a whiff of his cologne from time to time, which only goes to prove my point: he always wore too much of it, but I even miss his vehement denial whenever I mentioned the fact.

Who'd think that such a strong man had such a fragile heart?

There's a lot to get through, though, before the castle can go up for sale. It's really pretty amazing how much junk he kept here. I haven't set foot in the castle for twenty years, and the clutter has built impressively since then. The realtor thinks we can sell the house furnished, which certainly helps, but what about all his fishing gear, or the vintage books and radios that take up a whole room each?

I'll say this for my beloved uncle, he knew how to nurture his hobbies and went all in, no matter the cost. Clearing out his apartment in the city was nothing compared to this. I really shouldn't have come alone. I should have at least brought Erica.

Strangely enough, my old room is uncluttered. I remember Uncle John telling me once that he'd left my room ready for when

I chose to come back to F—, but I never took it seriously. Shame on me then, because the room is just how I left it at eighteen, even the magazine stack on the bedside table is the same, though slightly more musty and yellow. I just can't believe that he kept that room for me.

The kitchen is in good shape too. He always had that weird thing about old food, so everything is empty and clean, but there's plenty of canned food in the pantry, and I stopped at the grocery store on my way here to stock up on perishables. It just won't be the same being here without his poor cooking, though. I'll desperately miss those sooty hotdogs and greasy salads he made. I'm sure this house has never before seen a smoothie, which is why I brought my own blender from home. I also brought plenty of black bags and cardboard boxes, remembering only too well the chaos when we cleared out the apartment, and how heartbreaking it was to crate his paintings.

Hopefully, he didn't leave many of those out here. I just don't think I can take that kind of heartache again—all those glorious colors packed away and sent to storage. There are a few, of course, hanging on the walls downstairs, holding his blood and breath in the brushstrokes, but mostly this was his place to refill the well and soak up the woodsy energy. His place to do things *other* than paint, like building radios and fishing in the lake.

I really wish we could have kept his haven, but neither Erica nor I will ever use it. It still hurts bad to let it go, though.

It's the first time I've been here all alone and I have to admit it's not entirely comfortable, with the woods growing so dense and thick just a stone's throw from the house. I'm not sure if it's me being too used to city living, but I really don't like not being able to see what's hiding inside those woods. I also think the woods have crept closer, somehow, over the years, but that could just be me remembering it wrong. What I *do* know is that wildlife is still rife, as I was repeatedly disturbed throughout the night by some keening sound from the woods—very likely a fox. Every time I fell asleep, the sound came back and had me sitting straight up in bed, heaving for breath. I even went downstairs at one point to rummage through the cupboard for chamomile tea. Not that it would have helped much, but I've been trying to cut back on the sleeping pills. I also tried some light breathing exercises to calm down both body and mind, but in the end, I just gave up and took a pill anyway. It left me sluggish in the morning, but at least I could sleep.

The fox was still keening when I drifted off.

This morning, however, the sun was bright and flooded into the kitchen through the windows, revealing plenty of dust on the counter and the ornate carvings on the oaken cupboard doors. I'm so happy we'll have professionals in to do the cleaning, as Uncle John didn't spend much time worrying about practical things. While eating, I went through the house and looked through the windows, reacquainting myself with the "castle grounds." The old cherry tree is still there, though Uncle John told me once that it doesn't carry fruit anymore. It's ancient by now, dark in color and tilting to the left. The leaves are still budding, though, so there is still life. I wonder if it's a hazard, somehow, if it's soft and rotting on the inside. It seems to me an aging queen kneeling on the lawn.

Everything must come to an end, I suppose.

I snapped a picture and posted it. #thewisdomoftrees

Today, I'll start working in the living room and go through the contents of the bookshelves. I have no illusions that I'll be done in there today, and there's also the makeshift library upstairs. Had he been any other man, I could have just crated the lot and donated the books, but he kept some rare ones and first editions, so I'll have to go through it all.

I have to remember that I'm here to work as well—it's highly overdue. I really ought to put words to paper soon, or the world will forget about me. One thing is to succeed, something else entirely is to remain in that position, and my material feels a bit stale. It's not easy, though, to just come up with something new. Eva thinks I can just put a new spin on the SOUL voices and deepen what is already there, but it honestly feels done with, and my own SOUL has also grown hoarse of late, ever since Uncle John died.

I can't remember grieving like this even after Mom passed. It really hit me that hard.

I can't postpone work forever, though. I need to come up with something, preferably as compelling as my last concept. Hopefully the quiet and solitude out here will soon have the creative—and *spiritual*—juices flowing. I have set up a make-shift office in the dining room, trying not to think of all the meals we shared in there, Mom, Uncle John, Erica, and I. It's hard, however, as the worn blue upholstery of the chairs and the faded varnish of the walnut table tell of a place much used and much loved.

Nevertheless, I've made a spreadsheet with ideas for social media content, and a new posting schedule as well. It won't do to start slacking off now, not when I've come this far. If I truly want to keep succeeding, I have to keep at it, heart and SOUL!

It's just hard when you feel so fucking empty.

*April 30*

Why is it that it's so much easier to write in you, my trusted journal, than to do some *actual* work? I think I'm deluding my-self that by writing in here, by spinning these endlessly boring accounts and dissecting my lingering grief, I am at least writing *something,* even if it'll never translate into acclaim or money. I tell myself that I'm flexing my muscles—*writing* muscles, that is—while what I'm actually doing is avoiding the fact that I can't seem to be able to write. Whenever I try, everything I put down looks stupid and childish and utterly pointless.

Perhaps I've lost my knack?

I say to myself that it's grief that's holding me back, but I know that's not the truth. To be perfectly, utterly honest, this was a problem even before Uncle John died. I think I'm afraid of failure, of not getting it right this time around. Praise for *Awakening* online only makes it worse, as I am, at this point, at least 90 percent sure that I'll never write on that level again. It was a one-time thing—a fluke for sure, and I'll inevitably disappoint everyone who ever believed in me. Sometimes I even think that I should never have written that book at all, as if I had no right to do so. Who am *I*, after all, to tell others how to live? What *bliss* has my own system brought me?

It was nice there for a while, when I could hear the SOUL VOICE so clearly. I remember how I, instead of turning on the TV, could just sit there on the couch and have long conversations with myself in my head. I felt quite the Buddha, to be honest, quite the Master, as the VOICE and I discussed everything from dieting to the SOUL COLOR of the universe. I slept with so many crystals under my pillow that I woke up with raging headaches. I felt perfectly in tune then, with myself and with the world. The success only seemed to confirm that I truly was onto something big, and it was heady and exciting. I felt as if I had found a secret door and stepped right through it, into a similar, yet different, universe; another way of experiencing reality.

Did it make my ego bloat?

Maybe . . .

The only problem is that things still go awry. Milk still

expires and stinks up the fridge, and you come home from a yoga retreat with ticks on your bum. There's no room for yeast infections or forgotten bills in a state of bliss, and your SOUL can clearly not fix a faulty heart like Uncle John's. It all just seemed so *useless,* after a while, and whenever I asked my SOUL why bad things happened, it just went on a rant that said nothing at all ... *Remember that everything that happens happens for a reason, and that the milk in your fridge can be a manifestation of a number of things happening inside you, like old feelings or thoughts that ought to be discarded, an old friendship souring perhaps? The yeast infection might be nothing but bad or repressed memories of an old lover boiling over, and the forgotten bills only means you're not taking care of yourself enough—have you tried a facial mask with charcoal?*

My SOUL, clearly, has no sense of humor, and puts a lot of stock in skincare routines. I still forgot the milk, however. Still got those blasted yeast infections, though I've come to suspect my underwear as the culprit, and not some old lover haunting my spirit.

I still have to write, though. Come up with something new. This is what I do—it is who I *am,* and I don't know what I'd do if I couldn't do it anymore. If only this place could *heal me* somehow, unstick the words inside me and bring me some sort of glorious revelation.

I *yearn* for fresh inspiration!

### May 1

I went into town today for avocados and toilet paper. F— is such a picturesque little town, the main street lined with brick buildings and old-fashioned storefronts. There's even a park with a fountain and white-painted benches under the ash trees. I think the council here must be sticklers for rules and regulations, devoted to preserving F—'s charm. Even the grocery stores don't assault the senses with bright colors and fat fonts, but keep their business mostly inside the buildings, their presence only announced by discreet signs on the brick walls. I posted a pic online. #nostalgia #haven #theperfectlife

Parking is a bitch, though, which is why I suppose many people prefer to drive to the mall outside town instead. Uncle John never went there, however; he claimed that malls had no SOULS, and I agree, but it really is annoying with the lack of parking. Also, all my memories of the town center involve Uncle John, and I wasn't as prepared as I was with the house, so couldn't help being assaulted by them at every turn. There was the spot where we had ice cream in the park. There was the dry cleaner he brought me to once. There was the florist where we went to get sunflowers for Mom's birthday. There was the dentist where Uncle John and I had to wait for two hours when Erica's tooth split in half after a fall from the cherry tree. The waiting room was very warm, and all the magazines at least five years old. We didn't have smartphones then.

I couldn't even look at the town library, a large white building with impressive marble stairs, as Uncle John and I had spent so many hours there, treasure hunting on the shelves. Grief is such a bitch!

When I finally found a parking spot, another blast from the past hit as I sauntered down Main Street, and found myself uneasy all of a sudden, scanning my surroundings with keen eyes. At first, I couldn't figure why that was, but then I remembered the last few times I was in F—, and how I was terrified of running into Cathy. I knew she was married by then and unlikely to be interested in rekindling our friendship, but I guess it had really rattled me how rude she'd been the last few summers we were together. She treated me as if I had done something wrong, although we both knew that it was *she* who had scared *me* half to death, putting all kinds of creepy stuff into my head.

Then perhaps the memory wasn't a memory at all, but rather a premonition, because who did I run into in the checkout line but Cathy? My internal scanner was obviously off by then—my brain more concerned with the toilet paper and wine in my basket—so it came as a shock when I recognized the bony woman in front of me. She was wearing a burgundy coat, and sported large glasses with silver frames. She was busy hoisting large containers of yogurt out of her basket, and I would maybe not have recognized her at all if it hadn't been for the shape of her nose: thin and very sharp. Her hair had some gray in it, I noticed, and she had it pinned at the nape of her neck like a 1930s schoolmarm. When the yogurt was all gone, she dug out bottles of honey and tea bags.

It was only then that she turned back and saw me, her hands still clutching some jasmine tea, and her eyes went wide behind the glasses. She looked almost frightened, but then I probably didn't look so good myself, either. It felt like electric currents were running through my body as I stood there with my toilet paper, unsure of what to say. I had *just* thought of her—or at least the young woman she used to be before. Without really trying or wanting to, I noted that there was no longer a wedding band resting on her long, bony hand.

"Cathy," I managed at last. I'm sure my lips shivered when I smiled. In my chest, my heart set up the pace for no discernable reason.

"Elena . . . how nice to see you." She pursed her lips and didn't look very pleased at all. The years had clearly not thawed the ice in her.

"Nice to see you too, how are you?" I tried for another smile, but think I failed.

"Oh, you know," she cocked her head. "Good days and bad days."

"Sure," I nodded in agreement, a little taken aback by the unexpected candidness. "It's all we can hope for, I suppose." I felt as if I had turned into my grandmother all of a sudden as I stood there nodding like an idiot. I could all but feel the permed curls bounce upon my head.

Cathy's lips twisted up into something vaguely resembling a smile. "Yes, I suppose," she replied. "Some have it easier than others, though."

Was that a barb aimed at me? No, that couldn't be. "I suppose we all have something," I muttered, not quite believing how somber the moment had become.

"Are you here about the castle?" She changed the subject as she fished a large red wallet out of her sensible purse and set to finding her credit card. Behind the counter, the cashier, a young woman with long blond hair, chewed gum with a bored expression.

"I am," I confirmed. "It'll be put up for sale very soon. Let me know if you know of anyone who's interested." I added a laugh, dry and insincere.

"Hm," she seemed to think about it while paying for her goods. "It's in poor condition," she remarked, "and that ghastly green color . . . I'd be surprised if anyone bought it the way it is now."

I was immediately stunned—what kind of vehemence was that to aim at someone recently bereft? "I thought you liked the castle," I said. "You always did as a child."

A flash of a smile came and went upon her red-painted lips. "Yes, you always thought that, didn't you?" she muttered and readied to leave. "I do hope you find a buyer," she said over her shoulder as the sliding doors parted to let her outside.

I was so shocked by the encounter that I just stood there and gaped for a good long while before the cashier gently cleared her throat to call me back to reality.

"Never mind her," she chatted while scanning my avocados. "She's like that to everyone—nobody likes her. My mom says she's not right. She thinks everybody talks about her and is out to get her." She blew a soft pink bubble gum bubble that burst with a snap.

I refrained from pointing out that the cashier was indeed talking about her, so maybe Cathy was right. "It's definitely not a great way to make friends," I noted, still feeling frayed.

"Yeah, no—I don't think she has any," she helpfully informed me. "I'll tell people about the castle, though." She tossed her long hair. "There's lots of people coming in here, it'll sell in no time I'm sure."

I thanked her profusely before leaving, not only for helping me promote the castle, but for putting me at ease about Cathy, too.

How can a person be so utterly unpleasant? Whatever does she think she'll gain by spewing shit like that at people who are practically strangers? If this is how she usually acts, I'm not surprised at all that people talk about her and are out to get her.

I just can't believe we were ever friends!

# Fall

# 4

*An open letter to the people of F——, continued*

When I was taken to the police station after Elena had been fished out of the water, I honestly didn't think they suspected me of anything foul. Even when they sat me down in the interrogation room and served me lukewarm coffee, did I think they had murder on their minds.

It was Officer Rogers who spoke to me, and he had brought pen and paper even though the recorder lay there on the table between us, picking up every word. In hindsight, I suspect the paper was for me, in case I would've liked to confess. Needless to say, there wasn't a single word written in my hand on that paper when our long conversation finally came to an end.

At first, he asked me the normal questions, like what I had done in the woods, but when that didn't yield anything of importance, he started asking about Elena in more general terms, as if to put me at ease.

"Would you say you and Ms. Clover were close before your falling-out this summer?"

"No, not at all," I replied. In fact, I had only watched Elena from afar over the years, as she blossomed into her online persona, dripping with sugar-dusted spirituality and spewing sanctimonious life advice. I think we all watched her to some degree. She belonged to us, in a way, even if she had only been a summer guest in F——.

I'm sure I'm not the only person in town who regularly took her rambling videos with my breakfast, or a helping of her artfully staged photos with dessert. The latter were all enhanced with nifty filters and gentle lighting to erase her tired skin and fine lines. I'm not criticizing, mind you, it's just the world we live in, but I think it's a little pathetic for a grown woman past her prime to cling to beauty standards designed for women half her age. If nothing else, you are certainly setting yourself up for a losing game, because nature is hard and nature is cruel, and everything withers in the end.

Even Elena Clover.

"But you were childhood friends, isn't that so?" Officer Rogers asked.

"Sure," I confirmed. "But that was many years ago."

"You did read her book, though?" He looked up at me with an expectant expression. His chestnut hair fell down in his eyes. He truly has a poor skin color; I think he ought to exercise more. "Ms. Clover told us that you frequently commented on her blog," he added with some satisfaction, as if making a point.

"That is hardly a crime," I pointed out. "It's only natural, I think, when a childhood friend takes to the pen to want to support the effort. I'm sure there are many copies lying around in the homes of F——, bought by people with far less history with Elena than I have."

We all crave a little starlight, after all, and take it where we can, even if our claim to it is dubious at best. I can vividly imagine the chatter over coffee tables after the book came out: "She used to vacation in F——, you know. Her mother once had her hair cut in my aunt's salon." Or, "I went out to the castle once to sell her uncle some paint, and both Elena and her sister were there, playing on the lawn. You could tell even then that she was *special* . . ."

Now that Elena is dead, I suppose people will be eager to talk about how "special" she was again. We do that as a species, it's like a compulsion we have, as if people somehow become better or brighter just because they're dead. Except for Ilsbeth

Clark, that is. *Her* reputation has never recovered. It never will, either, as such a recovery would cost the reputation of everyone else, and nobody wants to pay that price. I think it's mightily unfair, though, that Elena's halo is so bright and dazzling, while Ilsbeth's is so dull and black. I'm not ashamed to admit that I don't think any of them deserve their fate.

"What did you think of Elena's book?" Officer Rogers poised the pen above the paper, as if what I was about to say next was of the greatest import. The question threw me a bit. This was hardly a time to be overly candid, but on the other hand, it *is* against my nature to lie.

"I suppose it served its purpose." I settled for a tempered reply, but in truth, that book, *The Whispers Inside: A Reawakening of the Soul,* was a complete mess. For the few lucky souls among you who have yet to consume the self-important drivel drizzled onto its pages, I will tell you to save your money and look elsewhere for spiritual guidance.

The premise of the book is quite simple: Elena claims that each and every one of us has a "voice" inside our head that is the soul. This voice is "mostly just whispering, other times shouting," according to the author. Through nine "simple steps" she shows you how to cultivate that voice to make it coherent and promote a "fruitful discussion" between yourself and your "voice of divinity," quite often aided by ill-smelling incense and crystals.

Personally, I think that if you hear whispers in your head the wise course of action is to see a professional, and not to write a book about it, but I suppose the latter option is more profitable. When she launched her public speaking career in the book's wake with such success and bravado, I thought the world had gone quite mad, but then Elena always had charisma—I should know that better than most.

It's a shame that she never used it for something of real value.

Officer Rogers was not appeased by my curt reply, but kept digging into the meat. "Why were you carrying raw meat around? Were you setting snares in the woods?"

"No," I snorted. "I'm hardly a trapper."

"Then what purpose did it serve?"

"That's none of your business," I replied. "It was only a few cutlets."

Officer Rogers sighed, and then deftly changed the subject. "Isn't it true that you frequently tried to discredit Ms. Clover's work by bad-mouthing it in your personal relationships, or giving it poor ratings online?"

I couldn't help but laugh. Telling the truth about something is hardly the same as "bad-mouthing" it, and I really did try not to let that book irk me, but it is hard when you see someone succeed having done so very little to deserve it. My family had little understanding in that regard and it caused some disturbance in our household, culminating with my son, Brian, accusing me of being unduly concerned with Elena's drivel. "No one cares about that fucking book, Mom! No one cares about it but you!" I remember him yelling once, but of course, I knew he was wrong.

That book was *everywhere,* following me around, and especially online, helped by clever algorithms. The cover was on me like a shadow, displaying a gaudy indigo sky with a spatter of glittering stars—and there at the bottom: a woman silhouetted in black, with one of said stars twinkling merrily in her head. It was quite the disco in there, I'm sure.

When I was quite done laughing, I answered Officer Rogers, "Though I did not personally like the book, I found the effort very inspiring." And I truly did! It was a *good* thing in the end to see her succeed with so little to offer, as it finally made me turn to my own words. Yes, it was in fact Elena's silly soul book that had me make up my mind about writing my Ilsbeth Clark novel at last! If Elena could do it, I definitely could as well! I, who had done my homework and meant to write a *proper* book, one to right a wrong and clear a name! I wrote for Ilsbeth, and not for myself, so surely I deserved the same success as someone who only wrote to sate their own ego—or so I thought at the time.

So you see, I have much to thank Elena for, and would certainly not do anything to harm her. If it hadn't been for her, my book might never have seen the light of day, and poor Ilsbeth would have gone undefended, so why would I want to see her dead?

As I said before, besides watching her online presence, which I'm sure *we all* did, and reading her book, I had nothing to do with Elena after our falling-out as teens. I honestly didn't think much about her at all, having enough with my own life.

But then, of course, she came back.

# Spring

# 5

*Elena Clover's journal*

*May 3*

Today I continued the immensely challenging, but hopefully re-
warding, task of clearing out this house, and just happened to
stumble across something unexpectedly delightful!

When I went through the rooms upon my arrival, I was focusing on the bedrooms and downstairs. I didn't go up to the
tower room then because I didn't think there was anything to
find there, but today I did, mainly to catch the sunset, but also
to make sure there was nothing of value stored up there in later
years. I fully expected the room to be empty, as it always was before. There was only ever the wall-mounted benches up there, as
white as all the eight walls. The only thing breaking the silence
of color was the bright red of the windowsills, paint glossy and
layered on thick. As I girl I thought it looked like fresh blood.

We used to sit up there with mugs of hot cocoa, under knitted blankets, looking out at the dusky garden at nightfall while
Uncle John read aloud from a book. Mom rarely joined us but
opted to have some quiet time downstairs, or soften her muscles
in a tub of hot water perfumed with drops of lavender oil. Uncle
John often brought a lantern up the rickety stairs, a shivering
flame behind translucent glass to keep us company as night settled. There was no electric oven there or anything, and late in
summer, it could be cold, but we still begged to go there before
bedtime—no matter how old we got.

We rarely went there in daytime though, even if the view was spectacular and one of the realtor's selling points when Uncle John first bought the castle. You can look in every direction from up there: acres and acres of woods, and then the town spreading out like soft-colored Legos toward the horizon. You can see the farms as well, closer than the town: four or five of them spread around the castle, resting on land that once belonged to Nicksby Farm. Each cluster of buildings rests upon its own quilt of fields; some patches are golden, others green. The sun glints off the glass in their greenhouses. Cathy's childhood home lies on the smallest quilt of all.

You can see the witch's well, too, from up there. As a girl I would always close my eyes when my gaze fell upon it, but not today. It's as if the years and the grief had worn the fear down to nothing, and I'm hardly the same person anymore that I was at eleven. I have seen things—*experienced* things—that perhaps make me think of that old story in a different light. I knew nothing of SOULS when Cathy and I ventured out there that night. I knew nothing of things unseen, but was a spoiled and untried little brat.

From the tower it appears as a circular empty patch, with the well at the center like the pupil of an eye looking back. It seems wrong somehow, that clearing, as if it's a wound or a scar upon the green skin of the woods. Uncle John once told me that the well water is toxic, so perhaps that's why the trees have stopped growing around it. For the first time since my unhappy outing to the well with Cathy, the thought of it didn't feel uncomfortable at all—in fact, it felt more like a delightful thread spun out from there, tugging playfully at my SOUL. It sounds cheesy, I know, but I don't know how to describe it better. Suddenly I felt curious about that place—about the things we had both seen, or *thought* we had seen. True, it had scared me at the time, that little cabin and the smoke, the door that swung open, but I now I found myself wondering what truly resided in that ancient structure, if it even was there at all. I have thought about it many times, how the dusky light and Cathy's words might have tricked me into "seeing things." "It's a secret cabin," she had said before we went. "Made of stone and bone. An old woman lives there, but she's not like other people . . ."

Perhaps, I thought, as I stood there in the tower, the untangling of that mystery was just what I needed to get out of my funk and set my head straight. If there is one thing working with the unknown has taught me, it's that what appears to be weird and scary really isn't once you learn more about it—we're all just parts of the natural world.

Perhaps it could even help with the new book.

Mostly, I think, it was that flash of delight, as pure and honest as that of a child on Christmas morning, which compelled me to go to the well. It had been some time since I felt anything close to joy, and being at the castle, among Uncle John's things, didn't help at all, so I followed the spark of bliss like a bloodhound on a trail, only stopping in the kitchen for some iced tea and a yoga mat before trotting into the woods.

The weather seemed to conspire with my newfound joy, and the sun was dazzling: sharp and bright as it filtered through the evergreens and dappled the path in flecks of yellow. The birds chirped in the treetops; shrill mating calls rose toward the sky, and as I walked there on the path, with my yoga mat under my arm, it seemed just ridiculous that I'd been so afraid to go back. The woods around me were teeming with . . . *something*. A promise of new life, perhaps, nature's brutal quickening—or maybe I'm just afraid to tell it like it was, to use that scary word: the woods seemed to be bursting with MAGIC.

My therapist would doubtlessly be fighting me on that, saying that it was only in hindsight—after my incredible experience at the well—that I remembered the journey there like that, but I still think that the day was enchanted from the moment I spotted the well from the tower window. No matter how hard I try, I can't remember my stroll as anything but eerie in the best of ways.

I think it was my SOUL guiding me there, my inner compass going haywire, pointing toward gold.

The well also showed itself from its best side today, draped in sunlight, glimmering with mica. Fresh green leaves covered the oaks' and willows' slender branches and made everything appear almost shimmering. It was definitely nothing like the time I went there with Cathy.

I rolled out my mat on the ground before the well and started doing my yoga routine. There's something so special about doing it out in nature; you really do feel at one with your surroundings, like the heartbeat of the Earth resonates with your own. I really could feel it as I worked on the mat, how the energy rose from the ground like a snake and slithered up from the base to the crown uninterrupted, just crashing through all my blockages! I fell tingly all over and every breath I took was a heady rush. It felt like being high on Earth alone.

It was only then, when I felt fully in tune, that I rose my gaze and peered across the well to where the stone cabin was—or wasn't—before. Despite all the beauty of the day, I willingly admit that a chill passed down my spine as I did it, as the childhood encounter has lived so vividly in my mind for so many years, tinged with my own fear of the unknown—but I had sworn to be brave, and brave I would be. I breathed deep and evenly and tried to remain open.

I sat there for a good long while, just staring, breathing—waiting for some sort of shift to happen to let my eyes see the same thing they had before. This, sadly, did not happen—but I did feel *something* as I sat there, like a strong charge in the air, something powerful and electric. After I decided to close my eyes and try for more of a visualization, I saw it vividly at once: the cabin as it was back then, only now there were flowers growing between the stones—not hair—and the bones that had been scattered on the ground had turned into leafy branches. I sensed nothing but goodness radiating from its battered walls, and couldn't for the life of me figure out why I had been so scared before.

I made a really great video after I came out of that trance, detailing my previous encounter there, and also my experiences today. I'll edit it later and post it tonight. #goddesspower #magic #weareone

The sense of contentment—of *wonder*—has still not left me as I sit here penning these words, and I just can't wait to go back there and continue exploring that magical place.

Maybe next time, the door will open!

# Fall

# 6

## *An open letter to the people of F——, continued*

It's been three whole years now since I started working on *Ilsbeth in the Twilight,* though in some ways I think I've been silently writing it my whole life. Yes, it was in the wake of Elena's horrid soul book that I decided to take to the pen in earnest, and it truly did feel like embracing my purpose at last. I am no religious person, mind you. I don't believe in gods or karma or, heaven forbid, *souls*! But I still couldn't help but feel a sort of inevitability when I first opened a fresh Word document and started to try to make sense of my thoughts.

Every small town has its stories and legends, and F——is no exception. We have all grown up with the stories about Ilsbeth who was drowned in the well at Nicksby in September 1862. I can vividly recall watching the other children "play witch" in the schoolyard. It was a crude and simple game where the appointed witch ran about trying to catch their classmates and throw them in "the well," which was a circle drawn in chalk on the pavement. Once in the well, the children were trapped by chalk and imagination, and though it was never spelled out per se, it was understood that the witch would eventually eat them. If, however, a brave soul managed to erase some of the chalk line, the children were magically transformed to a mob of angry townspeople who stormed from the well to catch the witch and throw *her* in the well in their stead.

The game was, in its way, a fairly accurate description of what happened in 1862, though Ilsbeth Clark never caught—or ate—

any children. It's important to note, as you'll see in my novel, that the law never accused Ilsbeth of witchcraft, as that particular craze had long since died down, but only of abduction, of which she was subsequently acquitted.

What happened to Ilsbeth was highly unjust, and I found it was time to state that fact. I also wanted to remind you all that behind our local legend, there was a woman of flesh and blood, and that is why I opted to cloak the truth in fiction and lend Ilsbeth my voice, to write a novel rather than a proper book, and thus forego all scholarly acclaim. I wanted you to meet the *real* Ilsbeth Clark, not "the witch in the well" or "the demon bride at Nicksby," but the woman that she was. A woman who carried the brunt of suspicion merely for being a stranger. She was a little too clever, perhaps, or a little too beautiful. What she most certainly was *not* was a "sorceress feeding off the blood of the innocent."

My own history with Ilsbeth started at an early age. Since I grew up on old Nicksby land, I was always aware of the well in the woods behind our home. I found it an intriguing thing, as cut from Grimms' fairy tales, and often went there alone to play. I didn't connect it to the schoolyard game, though, before I one day asked my grandmother about it. I will always remember her blunt reply, "A witch died there once. She killed some children and then they drowned her for it."

That little scrap of a story from my grandmother's lips moved me in several ways. First, it set off a series of nightmares, in which a hag in soaking-wet clothes rose from the well to come lumbering through the woods to eat me alive (though I laugh at it now, it was terrifying at the time). Later, a sort of fascination fell over me and I often found myself out there in the woods by the well, idling away the hours, even painstakingly making my way there on crutches.

I suppose I could sense the sadness hanging in the air even

then, and the atmosphere spoke to my young heart in a powerful way. Other children usually left me out, but I found a certain kinship with Ilsbeth even before I knew the whole story. We often joke that children are more perceptive than adults, and looking back, I think there might be some truth to that assessment, because I felt at that time a genuine sympathy for the poor witch who lived all alone in that well, and thought that we were the same, she and I.

Then followed my introduction to the town archives under the F— Library, and endless hours poring over dusty tomes and fragile documents, trying to connect my thoughts to facts. It was an exhilarating journey, a dive into unchartered depths, to try to separate truth from folklore and get a clear picture of Ilsbeth Clark at last!

It fed me that search—it *fueled* me—and I'm absolutely sure that no one in this town has spent more time immersed in its history than I now have. Every day after work, I would go to the archives with a thermos of tea and perhaps some soup to heat in the ancient microwave that resides in the kitchen nook down there. I had the janitor move an unused wooden desk from the fifties in among the wooden shelves, and made my second home there with my laptop, stacks of musty paper scribbled with fading ink, and a box of raspberry-flavored cookies. Sitting there with the past thus laid out before me, I could nearly forget that my real home was empty and dark, and that not even Brian wanted to stay with me much. It kept the loneliness firmly at bay, and I will always be grateful for that. Being a new divorcée is hard; it takes a lot of adjustment.

When the day's work came to a close, I would drive home with a deep sense of accomplishment, wash the cobwebs out of my hair and the ancient dust off my skin, and brew a nice, big cup of chamomile tea to see me into the night. In those late hours, I felt utterly content. I was at peace in a way I had never been before. Working to unearth Ilsbeth's story fulfilled me as nothing else had ever done. The fact that my research revealed how I'm myself related to Ilsbeth through her sister, Georgiana, did nothing to diminish my enthusiasm.

I would say that the book became my very life.

So *of course* I did mind when Elena appeared in the *F— Daily,* announcing her plans to write a book of her own. *Of course* it sent me puking down the toilet bowl. I wouldn't have been human if it hadn't. Was it a breakdown? Maybe. Did it rattle me to the core? Absolutely! There was *she* with her platform and connections, so confident that she could spew out a book in just one summer. There was *I,* with nothing but my passion and work ethics to carry me forth, and none of the latter have ever been applauded in a world consisting of "likes" and "follows." I was at a disadvantage, and I knew it. Three years' worth of work and my very being poured into that book and now she meant to sweep it all away?

I had every right to puke that morning.

It obviously didn't help one bit that it wasn't the real story of Ilsbeth she was attempting to tell, but one that was so twisted and convoluted as not to be recognizable at all. It was all so very moving, wasn't it? When she spoke of how Ilsbeth's story was *every* woman's story and that whatever Ilsbeth had done in the woods, it was surely both wholesome and good. I can assure you at once that Ilsbeth's story isn't *every* woman's story, but only the story of those of us broken and ostracized for being cut from a different cloth than the rest. Bitter fates like Ilsbeth's don't strike randomly but are tailored to harm those who stray from the flock. Turning this into some sort of universal feminist spiritual propaganda served nobody but Elena herself, hungry to follow up her previous success, and her rhetoric, of course, utterly missed the mark.

My stomach lurched violently when I read how she planned to examine local stories of witchcraft and nature lore to "place Ilsbeth within a broader context of female-driven spirituality." She claimed that there had existed a sort of nature-worshipping magical cult of which Ilsbeth had been a part. This is utter rubbish, of course, but I knew in my bones that no one would care one fig about *that* if Elena said that it was so. She could speak with her *soul,* after all—and for most people I'm sure it makes for a far more compelling narrative if the local witch was a goddess-infused tree hugger instead of a woman deeply wronged by the very citizens of this town. I'm sure the merchants on Main Street saw coins and bills at once, already planning for collections of witch-themed mugs and little cards with spells on them to sell as quirky souvenirs.

Ilsbeth would be no more than a joke.

My *work* would be nothing but a joke!

So *excuse me* if I got a little worked up there for a minute, but I think it was in every way just! To be honest, I'd known there would be trouble ever since I saw Elena was back, running into her at the grocery store on Main Street. It was as if the uneasiness I felt ever since she published her soul book suddenly bloomed into something red and vicious. She meant to harm me, that woman, though she might not even have known it. She meant to eradicate all my plans and leave me bereft, so what was I to do?

I'm sure that, in light of all this, you may better understand what happened next between us. Perhaps I wasn't so crazy after all. Perhaps I was merely defending myself, and Ilsbeth, too, from an invading force. Elena had no right to write that book— she didn't even *live* in F——. She certainly had no right to just rewrite history as she saw fit, just to make more money. She had no right to claim that her psychic "soul connection" to Ilsbeth (I feel sick just from typing the words!) was somehow more valid than my painstaking research.

It was just horrid, all of it.

*Of course* it had to come to a boil!

# Spring

# 7

*Elena Clover's journal*

*May 10*

Something has changed in me since I first went to the well. I can't explain just why or how that is yet, but the crushing grief seems to have lifted, and my head is much clearer than before. It is as if the very air I breathe is lighter as all my senses are sharpened; flavors, sounds, and scents are stronger, and I can hardly touch anything without noticing its texture. Even the sunlight has grown brighter, and the darkness more dense. Everything is somehow *more* than it was before. The very best part is that I no longer hate myself for not writing, and don't even feel anxious about it—or at least not in the way I did before.

Clearly, the well is good for me, and I go there every day now, bringing my yoga mat and plenty of fluids to spend all morning by the well. It's so much easier to ground myself there, to feel the energies move through me. I definitely feel like a part of a whole, and never alone, which should freak me out, but doesn't. Rather, I find that I appreciate the feeling of silent companionship, as if there is someone with me there—kind eyes upon me, as I stretch and breathe, find my poses, and plug my SOUL into infinity.

It all melts away then, the pain and the sorrow, the emptiness that Uncle John left behind. I'm not so worried about failing anymore, as the more time I spend by the well, the more I feel certain that my purpose in life stands firm, and that I'm just where I'm supposed to be. My SOUL speaks again and tells me that the path to true enlightenment often goes through pain, and I know that—have always known it, but perhaps I lost sight of that truth for a while. If there are no hardships, there can be no growth, and what I have been experiencing lately—the grief, yes, but also the doubt—is nothing more than stumbling blocks, a way to hone my *will*.

As I sit there by the well, that word often comes tumbling into my mind. WILL. It's such a big word—somehow more dangerous than "affirmation" or even "wish." The idea that one can use one's will to create actual change seems somehow preposterous—or selfish. It feels more innocent—of less consequence—to dress it up as hope. That is what my SOUL and I have always done, as visualizing change feels less like a "trespass" than claiming it. Yet, by the well, it's all about WILL. Even the treetops whisper about it, promising me the world, if only I accept the power. *You can have it,* they say. *The fame and the fortune, a heart that is light and full of joy.*

When I come home from the well, I feel high from the experience. I giggle and spin around the floor. Sometimes, I even sing a little. It is addictive, too, I can't help but go there, if only to have that feeling again—of being *seen* and accepted. It's as if all the world loves me while I'm there; as if I'm special and blessed and can do nothing wrong.

It really does feel like I am onto something new, something strong and shimmering. A golden thread to follow through the woods . . .

*May 14*

Erica called last night and pulled me down from the cloud I've been living on by asking me all sorts of questions about Uncle

John's things: if I've crated his fishing gear yet, or if I think any of the furniture is antique. I honestly couldn't care less. I'm very busy all the time, but not with the mundane. I know I can't say that to Erica, though, she wouldn't understand. She thought it was hard enough to wrap her head around the SOUL VOICE, and this new thing I'm exploring—this golden thread—is still so new and fragile that I don't even know what to call it yet. It's just something that speaks to me, *loudly*, but I still don't know what it means. I know it is an offer to change my life and claim my WILL, and hopefully will even result in a new book, but it's just like the first shoots in spring: something tender and green that must be tended with care. I can't tell Erica about it yet.

Instead, I lied.

"I have been through the inventory," I said, "but haven't found anything of value."

"Really?" My sister sounded surprised, and a little suspicious. "Not even the Witt sewing table upstairs? That has to be worth *something* . . ."

Guilty conscience sunk its claws into me and squeezed. "I meant Uncle John's things. I haven't found anything of value *there*," I quickly backpedaled. Of course Erica would remember the few pieces of furniture left from the Witts—the castle's first owners.

Erica sighed, seeing right through me. "Send me a picture of the table," she said, "and the dining room set. I'll have Lisa look at it." Erica's best friend is a huge antiques enthusiast and self-declared expert to boot. "I think there's a few pieces left in the attic as well."

"But shouldn't they follow the house?" It felt wrong, somehow, to separate the castle from what little was left of the original furniture—and the attic is cramped and dusty, and really not a place where I wanted to hang out.

"I seem to remember a children's bed," Erica continued undeterred. "Maybe some hat boxes, too."

"The house is not that old," I protested. "*When* did they live here? The thirties? It can't be worth very much."

"The furniture looks to be older," Erica argued. "They probably brought it with them when they came. Why don't you go up there right now? I'll keep you company." Her cheerfulness was highly unwelcome when all I really wanted to do was savor my state of bliss, but then I know better than to argue with my sister when she has her laser focus aimed, so up to the attic we went.

It was just as filthy and dark as I remembered, with the wooden roof beams garlanded with cobwebs and dead flies littering the dusty floorboards. Uncle John never really used the attic, but his predecessors had, filling it up with crates and cardboard boxes, broken lamps and worn-out furniture. It took me a while just to maneuver myself and the phone across the sea of stuff to where a tiny round window let in enough dusty daylight that I recognized the ornate headboard of the children's bed.

"The next time, you and Lisa can come here yourselves," I grumbled when a rusty nail snagged on my cotton pants. "I'd like to see the two of you crawl around up here—especially her with her manicured nails."

"You *volunteered* to go to F—," Erica reminded me. "You said that it was perfect for you, you wanted to work—"

"I did, and I *do*," I cut her off. "I just don't like the attic."

"I know," Erica chuckled, "but it's for a good cause. Perhaps the bed is worth something."

I finally arrived by the bed and squinted at the oaken frame, trying to guess at its value, but appraising furniture is just not my thing. "There's a lot of junk on top of it," I said while snapping a few pics.

"Well, lift it off," Erica commanded. "Just a few clear, good photos. That is all I ask."

With a sigh and a curse, I went to it. If I hadn't felt so bad for having done so little before, I probably would have refused, but I *did* feel guilty, and so I hauled a heavy chest and an even heavier wooden crate off of the bed to perch upon an ugly green couch instead. It was then that I found it: a slim folder of yellow cardboard, pressed against the bottom of the bed; caught there for decades by the weight of the chest.

"Hang on, I found something," I murmured to Erica.

"What is it?" she asked, all curious and excited.

"I don't know." I opened the folder to find five sheets of yellowing paper, brittle and old. "It looks like drawings," I said. "Sketches, like Uncle John's studies." He would sometimes fill a whole pad before starting on the actual painting.

"Are they his? Was he working up there?" Erica sounded in my ear.

"No, not at all," I mumbled and looked at the drawings in my hand. With a jolt of excitement, I recognized the scene. All the drawings showed the same thing: the clearing in the woods, and the well. "It's not his." I turned the top sheet over in my hand in the hopes of finding a clue to their origin, but didn't find one before I studied the third drawing from the top, which showed the well up close, surrounded by tall grass and wildflowers. "N.W.," I read the faded signature in the right corner aloud. "Who is that? The Witts' daughter?" I ogled the tiny bed, although the drawings seemed to have been done by someone much bigger.

"No," Erica said at once. "That would be Natasha Witt. The wife. What did she draw?"

"Oh, just woodland scenes," I replied, though I wasn't sure why I lied.

"Send me pictures." Erica still sounded perky.

"Sure," I replied, though I knew I wouldn't. It felt too inti-
mate somehow—as if showing them would be like spilling a
secret. One I had promised to never, ever tell. "I'll send you the
pics of the bed right away," I offered instead, and that promise I *did* keep. Erica forgot all about the drawings after that. She
was far too busy admiring the bed. I did not forget, though, and
brought them downstairs to study them more closely.

Natasha Witt was clearly adept at drawing, her lines are
strong and expressive. She has rendered the well from different
angles, but all the sketches are basically the same: the well and
the surrounding woods. Only one of them looks a bit different;
there's an animal or something in the background, behind the
tree line. You can't see it clearly, but it looks to be big, like a deer
or something; its hind flank is pale among the spruces.

To be honest I don't know what to make of them. At first,
I was all excited, as if finding the drawings was meant to be a
part of the golden thread, but now they sort of make me feel uneasy. I have spread them out on the dining room table, behind
my laptop, but I don't think I'll keep them there for long. There's
something *wrong* about Natasha Witt's drawings; as if the perspective is skewed somehow. The well doesn't look very magical at all, but more like a circular open maw. When I looked
at them in the attic, I thought Natasha and I perhaps shared a
connection—that we had sensed the same thing by the well,
but now I'm not so sure. In her pictures, I sense nothing of the
otherworldly bliss by the well; it looks more like a place of fear,
stark and slightly off.

Clearly, she didn't get the well at all.

At least I got a few good shots out of my trip to the attic. As
soon as I found the right filter, the bed looked all romantic and

nice standing there in a shaft of dusty light. #treasurehunting #atticjewels #echoesfromthepast

## May 22

Today it finally happened! The answer to the mystery has finally been revealed! I know now what—or *who*—it is that has been calling me to the well, and changed my life in so many ways!

Over the last few days I have been focusing on the empty spot between the spruces again, staring across that musty old circle of stones, all the while visualizing the cabin in my mind, and slowly, slowly, over days, the image has taken on a life of its own. The smoke came back, with *smell* this time, and the petals of the flowers set in the stone wall would move in a breeze I could feel on my skin. Sometimes there would be a butterfly in the scene in my head, and then, when I opened my eyes, a butterfly would really be fluttering in the air, just where it had been in my mind!

It was all very exciting!

When the door finally opened—well, I didn't *see* anything then. She didn't preen or pose before me, she just slipped out of the cabin and moved right into my head. Fit in there at once, like a piece of a jigsaw puzzle. I brought her out of that cabin and into myself!

I wonder if this is how spirit mediums feel *all* the time. Of course, I already know from having spoken with my SOUL at length that I have some channeling abilities—that I *sense* more than most—but I never really thought of speaking with the dead before. This is no Ouija board nonsense, though, not some poorly received messages delivered through the ether, she is closer than that—as close as my own skin. Her wayward soul has found a harbor in me and tethered herself to my being.

We are the same, she and I.

I know it sounds creepy, but it *is* how it feels, and it doesn't disturb me one bit! I want nothing more than to shelter her and let her borrow life from me. My body is healthy and strong and there's more than enough room for two. In fact, I love doing this for her: giving her a channel back to the world! She lost her own life so abruptly and violently, it's only fair that she's allowed to come back—and suddenly I know exactly what to do! Together we will write the book about her life. The *truth* of it this time and not that devil nonsense.

That is her gift to me: the next step on my path!

This is the first time I've connected with a SOUL not my own, a SOUL that doesn't even belong to a living thing but has drifted through the years like a shadow. We speak through images mostly, and thoughts. Through the MAGIC of the surrounding nature. Just this afternoon there was a robin at my windowsill pecking at the glass; then I found a circle of white pebbles in the gravel in the yard and a flower in the garden blooming way too early. I know that these things are gifts from her, small pleasures and impossibilities to let me know she is there, and that she cares for me. I took pictures of the stone circle and the flower. #witchgifts #soulspeak #magicwoman

So what does she want? What is it that drives her to such a degree that she opts to break her century of silence, and why does she speak to *me*? When I ask this question in my mind, I keep seeing roots, deep and tangled. I think that by showing me this, she means that we are somehow alike; that we come from the same soil, if only figuratively; that our souls are related though we don't share blood. I get a sense of love and sisterhood, a bond that runs deep. I think that me being here on my own at this point, after having already learned how to speak to my SOUL, has called her forth from the shadows and made her able to communicate with me. I think there's some sort of magnetism at work, as in "like calls to like" and all of that. I can sense a deep relief in her, that she's finally able to share her truth, and I am ready and willing, Ilsbeth!

I can speak for you!

*May 25*

I am trying to clear out the castle, I am, but I would be lying if I didn't admit to being sidetracked, always and constantly. It feels as if I've passed through the wardrobe and come out somewhere similar yet different to the world I've always known. Everything is enchanted, dusted with magic, infused with *her*: Ilsbeth Clark!

I can't help but think of how the grounds I walk on are the grounds where *she* walked, and how the view from the tower room must have been what *she* saw when looking out from the windows at Nicksby. My beloved cherry tree might even have been a part of her orchard! When I walk the path through the woods to the well, I wonder if the path is the same as it was then; and when I drink water from the tap, I know that it comes from the same source as the water *she* drank. It is all connected: the well, the lake, and the pipes that snake like veins within the castle walls. Every breath I take has her in it, and every dream at night holds her face.

It reminds me of when I had just discovered my SOUL and suddenly could feel it—*hear* it—everywhere, and *see* it materialize in everything I did. This is the same thing, only now it's another's SOUL that entwines with my own. One that has come from behind the veil, across years and other states of existence.

It feels powerful and mighty, and very, very real!

We share a certain loneliness, she and I, and she wants to let me know I am not truly alone, and neither is she, now. I will pay her back in words. I will tell her story in my new book! I won't even have to do much research, as I have Ilsbeth's own whispers to guide me. I've been to the library to pick up some local history books, though, just to know what people have been saying, how the story has been twisted over time—so I know what we are up against, Ilsbeth and I. What myths we will have to debunk!

Was she a witch? Most certainly, just as her mother before her. Was she a wicked child killer? No! To her, all life was holy and good, and she would never endanger a child! She lived in a sacred pact with all growing things and abided by the creed of "do no harm." Her actions have been judged as malignant and cruel, but that is just because people didn't *understand* what they were seeing. All rituals seem strange and even scary to the uninitiated, but once you have the key to decipher what you're seeing, it all makes perfect sense. This is what she wants me to do; she wants to show me what really happened by the well, between her and Owen Phyne, and with the children, to show me how acts of worship of the fertile land have become something ugly in simple people's minds.

Witchcraft is not evil—it never was!

It feels sacred to me, this mission I am on, as if I have finally found my new purpose. I can't wait to see what the days ahead will bring—what wonders she will show me. We are in this together, she and I, sisters in spirit and joined in a quest for TRUTH and MAGIC.

This book will change everything—it will change the world! There will be no coming back for humankind after this. We cannot turn our backs on the reality of MAGIC after Ilsbeth has shown us what it truly means to be a witch! This is just as big as finding the lost ark, or stumbling across a burning bush. Everything is about to shift!

I feel as if I'm about to burst out of my own skin.

I am powerful and strong—just like her!

## June 1

I'm not much alone these days, and I can't really say that I mind the change. Harboring a passenger who's been dead for over a century has its own challenges, though. This morning, for instance, at breakfast, she was craving oats made with full-fat milk, even drenched in cream if she could have it, while I only wanted fresh fruit. We compromised with a bowl of cereal topped with apple and banana slices. The latter is curious to her, apparently banana was a rare treat in F— back when she was alive. We'll doubtlessly have a similar discussion at dinner, as she has a craving for red meat while I try to eat mostly greens (which she thinks of as "poor people's fare"). She also thinks I wear peculiar clothes, my bra is to her a poor excuse for a corset, and at first she thought my jeans were pantaloons. She is learning our new ways day by day, though I don't think she'll give up on her beef just yet.

I do try to compromise as much as possible—we both live here, after all. I put my hair up off the neck, as she wants me to, dress in a flowery summer dress instead of my usual shorts, and I do get the impression that she's relieved not to have to sweat so much on sunny days as back when she wore heavy skirts. She loves TV and the internet, but is mystified by the lack of horses in the yard. It's a strange journey for the both of us, but I'm convinced we'll make it work!

She was really eager to go to the well today. I could feel her impatience like a restless tugging, a swirling unease deep inside. It had started already at breakfast, while I scooped the cereal into our mouth. Afterward, I tried to check my email, but found that I couldn't focus, as my gaze was constantly drawn to the windows; to the sunny garden outside; and behind it, the woods; and in the woods, the well. Whenever I blinked, I saw it, the well, but also not, because it wasn't covered in lichen, and the rim was not infested with black mold. It wasn't showered in sunlight, but the stones shone white in the silvery light of the moon. The ground in the clearing was riddled with white mushrooms, small circles, bigger circles—witch circles all around the well. I knew that it was a memory she showed me: the well as it had been, as she remembered it. When her memory became vivid enough that it appeared with sounds (a gentle rustle of leaves and a hooting owl), and I could actually smell water and dirt, I gave in and we went into the woods.

When we arrived at the well, I could feel her relaxing; all the restlessness just melted away and she became her usual, gentle self. We sank down on the yoga mat in front of the well and just sat there for a while, soaking up the energy. It was even prettier than in the memory; the ground wasn't covered in mushrooms but in soft emerald moss studded with gray rocks; a few feet from the well itself, the moss gave way to fat shards of grass, wispy straws, and delicate wildflowers in white and pink and blue. We lay ourselves down on the mossy ground and closed our eyes against the sun that burned in the bright blue sky. It smelled raw down there, like overturned soil rife with snails and worms.

*Why do you want to come back to where you died?* I asked, quietly in my head. Ilsbeth only laughed in reply and sent pleasant shivers running down my spine. She told me, in her wordless way that is really just knowledge appearing in my mind, that she had been to the well and used its power long before the townspeople came to throw her in.

*It's not the well's fault,* she said. *The well is pure and free from sin.*

We took several glorious pictures by the well, and especially one selfie that we're proud of. Our followers seem to like it as well. #earthmagic #wellofwisdom #twosoulsoneskin #soulsisters

I don't know why Ilsbeth chose me—if it's because I stay at

the castle, because we really have a "soul connection," or because I went to the well as a child—but either way, I'm so grateful that she did! She completes me and nourishes my soul, and I have never felt more vibrantly alive as I do after opening my home—my house—my body—to her.

I want her to stay with me forever.

## June 3

Ilsbeth means to make a witch of out of me! She means to have me find my WILL.

Every day when we go outside, she helps me discover something new. Things that were nothing but scenery before, like trees and dirt and flowers, are suddenly loaded with meaning and use, and I'm not just talking medicinal use either, this isn't some "chamomile before bedtime" type of knowledge. Suddenly I know that if I pick a rowan twig and wrap it in red cloth with a piece of iron, it will protect me, and if I pick waterlilies from the lake and put them under my pillow, they will inspire visions in my dreams!

This is similar to but also different from talking to my SOUL. Back then, I could get an acute sense of what my SOUL—and, by extension, I—needed, but with Ilsbeth, I am more like a student. As we walk in the woods, she can suddenly bring my attention to a tree or piece of greenery, have me sit down on my haunches and feel it with my fingertips, and only then will she reveal to me what exactly it does. Daisies always seemed plain to me, but now I know that they can be used to strengthen friendships. The oak tree gives me strength, while maple leaves bring me creativity. The dirt in the garden is different from the dirt by the well. The dirt at the castle speaks of safety and money, while the dirt at the well speaks of power of another kind.

Sometimes, Ilsbeth has me guessing before she reveals the items' true purpose. She wants me to use my hand and learn to feel it for myself. It's easy, she says, as long as you know how, and I'm starting to think that she's right, because sometimes I *do* feel something, like a tingle or a sense of what the flower or seed in my hand contains, what secrets it harbors under the surface. Decoding the world with a witch's eyes is like the world's most exciting game. Nothing will ever be the same again.

Soon, Ilsbeth says, we'll move on to bones.

My new exciting skillset can't fix everything, though. I know I should dedicate more time to clearing out the castle; I've barely made a dent as it is. When I came here, I had all these plans, I was going to rent a container and everything, but instead I've barely filled a couple of black plastic bags and half-heartedly packed up some books. I know it isn't good enough, but with the discovery of Ilsbeth and all, I'm no longer convinced that selling the castle is the best plan. Erica will be furious, of course, if I back down now. She's planning to buy a family cabin with her share from the sale, up in the mountains, far from F—. I need the money even more, though. I'd been planning to live off my cut while finishing my next book, and yet I'm having doubts . . . Maybe I'm afraid that Ilsbeth will disappear if I leave this place, and take all her secrets with her . . .

The plumbing is failing again. It's almost as bad as it was when Uncle John first bought the place. The toilet isn't working right and I have to carry buckets of water from the shower to flush it. Nothing a plumber can't fix, of course, but I have to admit it's putting a damper on my otherwise enchanted life. The pipes are rattling something fierce as well, threatening to come out from the walls whenever I turn on the tap in the kitchen. I'll have someone come out and have a look and let the estate take the bill. We can't sell a house without a working toilet. I wish there was a spell for it, though; I just can't relax with workers in the house.

If Ilsbeth's spells can't help fix my pipes, they can help me not to worry so much about them. Just tonight, as we were walking in the garden, Ilsbeth brought a stone to my attention: it is small and rounded and has a blue-gray color. I found it nestled on the ground in the blackberry thicket, just where one of the bushes came sprouting from the dirt. Ilsbeth told me—wordlessly, of course—to put it close to my heart to ease my worry. Once I came inside, I pressed the pebble to my heart and fastened it with Band-Aids. It works better than any expensive crystal I've ever owned, and I picked it just here in my garden! My pulse doesn't race anymore when I think about the plumber, and my stomach doesn't hurt when I think about Erica, so I'd say Ilsbeth knows her stuff! Just why this humble stone works so incredibly well, I don't know, and maybe there's no science to it, or at least not one we at present know. The only thing I can say for sure is that it does, and that's all that counts, after all.

All this new knowledge will be extremely useful when we start writing the book—which should happen soon, I know, but right now, I'm really satisfied with just exploring Ilsbeth's world, her essence and her craft. I feel like the more I learn and the more I understand, the better it will be when we finally put words to paper! This isn't just the story of one woman. It's the story of forgotten knowledge, about the bond between humans and the natural world, about unity and magic, and I want to get it right!

*Email Exchange Forwarded to the F— Library by Mistake:*
From: Elena Clover <ElenaSoul@elenasoul.com>
Date: Mon, June 5 at 3:31 AM
Subject: THE NEW BOOK
To: Eva Sommers <eva@xxxxxx.com>

Hi Eva,

I'm SO sorry that I didn't reply to your latest email(s), and COM-PLETELY understand that you worry about my progress, but I hope you'll be able to forgive me when I share with you the wonderful, AMAZING discovery I've made that will DEFINITELY make the wait worthwhile!

As you know, I've spent the spring months at my late uncle's summer house in F—, and while I've been here, I've had this CRAZY breakthrough that has completely upended my previous plans for Book 2 and put me on a new, *more powerful* path! For the first time, I'm in communication with a SOUL not my own, but belonging to no other than the "town witch" here in F—. Her name is Ilsbeth Clark, and she was drowned in a well in the mid-19th century—*killed,* to be more precise, by the townspeople.

I know that we spoke of an animal SOUL book, but I really think this is what I'm supposed to do right now! Ilsbeth has SO much to teach us, about being a woman, a healer, and a WITCH, and she speaks right into my ear, teaching me all kinds of secrets! I do think the world is ripe for this kind of knowledge—even if it never was before—and I feel both humble and blessed to have been chosen to awaken the world to magic at last!

As fate (or Ilsbeth?) would have it, I ran into a journalist from the local newspaper who had written about my uncle before, and we started talking about *Awakening,* and naturally also my next project, and before I knew it, he had typed it all up and the interview ran in the latest edition of the *F— Daily*! I hope you forgive me for this—I know I should have spoken to you first, but you know what it's like when I'm inspired, things just happen to usher me along! That's what it's like when you speak to your SOUL! You can read

the whole thing here: https://www.f—daily.com/elena-believes
-that-magic-is-real.

As I said in the interview, I'm envisioning the book as partially a
retelling of Ilsbeth Clark's life—in her own words—and partially
an introduction to magic, with exercises and anecdotes from my
own apprenticeship. I know that this is all very different from
*Awakening,* but I also just KNOW that it will the next big thing! I'm
absolutely SURE this time, that this the right project!

A preliminary outline is attached! I can't wait to hear what you
think!

Elena


From: Eva Sommers <eva@xxxxxx.com>
Date: Mon, June 5 at 1:22 PM
Subject: THE NEW BOOK
To: Elena Clover <ElenaSoul@elenasoul.com>

Hi Elena,
It is so good to hear from you! You had me worried there for a
moment, as I know how you struggled with the loss of your uncle.
I'm just thrilled that you are so motivated and enthusiastic, and
can't wait to see that energy transformed into another (wonderful) book.

I have read the outline—and the interview—and although I think
you have many interesting ideas, the subject matter is, as you
point out, pretty far from *Awakening.* I have to admit that I'm not
sure if it's wise to change your brand all of a sudden. You really

struck a nerve with the soul-speaking angle, and though I respect your personal journey, speaking to the dead and introducing magic might be a harder sell. People do want to explore their spirituality, but preferably within their own comfort zone. Perhaps it is better to stick with the animal soul book for now?

As you mentioned yourself, I would have preferred it if you had waited to speak to the press since nothing about Book 2 has been decided yet. *F— Daily* is a very small outlet, though, so hopefully not many people will have seen it if you change your mind. I feel like I should warn you, though, that with a following like yours on social media, there is a very real possibility that someone will dig it up.

I know that you are very enthusiastic right now, and also very inspired, but I would appreciate it if you didn't give more interviews right now, and perhaps also dialed back the magic stuff on Instagram, at least until things have been properly thought through.

Best regards,

Eva

# 8

*Transcript from the Nicksby Documents*

The burrow is not a place of beauty: the walls are damp, slick, and black. Fungus grows between the rocks. It reeks in here from rot and tallow candles, and no matter what we feed the hearth it smokes but gives off no warmth, only another foul odor. The clothes on my back are falling apart, ruined by water and time. I wear my mother's woolen shawl about my shoulders, but it gives no warmth either, as it will not dry.

I am a miserable creature of late.

My companion is not impressed with my struggles; she takes all my labor for granted. Every week I wash her hide in a basin of cold water. I scrub it with twigs and lay it out to dry. I make soup from her prey, polish her trinkets, and weave greenery into her coarse hair. Whenever I object to her unkind treatment, she gives me a dark look to remind me of a time when our roles were reversed, when it was *she* who was in *my* service—though I nary had any help of her. She was always mostly a burden, a chain to bind me to this cursed place.

My mistress is neither cruel nor kind, but a thing of hunger and a thing of awe. It is no wonder that Owen Phyne found her so irresistible, although I must say that her charms have tarnished in my eyes. A century of scrubbing and boiling bones will do that.

I have had ample time to regret my mistakes.

To be fair, I think my own light has also diminished in her estimation. When we first met, she was as affectionate toward me as a dog to his master, always aiming to please me, but that has surely changed. True, I always knew the agreement said that I would serve her as she had served me, should I go to my grave without signing her away, but I had stupidly assumed that it would never come to pass, full as I was of youthful brashness. I have the people of F— to thank for this cruel twist of fate; without their intervention, I would have had ample time to make arrangements before I died. Just like my mother did, when signing the beast over to me.

My companion has the right on her side, though, as she makes her countless demands, and that, in truth, is the worst of it. It was the deal that we made, after all, the one I signed with a bloody pen: *Until such time comes that there is another who will willingly enter a covenant . . .*

I never thought that it would extend beyond my years.

I never thought that I would have no rest.

Beyond these walls, the world has changed many times over, and I still have not found the one to take my place, though it is not for lack of trying. I find that people no longer have need for daemons, and I cannot blame them—the creatures are fickle beings, as my own circumstances surely prove, but I still would much like to be rid of mine.

We had both had such hopes for the girl who came wandering to the well with a pure and open heart. My companion, especially, much enjoyed the taste of her—but then the girl's heart broke, and she was gone for the longest time, nursing injuries to both body and mind. My mistress was very sad about it, and keened under the moon many a night. I mourned too, as I would much like to leave this house, but I did not care to wail and curse, rather I thought and planned.

Death may have bound me, but it surely has not silenced me, and there still is a trickle of power running through my veins. Enough, perhaps, that I can make yet another bid for my freedom.

There is another who had come to the well now, gazing through the veil. She is a thing of tangles and thorns, begging for release, like me. She is as open as a flower under the sun, as hungry as bear in spring, grasping for a hand to hold.

I can be that hand.

I leave the well in spirit form, and she is easy to reach as she dwells nearby. At first, I only aimed to whisper in her ear, but then I found that it was easy to slip inside her skin. She has no fear for her soul and is not guarded, I can flow into her like a hand into a satin glove to fill her every inch. It is good to be about again; smelling and tasting like before. I have surely missed the world above. I must take care, though, not to be seduced by the clamor and the trappings of flesh and nature. I must always remember my goal.

My companion is not pleased, as she is still dreaming of the taste of the other one—the bitter one—but surely she, too, must see that I am barely of use anymore. I am drained and feeble, staggering along. Surely she would want a new one to pamper and love before enslaving her soul. Surely she, too, must want for some novelty, someone fresh to enliven her spirits. I do not care if she thinks my choice is wrong, as it is not as if people are flocking to the well, begging to be bound to a creature such as her. People grasp for power in other ways now, and unholy covenants are rarely a necessity.

"We must take what we can," I tell her, but my mistress only huffs. "I shall bring her to you, and then you will see," but she remains as cold as a winter's day.

I shall thaw her heart, though. I shall make the new one come with a willing heart, and then I shall ready the blood for the ink.

# Fall

# 9

*An open letter to the people of F—, continued*

I know I'm not an easy woman to love—not even easy to like, and if I was ever in doubt before, these last few months have proven it to me many, many times over. I don't know what it takes, to be honest. I *never* knew how to please you all. Not even when I was little.

That was the biggest difference between Elena and myself; she always knew, with surgical precision, just how to make people like her. It was as if she could read them, or sense, in a way, what they wanted from her. Or perhaps I am giving her too much credit—perhaps it was always the other way around: she had a special something that *forced* people to like her. Call it charisma, warmth, bewitchment—whatever you like. A "winning personality," maybe. Whatever it was, I know two things for sure: *it* didn't help her in the end, and I don't have it.

I remember even now my first day at school, when I came strolling into the schoolyard with butterflies dancing wildly in my belly. How full of anticipation I was, how *sure* I was that everything would work out in my favor. Soon, I thought, I'd have lots of little friends like my sisters had. I'd be invited to every birthday party, and life would be nothing but song and dance and smiles . . . Well, we all know that's not how it turned out.

It was a giant failure all around.

As a teen, I went through a phase where I would think back and try to reexamine my childhood, and try to pinpoint just where I'd failed, but I couldn't come up with a definite answer. Perhaps I was too slow for you; I never did well with quips and sass. Maybe I was too shy; I never much liked to make a spectacle of myself. I daydreamed a lot, that I remember, and later, after you had rejected me, I would bring a book to school to transport myself away from there. That was after the accident, of course, after my damaged legs and crutches had made things even harder. Before it happened, I had never been outright bullied, but the crutches—and your ringleader, Jeremy James—quickly took care of that.

It was hard on me, I'll freely admit it. My confidence at that time was split in half: on the one hand, I let you get to me and felt my self-esteem crumble more every day. On the other hand, I always had a core of steel, a certain firm knowledge that good things were coming, that my destiny was *so* much greater than Jeremy James's—which certainly proved to be true—and that one day I would accomplish amazing things. As a teen, I liked to believe that you sensed that, that it put you off, so to speak, because you weren't worthy of me. As an adult, however, I realize how the belief that I clung to in order to survive might have come across as arrogance.

That never was my intention—but *you* put it there; you put cracks in me, and I had to glue myself together with whatever was at hand, and the only thing I found was anger and spite, and a wild, crazy hope that things would one day get better. I would show you all, I thought. I would show you all how wrong you had been, and how ten of you were worth less than one of me. I was just like Ilsbeth Clark, I figured, deciding to ignore her sad and violent end.

You never saw any greatness in me, though. You only saw a sad and damaged girl who was all too easy to anger. Torment like the one you put me through never truly goes away, but lingers behind as festering wounds, as ulcers and headaches and deep distain. So excuse me if I'm not always the most polite of persons. Excuse me if you think I am rude—if I roll myself up like a hedgehog, and proudly show off my spines to the world!

If you ask me how I'm doing, I won't lie to make you feel okay, but will tell you just how crappy I feel. If you ask me to help you with some menial nonsense, I will tell you right out if I don't think it is worth my time—and yes, I *will* enjoy watching you squirm as you digest the unexpected answer. We should all be forced out of our comfort zones from time to time, if only to be reminded they are there, and I don't mind at all being your local wake-up call.

I'm only telling you this so you won't jump to conclusions. Maybe I, like Ilsbeth Clark, am just a monster of your making. Perhaps I too have been wrongfully condemned. Perhaps there *is* no monster here but the one you have made up in your heads. Maybe my hands are just as clean as Ilsbeth's when your ancestors chucked her down the well. I think that you should stop readying your torches and think about that for a minute.

I'm telling you once again: I did not kill Elena Clover.

In fact, while you all conspired to make my life hell, she was the only good thing I had as a child—the one to make everything better.

At least she was that for a while.

# 10

For five summers in a row, Elena and I were as close as sisters, spending almost every day in each other's company. I remember vividly the thrill I experienced every year when I heard sounds coming from the summerhouse, and went through the woods to see her family's sleek black car parked in front of the ghastly green house.

John and Susan would be carrying bags and suitcases inside, while Elena and Erica went through the house opening every window to let out the stale winter air. I usually didn't approach them just then, as my mother had told me several times when my restlessness grew toward summer to "at least let them have a day to settle in." But I knew that the summer was on when I saw that car. I knew that my days would take on an enchanted quality, if only for a few months.

I could hardly sleep when I knew Elena had arrived but we had still not reconnected. It was anticipation, of course, that kept me awake, but a little bit of worry, too, because what if this was the year when she grew tired of me? What if this was the year when the magic didn't happen and Elena found herself some other summer friend to spend time with? I was very aware of my shortcomings; I had very little to offer. I was neither pretty nor exciting. I also quite often smelled of the barn, where I was required to help out now that I didn't use the crutches anymore.

The worry I felt beforehand only heightened the bliss when said worries were put to shame and Elena welcomed me back into her orbit, her family, and her presence. Every agonizing hour of waiting was erased when I saw the smile upon her face as I emerged from the woods and onto the summerhouse lawn. The summer lay before us then, with Uncle John's hotdogs under the cherry tree, card games with Erica, and swimming lessons in the lake. In the second year, John got a boat, a small one, and we were allowed to use it if we stayed among the reeds close to shore, and we spent many a lazy day out in that wooden rowboat. We took turns at the oars, learning how to maneuver on the green water while the frogs croaked around us and silvery fish leapt playfully as we slid through the shrouds of weeping willow branches.

So why did things change, you may ask. How did this summertime haven curdle and sour like a fresh glass of milk in the sun? When did anger and bitterness poison the well?

I can assure you it had nothing to do with Ilsbeth Clark!

The summer Elena was fifteen, she simply did not come to F—, and that was the first nail in the coffin, I think. Susan told me she had opted to go to France with her paternal aunt instead. I suppose that makes sense for a young girl, curious about the world, but at the time, it felt most like a fist to the gut. I felt so small and insignificant all of a sudden. While I had been ticking off the days for months, yearning for the school year to end so that Elena would come back, she had been reading guidebooks and practicing her French, not thinking of me at all.

I suppose that was the first time it struck me just how odd it was that Elena and I never spoke out of season. Surely, if we truly were friends, we would call each other sometimes, or send letters? Elena had never expressed any interest in that, though. Instead, she regaled me with stories about her friends in the city: Tessa, Karen, and Veronica, all of whom I thought sounded awful, but according to Elena were as sweet as peaches, with fat dollops of whipped cream on top. Though I had experienced the occasional stab of jealousy at these stories, I suppose I had always thought that it went the other way as well, and that Tessa, Karen, and Veronica had to suffer through stories about *me* come fall, where

*I* was compared to some scrumptious fruit and topped with something glorious. Now I started to realize that perhaps it was not so—perhaps she didn't think of me at all once F— disappeared in the rearview mirror. Perhaps her other friends in the city were just so sweet that she didn't need a small-town potato like me cluttering up her plate. How else to explain that she just went to France like that, without even trying to reach me to explain?

It occurred to me that Elena had always been more important to me than I was to her, and it hurt.

I was in for a long and terrible summer in her absence, mostly spent alone in my room, crying into throw pillows with horses on them, inherited from my sister when she moved away. I felt so very lonely.

The next year, Elena *did* come back, but she only stayed for three weeks, and with it being two years since our last meeting, things just weren't the same. I had grown some bitterness, too, I think; it had sprouted like thorny weeds in my heart. Not to do any harm, mind you, but to protect that sensitive soil from being invaded by careless people like Elena.

She did not seem to notice the changes in me, though, and kept talking about her boyfriend in the city, and the trio of Tessa, Karen, and Veronica, which had now become a square with the inclusion of a girl named Trina, who was "the best," of course, with sugar on top.

I hated them all just from having to listen—it wasn't rational, I know, but I was young and unused to friendships. My bad feelings from the summer before had had much time to stew and grow. The weeds in my heart had deep roots by then, and things were never carefree and easy between us again.

I suppose it made me cruel.

I remember one time in particular, on that last summer, when we were sitting outside under the cherry tree. She was painting her toenails blue, while I was just sitting there with my hands in my lap, acting unimpressed by her bold choice of color. John had made us hotdogs and the plates littered the table between us, heaped with greasy napkins and uneaten potato salad. The pitcher of lemonade was drained.

"Is that a city thing?" I asked her, to fill the silence between us. "Painting your toes blue?"

"No," she laughed. "It's a 'me' thing."

"No one can see it in the woods, though, so it really seems pointless." I pulled up my legs and cradled them in the chair but couldn't help but notice the pink scar that snaked down my skin, marring me for life. I promptly let my legs down again.

"Here," she tried to hand me the nail polish bottle. "You can try it if you like."

I laughed at her then, too loud, and too shrill. "I would never! It's the ugliest thing I ever saw." I rolled my eyes. "If that's a 'you' thing, I don't know what that makes you."

"Well"—she pulled her hand with the bottle back, looking somewhat puzzled—"if you don't want it, just say so. There's no reason to be nasty."

"I'm just being honest," I said, and sounded rude even to my own ears, but I just couldn't help myself. "If you can't take the truth, you shouldn't paint your toes blue."

"I don't remember asking for your opinion," she snapped back, probably both angry and hurt by then. "It's not like it matters anyway."

"Says who?" I wanted to know.

"Says me, and all my friends in the city." She started painting another layer; her toenails gleamed electric blue.

I felt like I should leave after that, but didn't. I still clung to a vain hope that somehow the skies would clear up and everything would be as before, that Elena would say the magic words to make the raw patch of anger inside me heal. "I'm sorry that I hurt you, Cathy. You know you are my very best friend." "I have missed you like crazy since the last time I saw you." "None of my other friends compare to you. You're like a sister to me and we'll always be best friends."

Childish, I know, but I *was* a child—and, of course, Elena never said any of those things, she just sat there painting her toenails.

The next year, she didn't come again, but by then I didn't care.

I was already married.

## 11

I suspect that you had all seen a different fate for me: forever a spinster, living at the farm with my mother and father, dedicating my days to tending livestock and cleaning house, but instead, I got hitched to "the butcher's boy" and moved into town proper.

It always amuses me how Bobby even now, after having had a career in insurance for two decades, is still "the butcher's boy" to you. It is as if time doesn't catch up in your heads, as if people will never truly be anything but what they were on the day of their hatching.

"The butcher's boy" doesn't much approve of this account, but thankfully it's no longer his business how I spend my time. That doesn't keep him from trying to meddle, though. Poking his nose where it no longer belongs. Just this morning, as I was readying myself to write these very words, he called me on the phone.

It was all very awkward; I was balancing my breakfast in my hands at the time when he called, and as I answered, the plate tipped over, sending my cream cheese bagel to the floor, and the scalding-hot jasmine tea splashing over my fingers. I'm not saying that it was Bobby's fault, but he does have a crossed way about him. Minor accidents and mishaps abound whenever he is near.

"You shouldn't be doing this, Cathy," he saw it fit to tell me. "You shouldn't be talking about the case at all! What do you think it looks like from the outside? You'll be able to tell your side of the story soon enough."

"Well," I replied while licking sweet tea from my fingers. "I don't see why I shouldn't talk, as I don't have anything to hide."

"But don't you see how this could be seen as a way of turning public opinion—as if you are trying to rewrite the facts."

"Why would I want to rewrite the facts, when *I don't have anything to hide*?" He always was very slow.

I could hear him groan on the other end. "I just wish you wouldn't be so honest, it's painful to watch how you just lay it all out. I think you'll come to regret it."

"I'm sorry if my honesty *offends* you—"

"It's not about me, Cathy. It's about *you*—and Brian, too. Just because we're no longer married doesn't mean that I don't car—"

I hung up on him then. What does he even know about me, about female friendships and all the ways they can go wrong? He's just "the butcher's boy," and currently seething, I'm sure, that his silly reprimands made it onto here. But that's just how it has to be. I swore to be faithful to the truth, and so I am, and I find myself enormously unconcerned with what Bobby may think or say about it. He has long since played out his role.

It was in the fall following my last summer with Elena that Bobby and I started dating. It began innocently enough with some flirting whenever he came to the farm to pick up a cow destined for slaughter. Then slowly, over the next year, it grew into something else. We were both awkward teenagers then. I still had some medical issues, and Bobby was a little pudgy and shy. I suppose our shared awkwardness drew us together. I remember being fascinated by his hair: all those tight yellow curls that promptly bounced back to their original position whenever I brushed my hand across his head. He was young enough to still be plagued by acne, and carries the scars to this day. It was a fascination between us more than anything else, I think. With each other and our own bodies. Neither of us had ever explored that side of life before, and we used to go on long drives on bumpy dirt roads, far into the woods, to be alone. Before you knew it, I was pregnant.

It shouldn't have surprised us, really.

My parents were aghast, and so were his. They started speaking of marriage, which I wasn't all opposed to. I had been worrying about the future and how to find my way, and now there was an option, ready furnished. It seemed a simple choice at the time. It would also take me away from the farm and the summerhouse, which seemed an immense relief just then. Everything at home reminded me of Elena, and even the air seemed laced with something bitter and broken.

I eventually lost the child, though, so our marriage was really pointless from the start, but by then it was too late, the knot already tied. My sweet boy, Brian, came along three years later, and I will never regret *that*—but the initial premise for the union between Bobby and myself washed out of me in one single night of blood and toil, which left me feeling betrayed—again—by my body, yes, but by fate as well.

Was I never to have and keep something of my own?

I'm not blaming Elena for the foolishness of my marriage, of course, it wouldn't be fair to put something so immense on a thoughtless teenager's shoulders, but if I am to be completely honest, I think she had something to do with it. What had happened between us had made me so raw, so very, very hungry for love and affection—someone to call my own—that I think I latched on to the first person who offered and clung to it with all my might, trying to heal my wounds. Bobby did that for a while. He soothed the aching pain, especially after we got married and I knew he couldn't just walk out the door. It calmed the fear that was Elena's gift to me; a deep and relentless anxiety that I would be left behind.

I can still feel it to this day, slithering down my bones.

A husband seemed a better option to me than any sort of friendship. The alliance between Bobby and me was sealed with words and fat rings of gold, and all of that felt secure.

Turned out I was wrong, of course. I'm sure I don't have to tell any of *you* about the events that led up to my divorce, as you're probably well informed already, but I will absolutely state for the record that I do not recognize myself in what Bobby says about me. I'm not a vindictive person. The only reason why our marriage ended after sixteen—*good*—years was that he couldn't keep it in his pants and had to go chasing Rosemary Adams to the point that her belly started to swell, just like mine had decades ago. You would think that after *that* whole debacle he would have learned to take preventive measures, but no! Stupid will be stupid, I suppose, and now it's *Rosemary* who feels safe and secure with vows and gold and a hefty mortgage. I wish them all the best.

I never thought I'd be a part of such a depressing statistic, though. Never thought I'd be such a cliché, but there you go. Perhaps I should have known better than to let myself be ensnared by "the butcher's boy." Perhaps I should have seen how it would end all along, but I have to admit that I'm better off on my own. I rather *enjoy* having the house all to myself, and I have my work to keep me busy: the job I keep at the school administration, but also the one I conduct at night within the deep belly of the historical archive. I am never idle! So you can just stop whispering at once about how "strange" I've become after the divorce, how "lonely" I must be, because I'm doing good work for the town and for myself. If you need further proof, I advise you to pick up a copy of *Ilsbeth in the Twilight* and see the fruits of my labor for yourself.

It's as if being married has somehow shielded me from ridicule, though, or at least you tried to hide it better back when I still wore a ring. Even the staff at school hide wicked smiles and roll their eyes when I come down the halls.

I tried to talk to Principal Myers about it once. I caught her in her office when nobody else was around. It was late in the day and she was tired, but I thought she ought to know. I will never in my life forget the condescending expression when she leaned toward me and said, "I have never heard anything wrong being said about you ever, Cathy. I'm sure the staff would never stoop to such a low. We have a good and inclusive workplace here."

When I stood my ground and told her about the sniggering that occurred whenever I stepped into the teacher's lounge, she merely replied, "They're on their break, they're allowed to laugh. I just don't think it's about you, Cathy. *Why* would they laugh about you?"

"Because my husband left me for another woman?" I suggested from the top of my list.

"Dear Catherine." She shook her head and took off her glasses, then set to clean them with a piece of flannel. "All we who work here are grown-ups. We do not engage in schoolyard bullying, rather we work hard to end it. A divorce is a serious matter that can hit a person hard, and I have problems believing that anyone on my staff would treat it as a joke . . . It *can* cause quite a crisis, though." She put her glasses back on her nose and her pale blond ringlets danced about her head. "Maybe you ought to talk to someone?"

I had gone cold by then; all my anger had dispersed. "So you think the problem is *me*?"

An expression of pity crossed her pretty features. "I think, in this case, it just might be."

I knew better, of course.

And you know better too.

# 12

I have to rectify something from my last installment. I have regretted the wording ever since I published it, and it's been riding me all day. It's about the miscarriage—the child that I lost. I made it sound as if it meant nothing, as if it was an insignificant thing, but it wasn't like that at all.

I had wanted that child, deeply. I had loved it ever since I knew it was there, and read countless books about pregnancy and childbirth. I had enjoyed watching my body change, crocheted socks and made lists of names. I had truly wanted that child, and saying that it meant nothing to me is a lie I cannot live with.

The night that it left was the worst of my life, and I will never, ever forget it.

We were so young then, Bobby and I, some might say too young—but in hindsight, I think we were protected by that youth too, because we weren't nearly as afraid as we ought to have been, not about the marriage, and not about the baby, either. We both took it in stride.

We moved into the apartment above Bobby's parents' garage and I decorated with doilies, knickknacks, and wreaths of dried flowers. I painted a dresser for the baby and set to fill it with miniscule clothes. Some of it gifts from nervous but excited grandparents, some of it things I had bought. I collected soft toys as well and lined them up on top of the dresser: a fat blue elephant, a pink giraffe, a yellow monkey, and a sand-colored lion. We never had many toys when I was a child, and I wanted my kid to have that: a room of its own with plenty to choose from. I wanted it to feel blessed from its very first day alive.

When it all went wrong and the bleeding started, I called Bobby at work at the abattoir. He came rushing home in his rusty Honda and brought me to the hospital. I remember crying and wailing all the way there—and he, too, wiped tears from his eyes, even as he squinted at the road before us. Neither of us had thought to call our parents, to have someone older and steadier with us, so it was just him and me as we parked at the edge of the parking lot and slowly made our way to the entrance, me with a towel squeezed between my legs. It was a lot of blood. I think I knew it already then that the baby was no longer alive.

I still held on, though, to a wild and crazy hope that somehow it would be saved. As I lay there upon the examination table, bathed in bright light; as they prodded and pressed down on my stomach; as my hand that clung to Bobby's turned white around the knuckles and my wailing gave way to a tired whining, I held on to that hope.

In the end, they couldn't do anything for me. "Nature takes it course," they said, and as women, we are expected to carry such losses with grace. We are expected to just accept and move on, and losing an unborn is such a quiet thing—you're not supposed to mourn, because the child was never there in the first place, so you didn't even know it—but you do! You know what it was like when it was in you, and you have woven a whole wardrobe of hopes and dreams and plans for it, cloaks of sunshine, mist, and moonlight that it will never get to use.

The child and what it had meant to me—the promises resting in its chubby little palms, of future and family and *life*—I couldn't just erase it. I went to a very dark place for a while, just as cold and deep as the well.

I remember—vaguely—lying in bed in the apartment, nested deep in a cocoon of green sheets, while refusing to even turn on the lights. Bobby would knock on the door from time to time.

"Cathy, are you hungry?"

"Cathy, won't you come out for a little while?"

"Cathy, we cleared out the nursery like you asked."

"Did you burn the toy animals?" I asked him back.

"No," he replied after a while. "We donated them—they were perfectly fine."

"You should have burned them!" I cried.

It was a very dark time in my life.

In the end, it was my sister Louise who helped me get up from that bed. I have honestly always loathed her brand of "tough love," but I realize that I needed it just then. She came bustling inside, threw open the curtains, and spoon-fed me canned tomato soup, just like when I was sick as a child. She brought me books from the library, too, and insisted that we read them aloud; among them was *Strange Stories and Legends from F—,* which has a few bits about Ilsbeth. When I was a little better, she wheeled a TV set through the door, and daytime TV became my new best friend. You can say what you will about those shows, but at least they ignited a spark of interest in me.

The best thing she ever did for me, though, was to convince me to try medication. Soup can only do so much, and sometimes you need a little chemical help in order to best help yourself.

When Brian arrived a few years later, I loved him even more for my ordeal, maybe. But I feared that love too in a way that I might not otherwise have, because of the one I had lost. The pain it had left behind never went away, and I was terrified of landing in that deep, dark hole again. I suppose all mothers fear losing their children, but having already felt some of that loss, my particular beast had a scent and a color. I knew what I was up against if something should happen to Brian; I knew that the pain had sharp and wicked teeth—and I felt, for a while, as if I just couldn't risk it.

They called it postpartum depression, and I went to see a psychiatrist, but I knew, even as I nodded my head and did as they said, that the beast had another name—grief—and that it couldn't be magically wished away.

It passed, though, in the end. Or at least I learned to live with it. I "bonded" with Brian, eventually, and everyone was happy. I had lost my window to breastfeed, though, and I honestly remember very little from his first year on this earth, but it got better. *We* got better. I bought him toys to put on his dresser: elephants, lions, and one giant kangaroo. I learned to make baby food from scratch. I carried him around on my back in a shawl, and made sure he got sunlight and fresh air.

I've never ceased to worry, though, that my failure at being entirely present for Brian in the first year of his life has somehow damaged him. I know only too well how fragile a child's psyche can be, and how important it is, developmentally speaking, to have a secure connection with your primary caregiver in those first tender months of life. Perhaps that's why I became such a nag as he grew older; always dressing him too warmly, riding him about his homework, and taking him to the doctor whenever there was a suspicion of a cold. I kept my eyes on him always. Maybe that's why he won't stay with me anymore; maybe it became too much—but then, can you really love a child *too much*?

I never quite healed, but we managed, although I won't pretend that it didn't hurt me, losing that first child. I have never dealt "well" with losses. I'm crying even now, though that might be over Elena.

When Bobby left me for Rosemary, it was to Ilsbeth I turned to appease the grief-beast. It worked, too, in the sense that I didn't have much time to think about my own dratted life as long as I kept busy with the book. Maybe that was what Elena did too, when she turned to the well after John died.

Maybe that is Ilsbeth's gift after life: to be a harbor for those who are grieving.

# 13

## *Excerpt from* Ilsbeth in the Twilight, *by Catherine Evans*

### I. Arrival at Nicksby

It was high summer when I first came to Nicksby.

There it lay, at the heart of a lush forest, a sprawling estate of white-painted wood and rust-colored bricks, barns crammed with livestock, and fields bursting with nature's bounty, and I, at barely nineteen, was to be the mistress of it all.

I know that I ought to have been pleased, and that to others my life must have seemed tremendously charmed.

The estate showed itself from its very best side as our carriage drove into the yard; the sun shone from a clear blue sky, and a scent of roses lay upon the air, having drifted in from the gardens. There was a flutter of activity as the news of our arrival spread, and the workers lay down their hayforks and shovels to come and greet their master.

The house staff came pouring out as well: the housekeeper, the cook, and the maids, all of them wearing sensible gray cotton dresses under their starched aprons. There were smiles and excitement everywhere I looked, as they had all been looking forward to meeting the master's new bride. I appeared to be the only one whose smile shivered, and whose heart felt heavy with doubt. Yet I put on my bravest face as I climbed down from the carriage to receive their congratulations, as they welcomed me and ushered me inside, as they showered me in praise and pressed hot tea into my hands.

To them, it must all have seemed so simple.

It was truly quite an arrangement my father had made on my behalf, and I knew I ought to be grateful. Besides the farm itself, the Nicksby estate encompassed a brewery, a sawmill, and a canning factory by the river. A couple of hundred people depended upon Nicksby for work. My father had told me all this, emphasizing the number, when trying to coax some enthusiasm from me, but all I could think of then was how Archibald Clark was the same age as him, and how the vigor that had helped him build all of it had long since seeped from his bones. To me, Archibald Clark had been nothing but an uncle, a friend of my father's ever since the war, a corpulent man who sometimes came to visit, keeping my father up long into the night while swilling whisky in crystal glasses and puffing on ill-smelling cigars. I always thought that he spoke too loudly, never even caring that we children needed sleep. His laughter would reach me through the floorboards, booming and obnoxious, as I lay next to my sister in bed, desperately trying to get some rest. Most of all, I associated Archibald Clark with annoyance, a disturbance to our otherwise so peaceful life.

"Your father only wants what is best for you," my mother said when I voiced my concerns. It was on the very same night that Father had shared his plans. "He trusts his old friend to keep you comfortable and safe."

"But I do not care for him as a wife ought to," I had protested, standing there beside her in the kitchen as she looked over the cook's budget laid out on the scarred table. The air in there smelled of hot woodsmoke and spices; a few plucked chickens hung naked and rubbed with lard next to the sprawling stove. Ceramic bowls filled with onions, beets, and carrots littered what remained of space on the table. I snuck a shelled almond from a cup and popped it into my mouth. My mother smacked my hand for it, but only very lightly.

"No one cares for their spouses in that way at first," she told me. "And you are thinking like a child, not a woman. Mr. Clark is old, that is true, but then he will not remain for very long. He already has the gout. He has also never been married before and has no children to stake a claim. Think of it, Ilsbeth, how all he has can be yours."

These were very new thoughts to me. I was not accustomed to thinking in that way, as if people were commodities, something to bring loss or gain. "But why would *he* do it? Marrying someone young, like me? Surely he will have little use of me—"

"He is still dreaming of a son, I think. They all do in the end, when fall starts claiming their bones. It is his last chance, and that is why he wants someone fertile and young."

"Like a cow," I remarked.

"Just that," Mother agreed, adding one of her wry smiles. "It will certainly be unpleasant for a while, but I am sure that you will grow used to it. If nothing else, you will surely have enough spending money to buy a few comforts to soothe yourself. I also hear that the kitchen at Nicksby is well kept, and so you will not starve."

"But what if I cannot give him a child?" I had heard of such cases before.

"Well," Mother shrugged. Some ink had fallen from the tip of her pen to soak into the paper below, obscuring Cook's scrawls. "It will be too late once you are wed. He cannot go back on it then—and he will make you a very rich widow."

"And then I can marry whom I like?" I stole another almond from the cup.

"You surely can," said Mother, "though by then you might be so tired of being a wife that you perhaps would rather be alone."

Mother signed Cook's budget with a strong, sure hand. It was strange to me to think of how she herself had worked in our kitchen before catching my father's eye. I found it hard to think of her as anything but the mistress to my father's estate, although I knew, of course, how he had been married before, and how I even had had two half brothers for a while. Mother had told me that it was for their benefit that the wedding happened so fast after the first Mrs. Willows's death. Sadly, they had both drowned in the millpond shortly after. Though I surely felt saddened by thinking of it, and bowed my head respectfully whenever we visited the boys' graves, it had all happened before I was born and so it seemed to belong to another world entirely. To me, the Willows family had always consisted of myself, my parents, my sister Georgina, and my brother Peter, and so it felt strange to me to think how another set of children had once inhabited our rooms.

I wondered, briefly, as I stood there by the kitchen table, with my heart full of doubt, if my mother had been as calculating then as she was now. If she had tallied the advantages and the discomforts before accepting my father's proposal. Probably, she had. She had arrived in this country as a very young woman— about the same age as me—with very little to her name. Though she always claimed that her family had been treated with much respect "back home," they did not seem to have had much in terms of riches. She would surely have had to keep a cool head to arrive at such a privileged position. Though another might find my mother's frank speech of such matters offensive, I always found it a comfort. I knew that I could always come to her for honest advice and good counsel, and that was why I did not argue with my father but bent my neck and accepted the proposal. It was why I donned the wedding dress and walked the aisle with Archibald Clark, even though he was twice my age.

We would surely both come to regret it.

# Summer

Summer

# 14

*Elena Clover's journal*

*June 6*

Catherine Evans can burn in hell! I have never been as angry in my life as I am right now! I am so upset that my hand is shaking as I write this. What gall that woman has! What GALL! She is utterly, utterly crazy and mad, and I don't even know how to accurately describe just how uncomfortable she made me today!

It had been such an interesting morning up until then. Ilsbeth and I had been to the well performing some sort of ritual that I didn't really get. I know it had something to do with Owen Phyne, Ilsbeth's lost lover, and finding someone like him. Apparently, this is important to Ilsbeth, so much so that I almost felt jealous as we sat there, cross-legged by the well, braiding supple twigs into ropes to "bind," she let me know, an "equal SOUL." As I said, I'm not exactly sure how the spell is supposed to work, but when the rope was ready, I could tell it was a bridle of sorts—a little strange and misshapen perhaps, but a bridle nevertheless. Ilsbeth sang the whole time, humming strange words through my mouth. Then we picked blackberry leaves and flower buds, and pushed them in between the twigs.

When Ilsbeth was all satisfied, we threw the bridle down in the well. I took a picture before it disappeared. #wildmagic #witchcraft #soulsisters

Needless to say, I was not exactly in a fighting mood when we came back to the castle. The magic that morning had been strong and my body felt as heavy as my head felt light. Everything seemed a little eerie: the blazing sun in the sky, the bright green lawn, the skeletal branches of the cherry tree that's sprouting far fewer leaves than before. To be honest, I felt a little high. To make matters worse, I was still wearing a nightgown, a ghastly salmon-pink thing with frills that Mom left here once and which I hate but Ilsbeth likes. I guess it reminds her of her past wardrobe. My hair had bits of greenery in it from our session by the well, and my bare feet were black with mud.

And there she was: Catherine Evans, standing in front of her golden diesel-guzzling car, clutching the car key in her hand, as if someone was about to come up and fight her for it. She had pushed her sunglasses up on top of her head and the amber-colored plastic had left gray track marks where it had combed through her hair. She must be dyeing her hair in her bathroom, alone, because it really is very uneven. Besides the sunglasses, she wore green plaid slacks and a red blouse with puffy shoulders that pretended to be more expensive than it was. Her shoes were brown, sturdy and sensible. She always wears very sensible shoes, probably due to her old injury.

She didn't even give me time to greet her, but came at me as soon as I rounded the corner from the garden. Her free hand curled up and pointed one sharp, wicked finger at me.

"How dare you!" she cried, striding toward me across the gravel while jabbing said finger in the air. "How dare you, Elena!" Her face was all twisted up, looking like wrinkly tissue paper, except for her brow, which was surprisingly smooth, like marble.

The welcoming smile I had plastered on my lips wilted and died like a flower in winter. "What do you mean? Cathy? I don't under—"

"Oh, you know very well what I'm talking about!" She almost spat out the words and her eyes narrowed to slits. She didn't stop her furious strides before she was right in front of me, and that finger came diving again, stopping just an inch from my frilly, pink chest. It was a good thing that it did, though, because I don't know what I would've done if she'd touched me.

"I really don't," I told her. "I have no idea why you're so upset—"

"Ilsbeth Clark!" she cried out, and I think she even stomped with her foot. "Ilsbeth Clark, of course! Elena, how could you?"

"How could I what?" I was still confused, still a little high from the magic. Deep inside, I thought I felt Ilsbeth wriggle and laugh a little. Clearly, she knew better than me just what was going on. "Cathy, I really don't—"

"She was mine!" bellowed the woman. "You knew very well that she was *mine*!"

Another moment of confusion then as I tried to make sense of her words, and her *anger*. Did Cathy have Ilsbeth inside her first? Was that what she meant?

Suddenly she started crying; angry tears came pouring out. "I have worked on my novel for *years*," she told me. "I have spent days on end in that cramped, musty archive and gone through everything just to get it right—and here you are! Come sweeping in like the vulture you are, just taking whatever you like! That story was mine to write!" She jabbed with her finger again, and this time I took a step back. "Why couldn't you let me keep it?" she cried. "*You* could have chosen *anything* to write to about but for me, it was always only Ilsbeth."

"Oh, Cathy." I threw out my arms. "It's not that simple . . . I didn't know you were writing about Ilsbeth too."

"Of course you did! Everyone does! It's all they ever talk about!" Her voice was a little hoarse by then, but she still kept shouting, waving her arms around, and accidentally pressing the key button so the car behind her unlocked with a beep.

"No, I swear!" I lifted my hands to appease her, which made me feel weak, and I loathed myself. "I swear to you, Cathy! I really didn't know about your book!"

"Well, now you *do* know!" she shouted. "So I'd *appreciate it* if you stopped!"

"Stopped what? Stopped writing?"

"Just that!"

"But Cathy, it's not that easy," I tried again. How could I explain to her that this was more than work for me? That Ilsbeth had moved in and was with us that very moment?

I couldn't.

"It's very simple, I'd say," Cathy croaked. "I had her first, and you can't just have anything you want."

"I don't— Cathy," I tried for my most reasonable voice. "Ilsbeth doesn't *belong* to you. She belongs to *everyone*—"

"No one knows her story like I do," she bragged. "No one has gone through the trouble of really digging *deep*. I have found things no one has ever seen before, things that will shine a whole new light on everything!"

"Well, so have I," I retorted, bristling a little myself. "You're not the only one who can make discoveries, Cathy!"

"What? Your *soul* nonsense?" Her lip lifted in a snarl. "That's hardly a discovery, Elena! That's just damaging to the story—it's ludicrous!"

*"Soul nonsense?"* I couldn't believe my ears! "Cathy, it was you who took me to the well that time! You know what we saw! Hell, you saw it first!"

A perplexed look appeared on her face for a second before it vanished just as abruptly. "I am sure I don't know what you're talking about," her voice was curt.

"Oh, don't you even try!" I hissed. "Just because you never wanted to talk about it doesn't mean it never happened. In fact, I think I have you to thank for discovering Ilsbeth and the magic in the first place—"

"If I ever did anything to provoke this . . . *insanity*," she retorted, "I deeply apologize! It was not my intention!"

"Cathy," I tried to appeal to her better sense. "The truth doesn't go away just because you find it *uncomfortable*—"

"The truth, Elena? The *truth*? You wouldn't know truth if it poked you in the eye!"

"I'm pretty sure Ilsbeth would disagree." My voice had turned cold. I could feel the icy needle of offense penetrate my core and unleash the rage. "You don't know what you're talking about, Cathy. You're in way over your head! You don't know the first thing about who Ilsbeth is—*was*!"

She laughed then. Laughed at *me*, who currently harbored the witch in question. "I don't know the first thing about Ilsbeth? I can assure you no one knows her story better than I do. Do you even know where her mother was from? What education she had? How many siblings she had?"

"None of that's important," I said, all the while willing Ilsbeth herself to speak up. She had gone very silent, though, curled up into a ball inside me. "I know who Ilsbeth is—*was*, and that is all that matters."

For a moment, Cathy almost seemed perplexed. "You really are something, do you know that?" she said at last. "You really aren't *right*." She shook her head as if dazed, as if trying to wake up from a dream.

"Cathy, does it really matter if there's two books about her?" I was still trying for reason, even if she had just called me mad.

"You'll ruin Ilsbeth forever," she informed me. "No one will take her seriously if you follow through with your idiotic book."

"Oh, but they will!" I informed her. "They will for sure! My book will be a gift to the *world*. Ilsbeth is sharing her magic with me—with *everyone*. We'll finally learn the truth!"

She shook her head again. "Elena, please, don't do this." She didn't seem enraged anymore, but concerned, which of course enraged *me* even more. "You'll ruin *years* of work! For old times' sake, for what you *did* to me, please, leave Ilsbeth alone—"

"Ilsbeth chose me, not you," I rubbed it in, and I have to admit that it felt sweet. "I can't say that I blame her either—"

"Ilsbeth Clark is *dead,* Elena. She has been dead for a very long time. All we can do is look at her story and learn what we can from all that went wrong." Something like compassion crossed her drab features.

"Dead doesn't always mean gone," said I.

"Yes," Cathy nodded once. "It does," she declared, and promptly turned her back on me to march back to her car, leaving me standing on the lawn like a fool, and no matter how hard I tried, I just couldn't come up with a retort to let me have that coveted last word.

Maybe I was just too happy to see her go.

What RIGHT does she have to come here and berate me in that way? What right does she have to say that I am wrong? What a pompous, ungraceful, unimaginative bitch she has become!

I can't believe I ever thought she was my friend.

And as certain as I was before, I'm even more determined now—I'll definitely write that book, and then I'll watch with glee as Cathy weeps.

# 15

*Excerpt from* Ilsbeth in the Twilight,
*by Catherine Evans*

### VIII. Owen Phyne

Perhaps it truly was boredom that drove me into the arms of the reverend, or maybe it was something more profound. What I know for sure is that it was strong enough to override all sense of obligation and whatever feelings of duty still bound me to my husband. What could he, with his aging body and thinning white hair, his boastful manner and lacking intellect, ever have to offer a woman such as me, compared to the many charms of Owen Phyne?

To Owen, I was not an animal to be exploited for offspring, nor a jewel to show off for the admiration of one's peers. Owen saw in me a human being—an equal. He admired my strength, my hopes and my dreams, as much as my physical assets.

After the first time he kissed me, on the bell tower stairs, he nearly cried with guilt; he clutched at the fabric of my gray dress as his handsome face twisted up with anguish. "Forgive me, Ilsbeth," he cried. "I never should have taken advantage—"

I placed my hand on his cheek to stop his flood of words. "Please, do not apologize. I wanted it as much as you did. I have been lonely ever since my marriage . . . My husband and I have so little in common, and you . . . you are everything I have ever wanted in a man."

I meant it, too, that sentiment. Owen Phyne, with his gleaming red hair, his lively green eyes and square jaw, had surely caught the eye of more than one lady in our congregation. It was more than that, though, because it was his spirit I craved, even more than his touch. I adored the way he saw the world: as an adventure to be explored, rather than a task to be endured.

"I felt a kinship with you," I continued my speech as he groaned and grasped my hand. "One that I have not felt to anyone before. I know there is no reason to it, but it feels as though I *know* you. Whenever you are near, if it is in this church as you give your sermon, or at Nicksby when you come for tea, I feel more vibrantly alive than I have ever since I left my father's house. I know I should not say such things, but I am not ashamed of it. You have my heart, Owen Phyne, and there is nothing you can say or do to change that."

Owen remained quiet for a moment; I could tell from his manners that he was struggling with himself. A fine sheen of sweat had broken out on his forehead. "As you have mine," he whispered at last. "My heart is yours to keep or discard as you like—but we should not speak such words to one another. You are a married woman, Ilsbeth, and I am a man of God."

"But surely God must have meant for us to meet. Surely he would want us to find each other." I dearly hoped that it was so. I truly *believed* that it was, because why else would two people, so strongly drawn to one another, meet at a time when they both needed it the most? I had my struggles with Archibald, while Owen was still reeling from the loss of his sister. "I think we are meant to comfort one another," I whispered in the cool stairwell.

He gave a short laugh, brittle and desperate. "Is that what you call it, Ilsbeth? Is comfort truly what we desire from one another? Had not my conscience bothered me so, I would—"

"Would what?" I asked him as our gazes locked. "What would you do to me, Owen?"

I waited with bated breath as the emotions flickered across

his face, from anguish to hope, then back again. "Nothing that a decent man would do to the wife of a benefactor."

"Well, think of it this way," I said. "Archibald is old, while I am still young. Before long, it is I who will hold the reins at Nicksby, and *I* will surely not hold the transgression against you." I could not help but smile as I said that last part.

Owen looked at me, aghast at first, then a smile came tugging at his lips as well. "You are too bold for your own good, Ilsbeth."

"No," I sighed. "I am just tired of waiting for my life to be happy."

"Meet me tomorrow," he said into my ear. "By the old Nicksby well in the woods."

"What will we do there?" I asked, while still relishing the feeling of his hand wrapped around mine.

"I will make you happy," he whispered, and then he kissed me anew.

# 16

I do miss Owen Phyne.

Sometimes I bring out what is left of him and place it upon the table, next to the tallow candles, and caress the rough arc of his skull. I gaze into the sockets that once held his eyes, and breathe into the hollow that once harbored his nose, as if trying to bring him back to life, though I know there is nothing but dust within. All that was Owen is gone.

Only his teeth remain undisturbed by time; I can still recognize his smile when I look at the crooked rows. He once had a molar pulled out, and I remember that gap from life. Some nights, when the longing is strong, I close my eyes and clutch the skull to my chest, trying—in vain—to coax *something* from the bone; a reverberation of the man whose thoughts and dreams used to fill the yellowing dome in my hands, but alas, I am always disappointed. Owen Phyne is lost.

My mistress was so smug when I first arrived, so eager to show me what she had done: there lay Owen upon the dirt floor, his flesh bloated and black, his hair wizened and falling out from his head. She wanted to show me how she had kept him in one piece, and not eaten as much as a toe. She wanted me to love her for that.

She never said how she had devoured his soul.

At least I learned that Owen had not deserted me after the trial, but had been in the well all along—although I would much have preferred if he had been alive so he could have aided me in my following predicaments. Mayhap it would not have come to such a violent pinnacle if he had. Owen always had a way with words, was velvety smooth when it counted.

I had warned him not to trust my mistress, though—had warned him many times—but he only ever saw her as a servant or a pet, and so she had taken him at last. Perhaps it was for me that he had come to seek her out that day. Mayhap he had wanted to ask her to use her sway in my favor—or perhaps he had come to care for her, as I was in no position then to ride into the woods on my own. I shall never know, because Owen Phyne is gone.

All I have left are his bones.

When we first met, he was like fire to my kindling. He was tall and well shaped, his hair was like a flaming mane. His eyes were a pale green, as birch leaves in spring, and his lips were as carved by Cupid himself, luscious and red, so soft to the touch. Mayhap I knew it already the first time we met, when he came riding to Nicksby as the new reverend to take tea with my husband and me, that there was something special about Owen, that he saw through me from the start, and knew what truly lived in me. Mayhap he had such blood himself, to see what is hidden from others; I always thought so as our friendship grew, that he was a kindred spirit.

But at first, I saw nothing but his eyes.

Oh, those first days of budding love. How I would find any excuse to seek him out in the church—how *he* would use any excuse to travel out to Nicksby. How our strolls through the graveyard would soon bring us to the woods, and there—below the trees—how our hands would touch, and then our lips. How warm his flesh was against my own as we found each other on the forest floor.

I shall never forget the taste of Owen Phyne: salty and sweet on my tongue.

Words, so many words, come tumbling from our lips, braiding cords between our minds and our hearts. Stronger than any wedding band. Stronger than any fear of sin. Stronger, even, than my name written in blood, and a promise made by someone too young to take on a creature such as *her*. I shall admire Owen always for taking my revelation in stride, and even offering to help me care for the beast I had taken into my keep.

"To protect the town," he said.

"To protect ourselves," said I.

In the end, we could do neither.

I shall always miss Owen Phyne.

My mistress shows no mercy when the sadness is upon me. She can only see her own pain, her own useless sorrows. She is a selfish creature and never does anything but take.

Had I known her true nature sooner, I would have taken Owen's hand and fled. I would have left her in F— to do what she liked, and though my fate would still have been the same in the end, at least I would have led a good life before I came here. Instead, my years were all squandered on duty, on feeding the beast by my side.

The bitterness runs dark and thick in me, and all the years since I died have not lessened the pain one bit. I cannot truly blame my companion, though, as she sits there on her heap of filth: soda cans and beer bottles, bike tires, plastic bags, candy wrappers, and condoms, all of it things that have been thrown down in the well, and which she believes to be her offerings. She is what she is and lives according to her nature. Raging against her, I have come to realize, is as futile as cursing the moon or the stars. So instead, I blame Mother for offering her so carelessly, and my own young and foolish mind, who would rather enslave my soul than live without a servant.

I shall not forgive her for Owen, though. Had she not taken

him, my life might have been worth the price of serving her after. As things happened, however, I knew nothing but loss in my life, so I can hardly be blamed for enjoying the respite of harboring flesh and blood again, if only for a little while.

Elena has not resisted one bit, but willingly opened herself to me. She is nothing but an empty vessel, a ship adrift without direction. She *welcomed* me inside, without even attempting to fight. I chuckle just from thinking of it! She *revels* in having me there, in not having to be alone with her mind.

No one thought to warn her, I suppose, of the dangers of letting a stranger inside.

Not all that knock are pure of heart.

I know I will not find Owen in this world, but I still aim to try now that I have Elena. Mayhap there is another lover woven from the same threads—not the same man, of course, but close?

What I would not give to have a love like that again.

I have to be careful, however, as such strong desires can cloud one's judgment, and I am not truly there to search for my lost love, but to bring Elena to the well—to have her name written in blood. Yet the temptation runs in me like a wildfire. Surely there can be another of the same temper and heart?

We shall have to wait and see . . .

I think it makes my mistress jealous to see how smoothly I get along with Elena. Whenever she gets a piece of meat thrown down the well like a bone to a dog, she comes to me, all smug, and throws it down on the table before me, as if it somehow proves that *her* choice has been right all along.

"She doesn't even know why she does it anymore!" I cry then. "She doesn't even know why she feels so compelled! What sway you still have is thin and brittle, she only thinks of *me* now. They both do!"

My mistress does not like me saying that, but not because

she is vain. She only wants the other girl so much that no other girl will do. Personally, I cannot stomach that dreadful creature, and would rather that she did not meddle in my—or Elena's—affairs. She is angry and loud and her heart is bleeding.

Yet I boil the meat she brings for my mistress's table and throw out the empty bones. This is what I do—what I have *always* done. Then I braid my mistress's coarse hair and listen to her singing, which only grows shriller by the year. The beast is growing older as my soul is growing tired. Nothing but young, strong blood can make her flesh supple and smooth again, and start her life's cycle anew—surely she must see it herself, how urgent it is that we find another!

Yet she keeps calling for the one that will not have her—the one that denies her very existence. She cries bitter tears as she keens under the moon. If she had mastered a human tongue, it would have sounded like her lost girl's name, cried over and over again.

"Catherine, Catherine, Catherine . . ."

# 17

*Elena Clover's journal*

*June 8*

As it turns out, Cathy really *is* writing a book. After she was here, I just couldn't stop thinking about it, wondering if she was lying for some reason. I don't know why she would do something like that, but she isn't exactly stable, so I thought maybe she'd just read about *my* book and made something up to embarrass or annoy me.

It bothered me, though, *if* it were true. I didn't *want* it to bother me, but it did. I had been so convinced that no one but me gave one fig about Ilsbeth, and that it was sort of *heroic* what I did, taking on her story. It really seemed unlikely to me that there should be two of us with the very same idea at the very same time, years and years after Ilsbeth died. I mean, what are the odds? So yes, I thought for a moment that Cathy was lying.

She *is* very strange, after all.

The day after our unpleasant encounter on the lawn, I drove into town. It was actually pretty nice to see some other people. Living with Ilsbeth can be very intense, and I had almost forgotten what the rest of the world looks like and how to maneuver among living people. I had taken care with my get-up, too, ignoring Ilsbeth's craving for lace and putting on a chic purple summer dress and golden sandals. If someone had seen me out in the woods, running around in my mother's old nightgown, I wanted to take the opportunity to rectify their impression of me—especially if Cathy was running her mouth, painting *me* as the mad one.

I started my quest for Cathy's book at the grocery store, mostly because I wanted some bottled water. I've become quite the regular there over the last few weeks, and Marion, the bored teenager behind the counter, has proven again and again to be treasure trove of information about the goings-on in F—. She is duly impressed with me being a writer and treats me like a celebrity, which is embarrassing, but also kind of flattering. After I appeared in the *F— Daily*, she even wanted to take a selfie with me.

After we had chatted for a couple of minutes, I asked, "Do you know about another book being written about Ilsbeth Clark?"

Marion stared at me blankly for a moment. "No," she said at last. "Should I?" Something frantic had come into her eyes, as if she were terrified that some tidbit had escaped her vigilant attention.

"I don't know," I shrugged, grateful that I was the sole customer just then. Somehow just asking about it made me feel self-conscious. "I heard there was another book, written by Cathy Evans. But the journalist from the *F— Daily* never mentioned it to me when we did the interview."

"Oh." Something seemed to dawn on her. "You mean the project she has in the town archive? I never knew that was a book; only that she spends a lot of time down there. I never knew what she was doing, though."

"Do you know who might know a little more about it?"

Marion winked at me and laughed, "Are you checking out the competition?"

I didn't find the question very funny. "No! Not at all. I'm just curious to know what sort of book she is writing."

"I would ask Brian." Marion blew a bubblegum bubble.

"Cathy's son?"

"Uh-huh," she nodded. "That's how I know about it. We're friends."

"God, how old *is* he?"

"Sixteen," Marion informed me. "He's working at his grand-dad's abattoir this summer. You can probably catch him when he leaves in half an hour. He works early shifts this week."

"What does he look like?"

Marion pulled out her phone and scrolled for a minute, be-fore presenting me with a picture of Marion herself and a broad-shouldered young man with Bobby's hair and Cathy's eyes, squinting at the camera. "He is *very* tall," Marion said. "Very hard to miss. I'll send you the pic just in case."

In hindsight, I can see that talking to Cathy's *son* of all people was probably not the best idea, as it's bound to get back to her that I am snooping, but I didn't really have the time to think it over then. Before I knew it, I was back in my car, heading for the abattoir, which was situated a suitable distance from the town center.

When I was a kid, the abattoir was new and freshly painted a startlingly innocent white. Now it had turned gray and tired; the plaster crumbled and dusted the row of workers' cars that stood lined up outside the wall. Behind the building the woods began, thick and dark. I knew that if I slipped in among the ev-ergreens, and kept walking in a straight line, I would eventually come to the well, then the lake, and the castle. It had bothered me as a child, while lying in my bed, knowing that poor pigs and cows were killed just on the other side of the woods. Ilsbeth did not seem to mind, though, and made herself known for the first time since we left that morning, only to remind me how she dearly craved beef, and to maybe bring a few steaks home.

I still had a few minutes to spare after I parked, and spent them looking for the staff entrance, but when I didn't find any, I figured he'd come out the main door, which incidentally was painted a dusty red that reminded me of uncooked bacon. As I stood there, slightly uncomfortable with my water bottle, I remembered when Uncle John first told me on the phone that Cathy was getting married. *To the butcher's boy*, he said. I always thought that sounded sickening. I wondered if young Brian heard that as well. If he too was *the butcher's boy*, or if the old nickname had died.

The workers came straggling out after a while. Most of them were grown men with beards, checkered shirts, and sensible shoes. A few were Brian's age, or close; they had better haircuts and better-fitting jeans as well. Some others were women my age, in washed-out T-shirts and poorly dyed hair caught in stringy ponytails. All of their faces were pale and tired after a long, hard day of butchering. One by one, they found their cars and drove away so fast that the plaster dust on their hoods flew like confetti. New cars immediately took their place, a few family-friendly SUVs among them, ejecting a new set of workers. They looked like the same people, only less tired. Quite a few of them gave me curious glances as I stood there in my purple dress, trying to blend with the white-gray wall behind me. I don't think I succeeded.

Finally, I caught sight of him. He really was very tall, yet otherwise an unremarkable young man in jeans and a T-shirt with a faded print. Besides his eyes, he didn't look much like Cathy.

Brian was about to walk right past me while giving me the same strange look as his workmates. He had no idea who I was.

"Brian?" I took as step forth, nervously fiddling with my bottle. It was nearly empty by then. I'd been stress drinking all of it.

"Yes?" He paused and gave me a closer look. Then his blank

face slowly filled with some sort of realization—or maybe even *dread*. "Fuck, it's you." I'm sure he paled, though I didn't really get why. "You're Mom's old friend, aren't you? The one that wrote that book?"

I gave a nervous laugh. "I sure am." I tried to be flippant, but the boy didn't seem impressed; rather he seemed spooked.

"What are you doing here?" he asked, sounding almost accusatory. His ungainly teenage limbs were suddenly all over the place, kicking a stone, flexing his fingers . . .

It dawned on me then that he must have heard something—something *unkind* about me, and doubtlessly from Cathy. Maybe she'd been complaining about my Ilsbeth book.

"Your mom came to see me," I said. "She was pretty angry with me."

He shrugged. "What does that have to do with me?" He seemed utterly unsurprised that Cathy had been visiting to vent her ire.

"Oh, I just . . . I wanted to ask about something, and I don't think your mom wants to talk to me right now."

"Okay." The boy didn't look at me but up at the clear blue sky. "I probably shouldn't talk to you, though, if you have a beef with Mom."

"Well, I don't *want* to have one," I told him. "I think maybe it would be easier to be friends if I knew a little more about why she was so upset."

"Yeah?" He looked down at me through an unruly fringe.

"I just wondered if . . . if you know anything about a book she's writing." I held my breath while waiting for his answer, hoping *so* badly that it would prove to be a lie and that Cathy had no book in the making.

"You mean the one about Ilsbeth Clark?" Brian asked, and all my hopes plummeted and crashed. "Yeah, she's been working on that novel for a while now, down in the town archives. She was pretty upset when she read about *your* book." He gave me a slight smile, as if apologizing.

"Fuck." It just came out. I didn't mean to swear in front of a minor. "I'd been hoping it wasn't true," I tried to explain. "I didn't know she was writing about her too."

He gave another shrug. "Good luck convincing *her* of that. She seems to think everyone is out to get her."

"That must be hard." I felt an unexpected jolt of sympathy for Cathy's ungraceful boy.

"It is what it is." He kicked another pebble.

"Maybe it won't be so bad if our books are very different," I said. "Do you know what hers is about?"

"Not really . . . She's afraid that someone will take her ideas if she talks about it."

Of course she was. "Do you know what she's reading up on in the archives?" Maybe that could give me a clue.

"Just old boring things, court transcripts and letters. She says she's going to 'restore Ilsbeth's memory' by giving her a voice."

"Really?" That sounded a little too close to my own agenda, and to my own great dismay, my heart started racing in my chest.

Young Brian seemed oblivious to my discomfort. "Yeah, I think she wants to prove that Ilsbeth Clark wasn't a witch. As if *anyone* believes those old stories anymore," he snorted. "*Of course* she wasn't a witch—and everyone knows that the townspeople killed her for no good reason at all . . . She never had anything to do with those missing kids."

"Is that really what people think?" I was genuinely surprised.

"Sure. But Mom still wants to prove it." He paused and bit his lip, looking very young and very vulnerable all of a sudden.

"Don't be too hard on her, okay? She didn't deal too well with the divorce, and—well, this Ilsbeth thing makes her happy. She just feels a little threatened, that's all."

"Yeah, I get that," and I did, but I still just couldn't let it go. "But does she have a deal with someone? Like a publisher? I'm sorry," I added when I saw his confused expression. "I'm just trying to gauge how serious she is about this thing."

"As serious as you, I'd think, but she doesn't have a deal as far as I know. I don't think she's even thought about that yet. She just wants to write the story." He added a disarming smile. I could see that his legs had grown restless again, moving on the ground. I knew I couldn't keep him for much longer.

"But is she thinking of distributing the novel only here in F—, or is she thinking bigger?"

"I'm sorry." He threw out his arms. "I really don't know, and I really have to go. I shouldn't be talking to you at all. She'd think I was fraternizing with the enemy." He paused to scratch his chin. "Just go easy on her, okay?"

"Of course I will," I said. "I have no interest in a fight."

"Don't let her provoke you either," he said over his shoulder as he headed toward a decent-looking car.

"Of course not," I replied, though it was far too late for that. I was already utterly, irrevocably provoked.

It was with heavy heart that I found my own car and sped away from the abattoir. All the way back to the castle, Ilsbeth laughed inside me, thinking us mortals silly, perhaps.

I have to say, though, that I strongly disapprove of Cathy's agenda—it's not what Ilsbeth wants! *She* wants to have her magic revealed to everyone and for people to know what a witch really *is*. She never asked to become a history lesson, a cautionary tale from a very weird woman who doesn't *get* Ilsbeth one bit. Thinking about it now, I figure Ilsbeth maybe chose me just *because* of Cathy . . . Maybe Ilsbeth knew what nonsense she was up to down in those dusty archives and decided to tell the story herself, using me as a conduit. It does make sense, though Ilsbeth herself won't tell me shit, but I think that perhaps I get it now, how important it is that Ilsbeth gets her say before Cathy comes trampling all over her story, obscuring the truth forever.

To be honest, it almost feels like a violation, as if Cathy is trespassing onto my turf and invading my space—like she's about to *rob* me! I know she doesn't have a publisher or anything, and that her book is probably poorly written crap, but with me and Ilsbeth being so close, it really bothers me a lot. It's like she's taking something holy and dragging it through the mud! Like she's making a mockery out of my experience—which is powerful and profound, and can change *so* many lives!

She's trying to put her stamp on something that never belonged to her.

What does Cathy know about Ilsbeth? Absolutely nothing! Whatever "facts" she has gathered down in that basement are nothing but sticks to build a fragile house that won't stand for long without a SOUL to make it strong—*Ilsbeth's* SOUL—which lives in me!

I'm trying to take comfort in that.

Ilsbeth chose *me,* not Cathy.

### June 10

Oh, Ilsbeth is growing stronger! She isn't just my passenger anymore but has power in her own right, and her magic is manifesting in the world around us more and more each day! It's glorious and amazing, and I can't do anything but move with the currents she's set in motion, take my cues and follow through. It's what she wants me to do.

Today I seduced the plumber!

I know, I know, it's a pretty big deal and I shouldn't be so flippant about it, but it's not exactly as it seems. And yes, the cliché does not escape me: lonely woman seduces workman, the only thing missing is a pair of fuzzy slippers on my freshly pedicured feet, and a fat wedding ring sparkling on my finger, and the set will be complete.

It's nothing like that, though.

His name is Will Morris and he's actually been coming and going for a few days already, but before yesterday he was just the plumber. I was immensely happy to see him, of course, even if I hate having workers in the house. The pipes aren't getting any better, and the whole upper floor smells a bit like sewer, so it was absolutely a godsend that he could make time for me. He has diagnosed the problem ("Old pipes, should have been replaced many years ago. I'm surprised the basement hasn't flooded already.") and has given me a sickening estimate of just how much that will cost. Thankfully, there's still money in the estate.

He is handsome, in a rugged way, with golden brown hair and a square jaw; quite fit, too, so he must be working out. He has a roaring lion tattooed on his shoulder because he is a Leo and a rose on his hip because his first girlfriend's name was Rose. He wears worn jeans and an array of solid-color T-shirts, which is a relief as I really can't stomach T-shirts with prints. On the first day he was here, his shirt was red, and then blue, orange, and, yesterday, indigo. Will is quite the rainbow!

At first, I only thought it comforting to hear him putter about upstairs, doing whatever plumbers do. Sometimes he'd come down for a break and I'd offer him cans of soda and a snack. I'd bring him outside to the cherry tree and install him in one of the old wrought-iron chairs, while admiring the slick fall of hair on his forehead. I really can't blame him for the latter; these are hot days and the bathroom is cramped. It doesn't even help to leave the window open. He is easy company, though, so I often stayed out there with him during the breaks, talking about F——, the castle, and my life in the city. Ilsbeth didn't seem to mind that at all, but curled up as content as a kitten in the sun whenever our plumber was near. It wasn't until yesterday I figured out just why that was.

*Everything* was different yesterday.

It started early in the morning, just after breakfast (oats today—I gave in to Ilsbeth's demands), and I was just pouring a glass of raspberry lemonade when I heard the fragile tunes of a flute coming in through the open windows. It was so eerie and so beautiful that I broke out in goosebumps.

Will arrived just then, stood there in the kitchen with his battered toolbox, decently dressed in the indigo shirt, unlike me, who was still in my sleeping wear: an oversized T-shirt with holes on one shoulder that used to be charcoal but had faded to ash.

"What is it? Is something wrong, Ms. Clover?" he asked, though I'd told him to call me Elena, and he usually did as well.

"No—not wrong, no! Do you hear that?" I asked him. "Do you hear the music?"

"Sure," he nodded his pretty head. "Sounds like someone is having a music lesson in the woods."

"Yes, it's beautiful, don't you think?"

"Sure is."

When he had gone upstairs to start working, I waited for an appropriate amount of time, and then I followed with a pitcher of lemonade, just to keep him company. I did help, too, sometimes, though he told me I really didn't have to. It just seemed stupid to let him tear down the ancient wall all by himself, its boards all soft and black with rot, when I'm absolutely capable of handling a crowbar. Besides, the sooner we get to those pipes, the sooner I'll have a working toilet.

I found him on the green linoleum floor, wedged between the sink and the bathtub, hands deep inside the interior of the wall. There wasn't much to see from where I stood just inside the door, only some rusty pipes and woodwork, but I could see *him*: the indigo T-shirt riding high on his stomach, exposing a trail of that honey brown hair. The single window in the wall was open, and a gentle breeze played with the white muslin curtain. The music went on, rising and falling. Sometimes it was quiet, and then it would be back again, flowing so prettily in through the window.

"I know that tune from somewhere, I just can't remember where," Will mused down on the floor, and I suddenly remembered a story from one of my library books, about Owen Phyne, who rode in the woods while playing the flute.

"Do you know how to play?" I asked him.

"Just from school," he grinned and blushed some.

"It's a sad melody," I said.

"It's about longing," said Will. "That much even I can tell."

"Longing for what, do you think?"

"A woman, most likely." He shrugged and picked a pair of tongs out of his banged-up toolbox. "One you cannot have."

"Why can't you have her?" I held my breath.

"Oh, she's probably married or something." He gave an embarrassed laugh.

It was then I realized that the spell Ilsbeth and I did had *worked*, and that Will, somehow, *was also* Owen Phyne, called back to life through the decades. It was also then I realized what I had to do—what Ilsbeth *wanted* me to do!

"Maybe she isn't," I said, moving a little closer. "Maybe she isn't unattainable at all."

"Really?" He looked up at me surprised, with an itsy-bitsy smirk curving his luscious lips.

I gently put the pitcher and the stacked glasses down on the floor and knelt beside him. Then I cupped his face in my hands and kissed him softly on the lips. His skin was a little damp, as he'd been hard at work before I arrived, and smelled faintly of sweat and the vanilla-scented soap from the dispenser by the basin. The music was all around us as a gentle ebb and flow. When I kissed him again, he wound a hand in my hair and pulled me closer. His breath was hot against my skin, his lips so very soft.

As I straddled his hips on the ancient linoleum, it really did feel like a homecoming—as if I had brought Ilsbeth back where she belonged. I don't know if it felt the same for Will, but he certainly didn't have a bad time. In fact, he said it was the best workday he'd ever had, but was also quick to point out that he wouldn't bill me for those hours we spent tumbling, first on the bathroom floor, and later in my bed.

I don't think this is reincarnation exactly, but I do think Owen lives in him now, just as Ilsbeth lives in me, and that through our union they are reunited too. I've been alone for some time now, and my stupid engagement didn't end well, so it's nice to be close to a man again. If it makes Ilsbeth happy too, nothing could be better.

What a book this strange journey will make when we write it—what an experience to render on paper (or screen)! Not many people are lucky enough to have the kind of adventures I've just had, and I feel so immensely privileged! I'm about to cry now just from thinking about it. Who would have thought the world could look like this, brimming with possibilities, because it really is that different from what we've always thought. It has all been true all along; the SOUL survives death and lives on,

MAGIC exists and so do witches. The world will be *floored* when my book comes out! I almost feel like a prophet in the making, chosen to spread the new word! In my head, I'm already planning what to wear to talks. I'm thinking pale blue or white, as not to invoke the gothic trope, and silver for a hint of mystery. I know Ilsbeth would prefer a bustle skirt, but I somehow don't think that will fly.

I've almost not thought about Cathy and her shitty book at all. Almost not thought of the *assault* (for that was what it felt like when she showed up outside). I'm trying to pretend that she doesn't exist, and considering how pathetic she's become, that *should* be easier than it actually is!

## June 16

This morning when I came downstairs, there were at least a dozen moths in the living room. I didn't see them at first, since it was daylight and they sat perched upon the furniture or hung in the curtains, but when I went to close the window, three of them lifted in a flurry of dusty wings. It was only then that I looked around and saw the rest of them, like little planchettes strewn about.

I read in one of the library books, *Strange Stories and Legends from F—*, that one of the reasons why Ilsbeth was suspected of having something to do with the missing children was that the windows in her bedroom were often crowded with moths. That doesn't have anything to do with kidnapping, of course, but her contemporaries saw it as a sign of witchcraft, which Ilsbeth now tells me is accurate. They are drawn to MAGIC, she says, as much as they are drawn to the light. I realize why the people back then, poisoned by both science and religion, might have found it frightening, but I myself find it thrilling. It's as good as solid proof that Ilsbeth is here and the MAGIC is real.

Why else would these lovely creatures come to say hello?

The house is no place for them, though, so I went to find an empty glass jar and a piece of cardboard ripped from the back of a cereal box, and set to gently removing them, one by one, and dropping them outside the window. I think I got most of them; there was only one that I could see that clung so high up on the bookshelf that I couldn't reach it.

The day continued to be magical: Will came to see me after work, and the two of us set out into the woods. He had told me he hadn't seen the well since he was a kid, and I thought that wouldn't do for Owen Phyne's mortal vessel.

Both the woods and the well showed themselves from their prettiest side today, flooded with sunlight. There was no eerie flute music, but the birds chirped in the trees, and everything smelled warm and green. We passed by the lake on the way, and I wondered if the boat was still there. If it is, and still floats, I might take Will out one night. We could make a picnic of it, out there on the water.

It was another sort of hunger I wanted to sate today, however. Both for Ilsbeth's sake and my own. As soon as we entered the clearing by the well, I made that obvious to my fresh-minted lover.

"It's a little morbid, don't you think?" he said as I tugged on his shirt, wanting to pull it over his head. "Doing it *here*, where it happened."

"*She* used to bring her lover here," I retorted and pulled the garment off. "Maybe it's just what this place needs, more love and less sad memories."

"Other people have died here as well." Something haunted had come into his eyes. "People come here to kill themselves."

"My point still stands." I caught his gaze in mine. "We can't change the past, and as romantic spots go, I think this one is amazing." I gave him my best smile and rose up to kiss him.

"Maybe we could do it by the lake instead," he suggested when our lips parted.

"Too many hikers and dog walkers." I shimmied out of my underwear, kicking the sensible cotton briefs into a blackberry thicket. "This is just perfect," I declared, and though the ground was very cold and smelled of mushrooms, it really, truly was. I think Will agreed too, after a while, forgetting his initial worries. Who can think about death and suicide when the sun is shining and flowers are blooming, and naked bodies are turning slick with salt?

No one I can think of.

When we got back to the castle, we ate shrimp and drank wine in the garden while watching the sunset over the treetops, rendering the sky blue and gold. A few moths came diving then too, dancing around the electric lantern. The air was still warm and fragrant, the dusk like a balm to the senses. When Will went inside to use the (perfectly functioning) toilet, I even had a surprise guest!

At first, I couldn't tell what it was, as I only saw a flash of pale drifting between the trees. My first thought—a stupid one—was that it was a person dressed up as a ghost, old-style, with a sheet. Then I thought it was a white deer for a moment, but it turned out to be a horse, so white that it almost seemed luminescent in the scant light.

It paused just where the woods meet the lawn and looked at me with dark eyes before stretching its neck like a swan. I knew right away that it belonged to someone, as I could see several braids worked into its snowy mane. For a moment, it just stood there watching me, and I, half-drunk, stared back, admiring its sleek form.

When Will closed the door to the house on his way back outside, I could see the horse's ears twitch, and then it took off, slipping in between the firs.

It didn't hit me before it was gone that the lovely thing could be a runaway. I'll ask Marion who it belongs to when I go to the store tomorrow, or maybe put up a note on the board by the entrance.

It really was a pretty thing. I wish I'd been able to take a picture.

*June 19*

Something really bad happened today. Really, really bad! I think I might be in shock still, but I also think I have to write it down just so I can wrap my head around it!

This morning started out just as magical as the last few days, with another eclipse of moths in the living room. This marked the fourth day in a row. I had also just discovered in *Strange Stories and Legends from F—* that Ilsbeth was said to be followed around by a magical white horse, and I was immensely excited by that fact, seeing that I had another nocturnal visit in the garden last night. This time, the horse came just as I was heading back inside after having lingered under the cherry tree while speaking to Will on the phone. It stopped just shy of the lawn like before, and it kept looking at me with those glossy black eyes. We stood there for quite some time, silently communicating across the expanse of grass, but when I lifted my phone to take a picture, it abruptly turned around and was off.

I regretted it at once, of course, trying to take that picture; it was dusky outside so it was bound to be grainy, but it was only to have something to put on the note for the grocery store. I had talked to Marion about the horse, but she didn't know who it belonged to, and so I was just trying to do my civic duty to reunite the poor animal with its owner, not knowing at that point that the owner might actually be *me*—or *Ilsbeth-in-me,* more accurately.

However that was, my mood was excellent when I stepped outside with my breakfast cereal to enjoy it in the garden, and almost stepped in something furry and brown draped across the stairs. At first, my mind couldn't make sense of what I saw: it was just too grisly. I went through several possibilities in my head: a roll of rotting cloth or a piece of old wood, before I had to accept what it truly was: a dead animal on the stairs.

I yelped and dropped the cereal bowl, which only made matters worse, with milk, ceramic shards and soggy grains showering the poor animal's matted fur and the cakes of dried blood. I danced on the stairs as if stepping on hot coals, making animal sounds myself. My heart was racing like crazy. I just didn't know what to do! I could tell by then that it was a rabbit; its long and yellow front teeth quickly gave that away.

Its gaze was void as it stared up on the sky.

With a shivering hand, I fished the phone from the pocket of my shorts and called Will. "A rabbit died on my stairs," I said when he answered. "It just died in front of my door! There's blood and everything—"

"Blood? Is it shot?"

"I don't know—"

"Was it shot on your stairs?"

"I don't know!" Just thinking about it made me feel cold. "Maybe it was hurt and came crawling up here for help?" I suggested.

"Not very likely," said Will. "I'll take an early lunch and come out."

After ending the call, I promptly went back inside and watched the yard from the kitchen window, averting my gaze from the stairs all the while. When I saw Will's blue truck come up the driveway, I was dizzy with relief. He parked and stepped gingerly toward the stairs, as if the poor animal would suddenly spring back to life and possibly attack.

When he had had an eyeful, he stepped across the carcass and came inside.

"Are you okay?" he asked when he entered the kitchen and put his arms around my waist.

"Shaken." I tried to laugh, but sounded mostly like a hoarse frog.

"We should bury it as soon as possible," he stated. "It reeks a bit, didn't you notice?"

I shook my head against his shoulder. "Can we just bury it anywhere? Aren't there rules about these things?"

"No, we can just bury it anywhere." He sounded slightly amused.

"Why did it die on my stairs?" I asked him, though, of course, he didn't know.

"I think it's very strange," he said. "We'll see what we find when we turn it over."

Never in my life have I been so happy to have someone to call for help. I usually scoff at the damsel in distress whenever she appears in a book or a movie, but just today, I was in dire need. Not in need of *a man* necessarily, but of *someone* who could find a shovel in the basement and dig a hole in the woods and help me get rid of the bloody thing, because I myself was useless. I waited in the kitchen while Will dug the grave, but stepped outside so as not to appear a total loser when he came back to the yard.

I didn't look down when I stepped across the rabbit.

Will prodded the dead animal a few times with the shovel before taking aim. I stood to the side of the stairs with my knuckles pressed to my collarbone, holding my breath.

"This is clearly roadkill, Elena," he said as he scooped the poor rabbit onto the shovel blade. "Look," he pointed to the animal's side and I pretended to see, all the while looking at the doorstep instead. "You can even see the tire marks."

"Uh-huh," I nodded my head with vigor, still not looking.

"Someone must have put it there."

That got my attention. "Why?" I was utterly befuddled. "Why would someone do something like that?"

"Beats me," he shrugged while still holding out the shovel, balancing the milk-and-cereal-spattered rabbit on the blade.

"Maybe it's a warning." It was the first thing that sprang to mind.

"A warning about what?" His eyebrows rose.

"I don't know—about Ilsbeth perhaps. Maybe they don't want me to write the book."

Will shook his head as he started walking toward the hole in the ground, and I trailed behind him. "F— is a quiet place. We don't generally put horse's heads in each other's beds, or—"

"Maybe they don't like that an outsider is here meddling," I suggested. "People are very weird."

"It *is* strange," he agreed. "That rabbit didn't land on the stairs by itself. It's been dead for a while, too, judging by the smell."

It was then that it all clicked into place. I don't know why it took me so long. Maybe dealing with the roadkill had slowed my brain.

"I know who did this," I said.

## June 20

When Will came after work yesterday, he was on foot, as we had decided it was better if his truck wasn't in the yard. We spent the night in the tower room, eating olives and chunks of white bread, flushing it all down with raspberry lemonade instead of wine, as neither of us wanted to be drunk for the event. Every so often, one of us would look out the windows to see if we could catch someone creeping around the house. When it got dark, Will whipped out his night binoculars, which he had brought from home, and I felt like quite the spy, kneeling on the bench with breadcrumbs in my hair and looking out on the garden.

It wasn't until then that I realized I hadn't felt Ilsbeth all day. Even when I reached out to her, she just didn't respond. This was incredibly worrying, and I found myself wondering if the dead rabbit was some sort of counter spell. Maybe it was a curse laid down to quiet Ilsbeth's spirit. I felt incredibly alone all of a sudden, even if Will was there by my side, solid, warm, and brimming with reason.

If the dead critter really was an attack on Ilsbeth, I hoped that our plan would somehow counteract it.

It just wouldn't do to lose her now, after all we had been through.

Will and I had set the scene downstairs, making it look like just another night. We had hosed down the front stairs, though, and picked up the shards from the cereal bowl. I just couldn't stomach seeing the stains on the steps. It didn't matter, though. Any reasonable person would clean up the mess, so it shouldn't set off any alarm bells for the culprit.

Will and I played checkers to pass the time, and when we grew bored of that, we fooled around on the ice-cold floor like a pair of giddy teenagers. We couldn't have proper sex, though, as we were still keeping watch.

It was well after midnight before anything happened. Will was at the windows just then, crouching on the bench with the binoculars. Suddenly, his body straightened with alert and he waved me over. I rose as quietly as I could, took the binoculars when he handed them to me, and lifted them to my eyes. The lawn sprawled out before me, black and white, and just by the edge of the woods, a small silhouette in a hooded jacket was creeping toward the house.

"It's time," Will whispered. "We have to go *now*."

We made our way down the two sets of stairs hand in hand like children, and didn't stop before we had crossed the creaking kitchen floor and were looking in on the night-dark living room.

Will positioned himself just inside the open door with one hand on the light switch, while I snuck as quietly as I could to the deep shadows by the bookshelves, keeping the windows in view. The white curtains fluttered in the draft. A twig snapped outside. The window to the left groaned and complained as it was forced more open on stiff and rusty hinges. Will and I exchanged a look across the room; my belly felt taut with excitement, and my hands around my phone were slick with perspiration.

A pale hand came in through the window, holding a mason jar. Inside the glass, I could see the flutter of gray wings. Quick as lighting, I whipped up my phone and pressed the red "record" button, just as Will flipped the switch and flooded the room in light. I ran to the widow, phone held high, and pulled the curtain aside. Cathy looked pale and wide-eyed when she stared up at me through the open window. She was hurriedly retracting her hand, but then Will was there beside me and swung the window shut, trapping the glass jar inside. She howled with pain, though it could hardly have been that bad, and before she'd regained her wits enough to drop the jar and free her hand, I'd had ample time to record her.

The jar, still with a few confused moths inside, dropped to

the floor and rolled to a stop against my toes. Cathy screeched like a banshee, from disappointment I suppose, before turning on her heels and running across the lawn, heading for the woods.

I heard the front door open and close as Will ran outside as well, meaning to catch the retreating bitch.

"You're fucking crazy, Cathy Evans!" I screamed after her through the window. "I'll fucking get you for this, you maniac!"

Will entered the garden just as Cathy disappeared from view, swallowed up by woods and darkness. He still tried to catch her, though, and sprinted quickly out of my sight.

He was gone for at least thirty minutes before turning back empty-handed. The night was too dark and the woods too vast. I have some glorious footage on my phone, though, with her face clearly in view, so she won't get away with this! She won't!

I'll see to it that she regrets it for the rest of her life!

# 18

*Transcript from the Nicksby Documents*

"It is you, is it not?" I cry at my mistress when I return to the burrow from a visit with Elena. I stand on the dirt floor with my hands at my side and stare at her as she sits there, surrounded by all her rubbish. "You have your foolish girl run fool's errands around the woods." Child's pranks—silliness, but it upsets Elena and we surely cannot have that. She ought to be spending all her time learning the secrets I have revealed to her. How else will I get her to sign? She is slipping, though, drifting away. Sometimes I cannot enter her at all, as her flesh is flooded with the sweetness of love and the rushing waves of anger—both anchoring her to the world around her, turning her to the mundane. This worries me greatly, as it is just what happened with Catherine, and with others, too, before her. Once the world takes a hold, they slip away, turning their minds from the well.

My mistress pauses her eager polishing of steel screws to shake her large head and let me know it was not her. She smiles at me between thick tendrils of gray hair. Her faceted blue eyes light up the dim darkness of the small room we inhabit. Her presence in my mind is like a gentle breeze, a rustling in wizened leaves. Her soft chuckling reminds me of a bubbling brook, pooling up from the earth, dark and poisoned. She is amused by her favorite's antics. She thinks it proves that her girl still loves her the best.

"It is *me* they fight over," I tell her. "Your girl doesn't even think that you exist anymore."

She shrugs at this. She does not believe me. She does not *want* to think that it is true. In my mind, she displays a series of pictures: a cutlet, a lamb shank, a pink and tender pig roast. Gifts she has gotten before. She also shows me a silver spoon and a bicycle handle, a candlestick shaped like a heart, and a wrench.

"I do not believe that she gave you that wrench," I say and slump down in my chair at the table; it is a rickety thing, made to fold out and with a seat of dirty striped canvas. My anger quickly fades, as I know it is useless. My mistress only sees what she wants to see and does not always understand. Of all the things that have eaten at me over the years, her thick-headedness has bothered me the most. How can something so fierce be so dull?

"I know you left the burrow," I say. "And not to hunt." This almost never happens anymore. It has become a rare occurrence. I know that has much to do with me. Before I died, all she could think of was her loneliness and sorrow, and I came to believe early on that taking her from her flock had perhaps not been a good thing. Mayhap the daemons thrive better in a pack. Now that she is not alone anymore, she does not often venture up to seek out company, but is happy to stay at home in peace. Before death, I would have been relieved by this, as it surely protects the townspeople, but now I am not much inclined to take pity on those folks, and so the relief escapes me. In fact, I would not much mind if she *did* peek her head up more often. It sure would serve them right.

I would rather she stayed away from Elena, though.

"What do you think you can accomplish by visiting Nicksby?" I ask her. "Elena is not so easily scared; she has *me* there with her. I am showing her our ways." My hand is restless, drumming out a jittery melody against the metal of the chair.

The beast sniggers at my words; it is a hoarse sound, like wind in naked branches. She lets me know, in her mocking way, that she has no faith in my ploy.

"Your girl is only bothering Elena because she wants to keep *me* to herself," I say in petty retort. "She wants to tell the world my story—they *both* do, hence their fight."

My mistress yawns, bored with my bragging. She pats her round white belly lightly with her fingertips. She is hungry again. She always is.

"Nothing but frogs," I warn her. "There is nothing but frogs in the well today." She looks very mournful at this tidbit. "If your girl loves you as well as you think, surely she would fill it with steaks." I cannot help but try to irk her. Sometimes the calm of her old age bothers me even more than the rage of her youth did. Back then, she only wanted to play, and would go to great lengths to amuse herself. Owen and I had to work at all hours to keep her somewhat satisfied. One would think that it was better now, when the playfulness has worn off, but it is not. Rather the trickle of time is a curse where nothing happens and nothing is done. I would rather go out like a candle flame than live in such a state.

"I'm sure Elena would feed you steaks every day," I try to tempt her to give up her foolish allegiance to her girl. "Elena would braid your hair and pick fresh flowers. She would bring you all the silver in the world."

The beast does not heed me at all, but makes a soft keening sound to express her hunger.

"Very well," I sigh and get to my feet, start looking for the copper pan. I have a stick for catching frogs with; it is black from years of use. Frog's blood is slick and sticks to the wood.

I get to work with a frown and a tangled heart, as my mistress and her girl's undue meddling is not all that has me in a foul mood. Besides Elena's recent distractedness, my attempt to find another Owen has badly failed. The worker who came to Nicksby had showed such promise, but in the end, he was nothing like Owen Phyne. Elena still believes that they are one and the same, though, as I planted that thought in her head early on—and now I simply cannot take it back. She has fastened on that idea like a fly on horseshit, and since she never knew the real Owen, I simply cannot persuade her to let that notion go, even if the man is useless and only turns her mind from the well. She forgets all about me when he is around—all she can think of is sating her flesh and basking in his company. Loneliness can make fools of us all, but truly, one would think that a knowledge of the hidden world would trump a lover's caress?

Men come and go, while my gift to her is rare and highly underappreciated as it stands. Yet I let myself be blinded by my desire to find another Owen Phyne, and so I suppose it only serves me right to be waylaid by the power of her passion.

I do not like it one bit, though. It is not how this was supposed to go. Elena ought to be on her knees at the well by now, eager to put a bloody pen to paper, but instead, she is frolicking on cotton sheets and serving her lover lemonade by the pitcher—and yet the girl is all that I have. She is still my only way out.

I better work harder, faster.

# 19

*Excerpt from* Ilsbeth in the Twilight,
*by Catherine Evans*

### XIII. The Disappearance of Margaret Thomas

That spring, I finally took Owen's worry to heart and made a conscious effort to remedy my undeserved bad reputation among the townspeople. I knew this was wise, although I could not help but rage against the injustice of it. What had I ever done to them but been a stranger? Surely it was not my fault that Nicksby owned the land that they lived on, or that they rented their labor to the farm, so why was it I, and not Archibald, who was resented for it? Could it be that it was merely my youth—or my perceived beauty—that was to blame?

However that was, I did not like the rumors any better than Owen did. It was very unfortunate that we had been seen by the well, locked in a lovers' embrace, and though Archibald thought very little of peasants and would surely not pay the whisperings any heed, he was also no fool, and so I was surely worried. I did not want Owen's good name to be tainted by a scandal on my account, and I did not want the unpleasantness of Archibald's rage unleashed upon either of us. I figured there perhaps was wisdom in Owen's advice that people would gossip less if they liked me a little more.

I thought long and hard about what I could offer to do good in the community, and found that of all my honed talents, fine needlework—embroidery—was a skill often sought by women of standing. Knowing such an art would surely open doors for the young girls of F— should they wish to leave our humble town and seek service elsewhere. Since my own marriage had been such a disappointment, I thought it important to equip women with the skills to always have options other than home and hearth. Many a woman has walked the aisle simply because there was no other choice, and very little happiness stems from such unions. It surely felt like a worthy cause, and so my little circle came about.

I invited all the young girls from the surrounding farms to come to Nicksby every Tuesday afternoon, and equipped them with needles and thread. We sat in the blue salon, on straight-backed chairs, the likes of which I thought none of the girls had ever sat on before. They marveled at the furniture's white finish, the velvet upholstery and the gilded details, and relished drinking tea from china cups. They felt like quite the little ladies, I think, while sitting there in their rough woven skirts, threading the needles with calloused hands. There were thirteen of them in all—an unlucky number—ranging from age five through fourteen. The older girls were more skilled, of course, but then the younger ones had the benefit of early learning. They would surely be excellent seamstresses in time. After our first session, my new maid, Evelyn James, served them little jam-filled tarts, and judging from the bliss on their little faces, I felt sure that it would help to remedy my somewhat tainted reputation in F—.

Owen told me later that they scoffed, though, after church. Not the girls, of course, who were perfectly pleasant, but their parents. They thought it a waste of hours for their daughters to attend my embroidery circle, and had it not been for Archibald owning the land they lived on, they would never have encouraged such folly. This grieved me, of course, as it was not the intended outcome, but by then, the girls' education had become important to me, and I tried to cheer myself up by thinking on how greatly my lessons would broaden their prospects.

"You have a kind heart, Ilsbeth," Owen said to me as we met in the darkness by the well, ever more cautious now not to be seen, after the unfortunate event when Carl Morris came upon us. "Just make sure that warm heart of yours does not burn you," he warned me, and I had cause to think of those words many a time after Margaret Thomas went missing.

Of all the children who frequented Nicksby, young Margaret was always my favorite. The girl had such a sunny disposition, and a head full of nut-brown curls. Naturally, the girl was a part of my circle, but since Ella in the kitchen was her aunt, she quite often came to see me on other days as well. I would spoil the girl with treats, have her sit for a sketch, or try to teach her the piano. She was six years old when she disappeared, and her misfortune shook me greatly.

It was a fine day in June when Margaret came to Nicksby to barter for eggs on behalf of her mother. Ella accommodated her in the kitchen, served her some milk, and saw her leave with an apron full of smooth, brown eggs. In trade, Ella had taken a couple of pigeons for the Nicksby kitchen, poached no doubt on Nicksby grounds, but Archibald rarely fined for such trespasses, thinking them a little beneath him. No one at Nicksby knew that the girl had gone missing until later, when a ruckus in the kitchen disturbed me just as I was readying myself for bed.

"Will you see what it is about?" I asked Evelyn when I could see several lanterns moving in the yard through the window.

Evelyn put down her needlework and rose from her seat at once, and I anxiously awaited her return, feeling already then that something was terribly amiss.

When Evelyn returned, her pale visage set my heart aflutter in my chest. "What is it?" I asked at once. "Speak, woman, what did they say?"

"It's little Margaret Thomas," she replied in a shivering voice. "She never came home from Nicksby today, and now they fear something might have happened to her."

"Happened? What do they think has happened?" I did not even care if my voice rose a little. The fear for the girl was sudden and strong, and licked at my insides with fiery lashes.

"They speak of a bear . . ." Evelyn sounded uncertain.

"A bear?" I was as puzzled as the maid. "There have not been bears in these woods for quite some time." Archibald often boasted of that fact, having taken most of them out himself, dragging the cubs out from hibernation to slay them on the ground.

"Yet it is what they suggest. The eggs she carried were found crushed by the Nicksby well," Evelyn informed me. "Her parents did not rise the alarm at once, thinking the girl had been sidetracked on her way home, although they noted how it was unusual for Margaret to stray when she knew that her mother was waiting. But Mrs. Thomas has six other children to care for," she added, as if to excuse the mother's negligence. "It was only when she did not arrive home for supper that they started to worry about her whereabouts."

I swiftly rose to my feet, nearly toppling in my haste. "Have them ready my horse," I declared. "I must join the search at once!"

We did not find her, though, even if we traversed the woods all night, calling her name, and shone a light down every ravine and hollow. We even searched the soft dirt around the lake for footprints, but the girl remained utterly lost.

# Fall

# 20

*An open letter to the people of F——, continued*

I think it is appropriate that I say a few words about mine and Elena's so-called dispute, since it—*by error*—has become such a big part of the ongoing investigation. I have tried to tell the authorities many, many times that the disagreement was minor and really of no consequence, and absolutely *not* connected to what happened to Elena. I do see why they would look to me, of course, having Elena's own words on file. It also doesn't help, I suppose, that I was the one to discover her body, but I assure you—again—that it was merely a coincidence.

I was only going to scare her a little. That was the whole plan. I never meant to cause any real damage. I just wanted her to pack up and go, or at least leave Ilsbeth alone. I figured it wouldn't be all that hard to chase her off; she might be speaking to her soul (or allegedly so), but I suspected that she was a coward at heart. If only she was nudged in the right direction, I felt certain that she would abandon both her book and poor Ilsbeth in a heartbeat. That was how she was, after all. You only had to look at how our adolescent friendship had played out to know; one moment we were sisters and the next, I was nothing. I callously exploited that weakness of hers, but I never thought it would have any serious consequences. All I did, after all, was to protect my own work and Ilsbeth's reputation. Life is like that sometimes; you have to play dirty to get what you want.

I honestly can say that it was innocent at first. I figured that Elena would have heard the better-known stories about Ilsbeth, or more accurately: the hostile rumors. She would have heard about the lost children of F—, about Owen Phyne, the little dolls and the moths that beat their wings against Ilsbeth's window. My first little "prank" was nothing at all. I found Brian's old recorder in a cardboard box in the attic and brought it out into the woods. Seated on a tree stump close to the castle, I dusted off my limited musical skills and played a little. That was all. I was banking on Elena having heard the story of how Owen Phyne rode through the woods playing a flute, and wanted her to make the connection. If she did, I'll never know, but at least that little charade of mine made *me* feel better for a while.

I felt like I was taking control of the situation.

Looking back, I realize that scaring a mentally unwell woman was perhaps not a wise course of action, but on the other side, just the fact that she harbored such "magical" delusions made me even more convinced that she should never be allowed to write a book about Ilsbeth. I have to admit, though, that her state of mind also made me satisfied that the ruse could actually work. Wicked, I know, but I swore to be honest, so that is what I'll be.

I spent about a week like that, driving out and playing in the woods. I always parked my car out of sight on the old dirt road where Bobby and I used to make out. It might seem like a worthless endeavor to you, but my intentions were nothing but sincere.

I really, really wanted her gone.

It was not as if I had much else to occupy my time, either. School was out for summer, and Brian preferred to stay with Bobby. No one cared what I did with my days and so I was free to do as I liked. I felt quite the crusader, to be honest, fighting a righteous battle for Ilsbeth Clark's tarnished honor.

I always brought a thermos of tea with me and sandwiches in a lunch box. I brought cookies, too, and split them with a squirrel that sometimes came to see me, as I sat there on my tree stump.

It didn't like the playing, however, and quickly ran away once I started. I don't think I've ever spent as much time outdoors as I did this summer, and I doubtlessly benefited from it. A bad cough I had been struggling with for months disappeared, and my skin looked healthy and radiant. I also had ample time to observe the wildlife. Besides the squirrel, I saw several deer, one fox, and even a few dusty rabbits.

Sometimes I walked by the well, too, just to be in its presence, or visited my father's old farm, though there are new owners there now so I stayed on the outskirts of the fields. They don't grow oats anymore, only pumpkins. I don't miss the farm in the way I miss the castle, though. Nothing much good ever happened there.

After several days of playing in the woods, I was forced to admit that my little prank had likely not worked, because Elena was still at the castle, and according to her social media, she was still meaning to write her horrible book. It was then that I figured I had to bring in some more powerful cannons, or "up my game," as they say.

It was then that I thought of the moths.

The stories of Ilsbeth and the moths are vague and inconsistent enough that they can safely be disregarded as fabrications. They do, however, claim that she was a magnet for the things. Evelyn James, that lying wench, said at the trial that she often came into Ilsbeth's bedroom only to see them crowd the glass of her windows. The horse breeder, Mr. Morris, said that he saw a torrent of moths rise from beneath the hooves of Ilsbeth's horse one day when she was out riding. Furthermore, the cook at Nicksby said that the parlor was infested with them, and that they seemed to find their way inside even when all the windows were closed. A modern-day scientist might have an explanation for it.

I was doubtlessly gambling—again—when I assumed that

Elena knew these stories, but I figured she couldn't be entirely un-informed if she was to write a book about Ilsbeth. She must at least have read *Strange Stories and Legends from F—,* by Benjamin El-don, as that terrible publication is a staple of every F— household, and contains a few stories about Ilsbeth's moths. Personally, I'm not a big fan of those flying critters, and even found them a little disturbing to handle, but I kept thinking of the greater good as I placed lanterns in my garden at night and then went out with a glass jar to collect my catch, wearing leather gloves, of course. I would never actually touch one.

I also happened to know that Elena's habit was to air out the house during the night, as I had noticed open windows when I passed by on my way to the well. This is a staple of people of great privilege, they are so convinced that they are shielded from harm that they never truly fear intruders, but leave their doors unlocked and their windows wide open. It's as if they think they have a special "something" that wards off all pain and discomfort.

In this case, it served me well, as I could easily cross the lawn with the moths banging their wings against the sides of my mason jar and their knobby heads bumping against the lid, and set the creatures free inside the castle. I always made sure to push the window closer to the frame when I was done, in the hopes that not too many of them would escape back to the balmy night.

This, I thought, would surely work. If nothing else, it would at least force her to question her own sanity—in which case I would really be doing her a favor, as the woman needed help. My whole idea was that this "bleed" of elements from stories about Ilsbeth into hard reality would scare her enough that she left and never again wrote a word about "the witch in the well."

If it would have worked or not we'll never know, as I was caught pretty early on. I still think it would have if given time, as someone who claims to speak with her soul is doomed to be highly superstitious. I blame that stupid plumber, Will Morris, for the plan's failure. If only he had kept from meddling, Elena might have left F— and still been alive in the city or something. I hope he feels guilty now that she's dead.

Lastly, the rabbit—yes, that was me as well, but it was just a product of chance and happenstance. I would never have thought of something so grisly if I hadn't come across it lying in a ditch. It's not something I would have actually *planned*. I found it one night as I was walking back to my car after having deposited some moths at the castle, and it seemed like a stroke of luck then. Had I stopped to think at all, I might not have done it—I *should not* have done it, but brought it to the well instead. But I was tired and discouraged and frustrated in equal measures, and the rabbit was there and the castle was there, and the night was dark enough to hide in.

To be honest, I didn't even look at the animal properly before wrapping it in my jacket and carrying it off to the castle stairs. It smelled horribly, *that* I know, and I had to throw the garment away when I came home, but I didn't really inspect the rabbit. I should have. I know that now. I didn't know that it looked bad enough to really put the fright in her—or maybe I'm just deluding myself. Perhaps a dead animal on the stairs will be terrifying no matter the carcass's state.

What I am trying to say with all this, is that it was purely a spur-of-the-moment action, which I've had plenty of reason to regret. It was a momentary lapse of judgment—a horrifying act, for which I should be punished—but I feel like a strong talking-to would have sufficed to set me straight. A restraining order is a serious matter, and I still can't believe that she did that to me. The animal was already dead, after all, it's not like I slaughtered it there on her steps. It's not like I am some criminal delinquent, either, I'm an upstanding member of this community. Had I only gotten the chance, I would have said my apologies and sent her some flowers. Getting the police involved seems like such a drastic step.

Not to mention how it made me look later, when Elena turned up dead.

# 21

For the first few days after my last misadventure on the castle lawn, I didn't hear anything, though I certainly had expected to. I had, however, been imagining a reaction in the form of an angry Elena at my door demanding an explanation, and not a phone call from Officer Rogers. This turn of events was very unfortunate, as I had already prepared just the perfect speech to give Elena, conjuring up a fond childhood memory: "I just wanted to remind you of the time we stole your Uncle John's bucket of fish and threw them down in the well." I had in fact perfected this flimsy defense while waiting for her to arrive, by reciting it to myself in the mirror.

The speech was, however, not right for Officer Rogers, who was overall more concerned with the dead rabbit than the moths. This was not something I had expected either—I had almost forgotten about that dratted roadkill. I had only thought about the humiliating moment in front of the window, and hadn't realized that the carcass would become an issue.

"But it *was* you who put it there?" Officer Rogers asked me on the phone.

"Yes." I didn't even think to lie. Surprise will do that to you. "But it wasn't a threat or anything like that."

"What was it, then? Do you deny that you put the rabbit on Ms. Clover's steps to scare her?"

"No." I was still so foolishly honest. "But it wasn't a threat as such, as I never implied that any violence would be done to Ms. Clover. I merely put it there to—" I finally managed to stop my own unruly tongue, realizing that my words were not saving me, but only digging the hole deeper.

"Then what could possibly be your intention, Mrs. Evans?" Officer Rogers sounded sardonic.

I had no ready answer to that. Whatever could I say to improve my situation? Sometimes in life, the best thing you can do is just lie down and accept defeat.

"She has filed a restraining order against you," said the officer. "I think you'll do wise in heeding that piece of paper."

"I can't go to the castle at all?" Somehow, that struck me as such a loss.

"No. You cannot go to the castle," he confirmed. "You are lucky that nothing more serious will come of this—and Mrs. Evans, please leave the roadkill alone. You never know what germs and other nastiness those critters carry."

At that point, standing there with the phone in my hand, just digesting the unpleasant words, I felt utterly, devastatingly beaten. I cried for myself, for my book, and for Ilsbeth, as it felt as if everything was ruined.

Elena would write her drivel, and Ilsbeth's reputation would never be restored.

I had utterly failed in my mission.

I slept uneasy for the next few nights, tormented by nightmares I hadn't had in years. First came the dream about the car crash that broke my legs when I was eight. It always started in the same way, close to my real memories of the events. I was upstairs in my room at the farm, and I could hear my parents quarreling downstairs. They were arguing about things going missing: gold rings, watches, and a Sunday roast left out to thaw.

My mother accused my father of taking the trinkets, believing him to be back at gambling, a habit that, unbeknownst to me, had nearly broken them apart years before. She shouted about my sisters' jewelry being missing from their rooms, little cherubs and hearts of silver that they had been gifted over the years. My father then replied that even if he had taken the jewelry, what on earth would he need a Sunday roast for? She called him immoral to steal from his children. He said she was insane to suggest such a thing. One of them smacked the other. I could hear the sound of a palm meeting flesh, but I didn't know which one had been hit. My mother was crying. Then the door to the pantry in the kitchen opened, suggesting that one of them was going for a bottle.

All the while I was lying in the dark on the floor in my room, all curled up like a caterpillar—or that was what I envisioned in my head. My cheeks were wet with tears, my tummy hurt, and my heart was beating painfully in my chest. I thought about the well and the treasures inside: cherubs, hearts, a roast . . .

Then we were suddenly in the car, speeding along winding country roads. My mother was crying at the wheel. I was in the front seat next to her, while my sisters crowded the backseat, bickering and sulking. I felt quite proud to be in the front, though the privilege merely stemmed from me being the first one to enter the vehicle. We were going to my maternal grandparents' house, leaving Dad alone back home to empty his bottle in peace. The night around us was dark. It was fall, so the trees were devoid of leaves, their bodies pressed in on the narrow road like lopsided insects waving their legs in the air. Despite the heat being turned up to max, the car was very cold. I was shaking from a combination of chills and fear.

"This is so stupid," Louise said from the backseat.

"We should just go back again," Christine agreed. "Grandma and Grandpa are probably asleep already." We were all wearing pajamas under our coats.

Mom didn't answer, she just drove—too fast—with tears in her eyes.

When we missed the next bend and the car went flying, I woke up in my bed, sweat-drenched and shivering.

The other dream was also familiar. It was the same one I so often I had as a child, about the hag climbing out of the well. Her long, white-gray hair fell around her face in tendrils as she emerged. Her dress, made from pale animal hide, was sopping wet. It almost looked as if it had rotted on her body, and smelled like it too. The hide also didn't look properly prepared, as I could see all sorts of gelatinous membranes and thick veins where the insides of the dress could be spotted between her knobby legs.

Beset by a sudden terror, I turned around and ran fast through the woods, but the hag behind me was running too, and I knew for a fact that she was faster than me. I rushed past evergreens and leafy branches, jumped across windfalls and rocks in the path. My skin was slick with perspiration and my heart was racing madly.

All the while, I heard her behind me, her heavy feet hitting the ground.

When I just couldn't stand it anymore, I stopped in a small clearing surrounded by thorny blackberry brambles, and I turned around, panting all the while. She stopped too, and her thin dark lip lifted in a snarl. Her eyes were small and beady; the irises were fractured, faceted almost; they reminded me of crushed blue glass. A pair of knitted pink mittens covered her hands, looking horribly out of place. As I looked on, her wrinkled face suddenly started to change, becoming elongated and smooth, and sprouting short white hairs.

Her blue eyes bled to black.

Then I woke.

## 22

*Excerpt from* Ilsbeth in the Twilight,
*by Catherine Evans*

### XVI. Tobias Green's Shoe

As summer arrived, I could not stop thinking of the two missing girls. Margaret and Elsie were always in my prayers—and in Owen's, too, that much I knew. Archibald had set up a prize of a calf to any man who shot the elusive bear that they all deemed responsible, but so far, no one had claimed it. The Nicksby woods seemed as devoid of such beasts as before. I was starting to think that the monster we were looking for was perhaps not the sort with teeth and claws, but so, sadly, were the townspeople, and what the girls had in common was me.

"You cannot let them unnerve you," Owen warned me as we met one night by the well. Though that place had taken on an uncomfortable eeriness ever since Margaret's eggs were found there, we still deemed it the safest place to meet. Owen had brought his flute with him and had been playing for me, a sad and mournful melody. Now we sat with our backs against the rough surface of the well. He had wrapped his hand around mine, and my lips were still swollen from his hungry kisses. We needed each other even more than before, with all the unpleasantness happening around us. "*All* the girls are in your circle," he said, "it had nothing to do with you."

"But they both disappeared on Nicksby grounds," I complained. "And they all know that both girls were favorites of mine."

Owen only scoffed at this. "Nicksby owns *all* the land around here. You would be hard pressed to find a spot of dirt without Archibald's name on it." A hint of bitterness bled through in his voice.

"But the dolls," I fretted. "What about the dolls?" *Of course* the townspeople would look to me after they found those dratted things. Made of only sticks and moss, there was no denying that the scraps of fabric they wore as clothes were made from the finest silks and laces. No other household kept such things around.

"Probably the girls have been pillaging Evelyn's basket of scraps," he assured me. "Or perhaps she simply gave them away, wanting to amuse the little ones."

"Of course," I agreed, "but how come they ended up here, by the well?"

"Children's play," he shrugged. "It was only unfortunate that Mr. Morris and that washerwoman found them."

"*Witchcraft.*" Now it was I who scoffed and spat out the word as if it were distasteful. "How come they think of witchcraft?"

Owen sighed and squeezed my hand. "They only think it is mysterious that the dolls appeared where Margaret vanished, and they *do* look quite frightening."

"Evelyn said that *she* has nothing to with it," I told him, "although I think she is just frightened to get blamed."

"It is not fair that you are the one to take the brunt of their suspicion, though." He squeezed my hand anew. "You only ever wanted to do good for those girls."

"Yes," I said, with tears in my eyes. "I truly did, but now it has come to naught."

It was only the next day that the lightning struck again. I had already gone to bed, but was greatly disturbed by a ruckus downstairs. I rang for Evelyn, but when she failed to appear, I found a simple dressing gown and made my way down the stairs. I could see through the windows that the yard, once again, was teeming with lantern lights, and several horses milled about, some of them from our own stables.

Down in the hall, I found Archibald and a handful of men from town, as well as Mrs. Engel, who was greatly distressed. The frilled nightcap sat askew on her head as the large woman dried her eyes with her handkerchief and sobbed uncontrollably.

"I only saw him today," she complained. "He came into the kitchen with feet as black as soot . . . He had waded through some mud, he said. His toes were cold as icicles."

"Calm yourself, Mrs. Engel," Archibald berated the cook. "I am sure we will find the boy in no time." It was then, by those words, that the situation became clear to me, and my heart instantly plummeted with dread.

"Oh no," I complained as tears quickly filled my eyes. "Who is it?" I demanded to know. "Who is it that has vanished?"

None of the townsmen looked at me; they only stared down on the floor, and Archibald barely offered me a glance. In the end, it was Mrs. Engel who answered me.

"Tobias Green," she said through a fresh bout of tears. "That fine young man," she complained. "I gave him my own boy's shoes, rest his soul," she rambled. "I went into my chest and brought them out for him. They were fine leather shoes, and barely used before he passed. Tobias was proud as a rooster when he left the yard with them on." Her voice rose to a pitch as she continued, "Now I'm thinking that maybe it was not very wise, for what if they brought him bad luck, those shoes—"

"Nonsense, Mrs. Engel," Archibald huffed, and for once I agreed with him.

"You did him a kindness," I added to his words. "Do not for a second think differently, Mrs. Engel."

"But you spoke to him too." Her watery blue eyes landed on me with something like vehemence, and I almost took a step back from astonishment. "I saw you feeding him sugared apples out the drawing room window," she accused me with a shivering finger hovering in the air between us.

I quickly thought back and recalled that I had indeed given the boy some sweets, but then I often did when the little ones came running errands for their parents.

"Now, now," Archibald started, sounding about as exasperated as he looked. He did not much like how this business with the children interfered with his schedule.

"Surely it is no crime to be kind," I answered her myself. I was highly surprised by the cook's hostility—and toward *me,* her mistress, the very one who kept her clothed and fed. Surely she overestimated the value of her rhubarb pie.

"It seems you always have dealing with the ones that go missing," she accused me next, and a sharp pain erupted in my belly.

"I have dealings with *all* who dwell on the estate," I said curtly, trying my best not to lose my dignity, but it was hard while standing there in the middle of the night with her furious gaze upon me. The townsmen shot me sly glances, while their lips twisted into hard lines. "How come you look to *me*?" I snapped at them. "Should you not be out there looking for the boy, rather than wasting your time in here? I will ride with you myself."

"We would rather you didn't," one of the men said. His eyes were as dark as his voice was cold.

"Of course she will not," Archibald agreed. "It is hardly fitting for the mistress of Nicksby." His gaze was just as laced with ice as he briefly turned it upon me. He offered Mrs. Engel, whose sobbing had resumed, a comforting pat on the shoulder, but for me, he had no warmth. "Go back to bed, Ilsbeth," he said. "Mrs.

Engel, why don't you serve some tea, and something stronger, too. The search is likely to go on for some time."

"But I can help," I protested. "I know these woods well enough, and I am an excellent rider!" Better than my husband, truth be told, and a better marksman, too.

"We do not want your help," grumbled one of the men from town. The other ones nodded their agreement.

There was nothing I could do then but make my way back upstairs, with hurt and worry at war in my heart. The news about the boy was terrible, but I still smarted from the callous treatment I had received downstairs. I just could not understand why they would look to *me*—I had done nothing but try to please them, and I was certainly not in the habit of abducting children. What on earth would I do that for?

I spent a long and sleepless night tossing on the sheets, while listening to the clamor outside as ever more men came to join the search, equipped with lanterns to hold the darkness at bay. I prayed more passionately than I ever had before, that they would find young Tobias, and the missing girls, too, although in my heart, I had doubts.

The next morning, as Evelyn served my toast, she told me they had found one of Tobias Green's new shoes discarded by the well. Next to the shoe, there had been another ugly stick doll, wrapped in the same blue silk as my new evening gown.

# 23

It seems silly now, of course, having been so upset about the restraining order. Obviously, things have changed to the worse for me since Elena went and died, so what seemed like such a catastrophe then is merely a trifle now.

Funny how that works.

None of you are surprised, I imagine, or at least that's what you'll say. I can all but hear you at the salon, gossiping from pink suede swiveling chairs, with your hair caught in plastic caps and your hands wrapped like claws around lukewarm cups of coffee.

"We always knew it was just a matter of time . . ."

"She had to go off the rails eventually."

"It was probably the divorce that broke her—"

"They say her son won't even talk to her anymore."

Oh, how you must love it, that I finally came tumbling down, that all your predictions were proven right. I don't think a woman has been so collectively scorned in this town since—yes, well, since Ilsbeth Clark.

I will have you know, though, that this battle is far from over. I will also have you know that you are *wrong*! I never went off the rails, the divorce did not break me, and my son still speaks to me from time to time. I will admit, however, that he isn't *pleased* by what's happening. Neither is he particularly thrilled about me writing this account for you all to see, but since the editor at the *F— Daily* refused to print it after all, Brian can at least no longer accuse me of going to the press. Not that it is making his mood any better.

"I just don't see what the point is," he said only yesterday, as he joined me for a simple meal of spaghetti with spring onions and an ungodly amount of cheese. I find I've had a craving for cheese lately. I think the fat and salt reminds me that there are still good things in this world to be savored and relished. Perhaps I'm preparing for leaner times by adding some flesh to my bones like a bear. I don't know much about prison, but have heard some worrisome things about the food.

Not that it will come to that, of course.

"I'm writing it so that I've had my say," I told my son between forkfuls of spaghetti. "I'm not so sure that they'll give me time enough to tell the whole story at the trial and I want my story to be heard."

"People mostly think it's weird." His head was bent over the plate so all I could see was a mass of yellow curls.

"Pah, who cares about people," said I, having had a little too much chardonnay. I find I've developed a taste for wine ever since Elena died.

"*You,* obviously." He looked up just to glare at me before his head dipped down again. His fork spun in the spaghetti, round and round and round . . . "You wouldn't bother to write it if you didn't care."

I took a moment before answering, debating with myself how to best reply in a way that he would understand. "You know when Ilsbeth died, no one cared to hear her story—"

"Who the fuck cares about Ilsbeth Clark? You have to stop this, Mom! You have to stop being so fucking obsessed!" He threw down his fork so it clattered against the china, rolled his eyes, and drew a hand through his curls before giving a deep and dramatic sigh.

"No, wait!" I reached a hand across the table to calm him down. "Let me finish, please! You young people are so impatient!"

"I don't think there's anything you can say that will—"

"No, listen, Brian, please! This is relevant!"

"If you say so." He still sulks as he did when he was a little boy, with his face set in a scowl and his lower lip jutting out.

"When Ilsbeth died, no one wanted to hear what she had to say. People were deaf to it then, having found themselves a culprit to blame for everything that went wrong. It was convenient, you see, to have someone to blame. Now, however, in a more enlightened age, when we *know* there's no such thing as witches, it would have been amazing to have Ilsbeth's own reflections about the case. What little we *do* have is dry court transcripts, and that's why I'm writing my book about her, to try to imagine what she *would* have said, and I want to write *my* story down too, in case the same thing happens to me." I contentedly sipped my wine, pleased with my own answer.

Brian didn't speak at once. His restless fingers toyed with a paper napkin, while his eyes were glued to the table. "What do you mean 'the same thing'?"

"Oh, I only mean that—"

"They won't throw you in the *well*, Mom!"

"No, but people are wrongfully accused and mistreated even today."

"I knew it!" He straightened up in his chair. "I knew it! You don't think you'll win, do you? You say that you do, but you really don't! You think they'll convict you for the murder!"

"Brian, please! Of course not!" I could feel a hot flush in my cheeks as I poured another glass of wine.

"Then why do you want to 'tell your side,' if it's not because you think that in two hundred years you'll have become a legend, like Ilsbeth Clark?" The scorn was apparent in his voice, and it hurt me. "You're not *her*, you know. You're not 'destined' to follow in her footsteps." To my great astonishment, I thought he perhaps was about to cry. "This isn't some *joke*, Mom. It's not some *fantasy*—"

"Don't you think I know that?" If he was about to cry, *I* was about to laugh. This was, after all, just what had been at the heart of my beef with Elena. "*I'm* not the one who can't tell truth from fiction!" I paused to take a deep breath. "Besides, Ilsbeth Clark was acquitted at her trial, if not in people's minds."

"Let's hope you have *that* in common, then." He still looked surly, but the tears had receded. "I still don't see why you have to post things online."

"What other choice do I have?"

"Save it on your computer. If—*when*—you are cleared of all charges, it'll only look stupid that you published all this stuff."

"I just don't want people going around saying all sorts of things—"

"I thought you didn't care what people say."

A heavy silence fell between us.

"More spaghetti?" I offered. He shook his head. "People can be dangerous when they're convinced that something is true," I told him.

"They *won't* throw you in the well, Mom!" He rolled his eyes again.

"They could do other things—"

"Like what?" He sighed, marveling at my foolishness. "This isn't the old days. We have laws and stuff."

"So did they in Ilsbeth's time, but that didn't really help." I had all but abandoned my spaghetti for more of the delicious wine.

Another deep sigh from my son. "Just don't write anything else about me," he begged, obviously in vain.

So you see, he does still speak to me, even if it's mostly to complain, and he's not the only one, either. Bobby just won't *stop* talking, even if I beg him to. He calls me on the phone almost every day, mostly to check if I've spoken to my lawyer; a breezy cool woman with white-blond hair called Nora Green.

Since Bobby is paying for the latter, I suppose he feels like he has a right. Rosemary can't be thrilled that he's spending so much money on his ex-wife's defense—or perhaps she is one of those *good* women who thinks it's her duty to help the less fortunate. If it hadn't been for Brian, I'd gladly throw the money right back in her face, as being at the bottom of the ladder is certainly no picnic. Being someone's charity case holds no glory whatsoever. That's not to say that I'm not grateful, I'm just pointing out that it's not a great position, but beggars can't be choosers, so there's that.

I guess I should be glad for every scrap I got.

# 24

I had another dream again tonight. I was running through the woods with the hag hot on my heels, until we came to the clearing, where we stopped. I turned to face her, I could hear her coming closer, rushing through the underbrush. The branches on the needle trees swung back and forth as if caught in a violent storm. Soon she would be there with me, and I willed myself to turn and run, but had suddenly lost all use of my limbs. I was frozen on the spot—helpless—as the creature drew closer.

I looked up and saw the sun above me as a disk of blazing white. As I watched, the darkness came though, bleeding in from all sides, swallowing up every inch of blue sky, and then the sun itself, until nothing was left but the tiniest pinprick of light. Then there was silence, sudden and complete.

The hag had arrived at the clearing.

When I woke up, I was drenched in sweat as always, and had to pad to the bathroom for water. I had to change my pajamas, too, as the ones I was wearing were soaked through. I even considered changing my sheets, but was too tired to bother. I don't like that they're back, these exhausting dreams. I had been hoping I had left them behind in childhood. I wonder now what it was that kept drawing me to the well when I was little, over and over again. I wonder, too, if the dreams' return is a sign of menopause, the copious amount of perspiration considered. I'll have to ask my physician about that.

This time the dream came with an unexpected twist, though, as just as I woke up, I knew the hag's name—or at least what I used to call her before. *Horse lady.* She was the horse lady, and just as I remembered her name, I remembered other things, too;

memories of other dreams came tumbling into my mind, as if I'd just cracked a hole in a nightmare piñata. Not all the dreams were uncomfortable, though. As they came back to me, I realized that there had been a time when I found them pleasant— *comforting,* even—as they weren't nightmares then. They all took place at the clearing by the well. I was there and the horse lady was there, usually looking like the hag with her crushed blue glass for eyes, but sometimes different, more like a horse.

In one of these dreams, I sat on a fallen log in the woods. The tree bark was littered with deep green moss, lichen, and stacks of fleshy white mushrooms. The horse lady was sitting beside me; her face was only a little long that day, and only dusted with fine white hairs. She was holding my hand in her gnarled one, and her long white mane was braided with wildflowers.

"You are my girl," she said—not with words, but like a whisper of sorts in my head. "You are my own special girl."

Then she proceeded to show me her treasures, gathered up in a sack of cloth and placed on the ground by her hooves. She pulled up a necklace with a locket that looked terribly old, as the silver was all black. I wanted to ask her if I could look inside, but she put it away before I had the chance. Next, she showed me a mirror, set in tarnished silver as well; the surface was cracked and broken, but the horse lady didn't seem to mind. She kept pulling things out of her bag: a crucifix on a chain, a cowbell, the lid of a tuna can, a silver-colored fish lure, and a pocketknife. I got the impression that she was proud of her collection, and promised that I'd bring my stickers next time, so she could see *my* collection in turn.

I also remember thinking that I should bring her something shiny as a gift. My grandmother's ladle sprang to mind, as it had a beautiful, twisted handle. In my young heart, I felt convinced that the horse lady would treasure it more than my grandmother ever had.

In another dream, we were sitting in the clearing again, but there was a table and tree stumps to sit on. I even remember seeing coiling roots, so the furniture must have been the remains of trees that had once stood there. There was a tablecloth of graying lace, and teacups made from brittle china, painted with blue flowers and with dainty golden rims. There was cake on the table as well, a yellow sponge and blackberries bleeding purple onto the whipped cream. I remember tarts as well, brimming with fat strawberries, and little pink cakes on a china plate. When I brought the cup to my lips, the tea tasted strongly of honey.

The horse lady sat on the other side of the table from me, dressed in her usual hides. She was holding a cup as well and was sipping it almost daintily. It must have been fall, because golden leaves drifted down from the sky to litter our little table, marring the cake with brittle decay.

As I looked on, the horse lady's face elongated and turned into a muzzle. Her hair, too, became longer, coarser, and her eyes slowly turned black. Her hands were still human, though, as she put down her cup and reached for my fingers. I don't recall feeling afraid, which is a little strange in hindsight, but gladly gave her my left hand to hold. Dreams are like that sometimes, you just don't react in a rational way.

I did hiss, however, when the thick nail of her thumb sliced into the skin of my wrist, and she bent over the table to lick the wound with a long maroon tongue, foregoing all the sweet delicacies on the table to sup on me instead. It didn't take that long, though, before she was satisfied, and when she let my hand go and retracted, she was all human again. Her eyes were as blue as before. She gave me a wide smile. Her teeth were very large, very square, sort of gray.

I could tell that she was happy with the taste of me.

In the last dream that I remember, the horse lady was crying.

She was kneeling on the ground in front of the well, and I was kneeling in front of her, comforting her with my clumsy children's hands, patting her shoulders, stroking her hair. I was wearing a nightgown with a star and moon print; it was dark around us, but I had brought a flashlight, which was propped up against the well, shooting a beam of golden light into the night.

The horse lady held my little body to hers; I could feel the bones shift under her hide as she cried, hoarse and ugly, into my shoulder.

"I am hungry," she wailed, though again the words were more like a feeling and not actual sounds. Then she made some ugly noises, high-pitched and keening.

"Not to worry," I said, and patted her shoulders. "I will feed you, horse lady."

I reached into my red backpack that was resting on the ground to find the necklace I had brought from my sister's dresser. It was a swallow in flight, made of real silver. I was hoping that it would comfort her. The horse lady grasped the necklace with delight, but I could tell that she wasn't satisfied.

"I'll bring you a roast next time," I promised. "A big one with lots of fat."

The horse lady smiled at that.

At least I *think* these were dreams. I cannot help but wonder, though, at the vividness of the scenes. I remember it sometimes being cold; I remember an ant in my tea. I remember a smell of blood and stagnant water. The sweetness of cake on my lips, like a kiss.

Can you be so aware of your senses in a dream?

I remember how I was lonely, and the horse lady was lonely too, and we comforted each other, I think. I know that's why I started stealing things, shiny things, the sort of things my dream friend liked, and slipped them into the well. I stole food as well, meat mostly, because I knew that she wanted that. I also quite often brought my recorder out there and sat down by the well to play for her, as I had a strong sense that she found it soothing. Never once did I question the ethics of my actions, trekking into the woods with my loot felt almost like being in a dream as well.

Those were twilight days, strange times—as if something had hooked a claw in me that kept me from being truly alive.

After the car accident, the dreams more or less stopped, and the world around me became more solid. Perhaps the pain and discomfort of my injuries left little room for fantastic beings. Although it must have been with my old friend in mind that I brought Elena out to the well one night. I think I wanted to share my childhood wonder with her. Of course, Elena only went and cheapened it with her theatrics, running away as if the devil were hot on her heels, claiming to have seen something scary out there. I thought even less of the horse lady after that, ashamed that my "magic trick" had provoked such a strong reaction. I was very concerned with what Elena liked or not back then—and yes, I do find it ironic that she later made up her own slew of parlor tricks to dazzle with based on what she thought had happened that night.

My childhood dreamscapes considered, I was naturally quite taken aback when, as a teenager, I first read in *Strange Stories and Legends from F—* about the white horse that haunted Nicksby Farm. According to Benjamin Eldon, a white horse was said to have been keening in the orchard at Nicksby for seven nights after Ilsbeth's death. He then went on to tell the story of two farmers who were on their way back home after having worked all day at Nicksby. Just as they came upon the well, they saw a figure dressed in a hooded cloak seated upon a white horse. As they looked on, naturally terrified, the figure rode in circles around the well while "emitting sounds of grief." It was at the time assumed that this was the ghost of Ilsbeth herself, who was lamenting her terrible fate. Another theory, also mentioned by Eldon, was that the cloaked rider was no ghost at all but Owen Phyne, come back to mourn his lover. Whatever the truth was, the two farmers apparently watched in "stupefied silence" until the figure was done "emitting sounds" and rode away.

Finally, there was the story of a married couple who had been to Nicksby for some apples when they came across the horse grazing by the well. There had already been much talk about the white horse, and so the couple knew at once that what they were looking at was a specter.

The story continued that the woman became spooked and refused to pass the beast. The man then started throwing their precious apples into the woods in the hopes that the horse would be hungry for fruit. At first, this seemed to be working; the horse lifted its head and went in between the trees to investigate the noise, leaving the path unguarded, but just as the couple had started moving again the horse came running after them, eyes black with fury and hoofs shooting sparks. It had no taste for apples after all. Not until the woman dropped a lamb shank she had bartered for in the Nicksby kitchen did the fearsome horse end its chase.

Both husband and wife later swore on the Bible that the animal had stopped to eat the raw meat. They believed it to be a horse from hell, raised up by Ilsbeth's wicked magic.

It did seem rather fantastical that I should have imagined meeting with a horse-like creature, and then something similar appeared in a book, but then the world is a strange place, and coincidences happen all the time, without any need to read something into it.

# 25

*Excerpt from* Ilsbeth in the Twilight,
*by Catherine Evans*

### XXI. The Witch in the Well

I had truly believed that things would be easier after the acquittal—that it would *mean* something to the people in F—that a judge had declared my innocence at a proper trial, but alas, I was sorely mistaken. People barely tried to hide their scorn when they met me; they spat on the ground behind me when I passed them by, and even at Nicksby, things were dire. Hardly a day went by without me finding some uncooked piece or gristle, or even gravel, in my food. After a venison dinner, I was sick all night, heaving so violently that I thought I should die. I suspected that Mrs. Engel was the culprit behind my gastric upset, but could hardly accuse the woman without evidence, having learned the hard way just how dangerous such accusations can be. I was always fearful, though, feeling unsafe, and especially at home, with the servants having turned against me. Never will I forget the terrible moment before the judge when it became clear that even my dear Evelyn had chosen to speak against me, telling all manner of lies.

Archibald's mood was foul. He wished nothing but for the unpleasantness of it all to go away. As mortified as he had been when it first became clear there would be a trial, he was just as aghast afterward, unable to accept that something so scandalous had happened to him, and that his money had been unable to prevent it. The shame of it was almost more than he could bear.

"You should go and visit your sister," he told me one day over dinner. We were having a beef roast and I had carved it myself to make sure it was not poisoned. I avoided the vegetables entirely, and drank but small sips of wine.

"I will not leave," I replied to my husband. "Not yet, anyway. The rumors would only grow stronger then, and I might not be able to return."

He gave me a look that said it might well be for the best. "It would be better for your health to be away for some time," he noted, subtly letting me know that he did have an inkling that my food had been tampered with.

"I won't bend my neck for them," I snapped, though the real reason why I wanted to stay was of course Owen.

I knew well that people said the reverend had left F— after the trial due to a fear that our affair would come to proper light, or even of shame that he had ever associated with me, but in my heart, I knew better. Owen would not have left me like that, or if he had, he was sure to come back, or that was what I told myself while stubbornly holding on to the hope that I one day would see my love again, that he was just busy building a life for us, a refuge where we could be safe and together.

Without Owen, there simply was no future to look forward to, nothing to infuse my days with joy. Not even the prospect of inheriting Nicksby could enthuse me, as I feared I would never sleep soundly there again.

My mood was bleak and volatile, and I knew that my tongue often got the better of me as I screamed at the servants and lashed at them with my riding crop, unable, at times, to contain the anger and resentment from them having treated me so unfairly.

Yes, I probably should leave. Archibald was right about that, if nothing else. Yet I simply *could* not. Not before I knew where Owen had gone. I clung to the conviction that he would never betray me, and so he *had* to come back. I never even dared to consider that something might have happened to him.

If Owen was gone from this world, the last of *my* light would die too.

It was only a few weeks later that the tension came to a head. The townspeople arrived in the night, hammering on our front door and screaming for the "witch" to come out. Next, I heard Archibald out in the hallway and saw his flickering candle light under the door as he passed by. He, if anyone, would surely be able to talk some sense into them, I thought, while struggling to calm my thundering heart. I could tell from the way he walked that he was mightily cross.

Then, as I lay there, shivering in the darkness, a desire came upon me to know just what was transpiring downstairs. I was no coward, after all, and though I was frightened, and even feared for my life, I did not value that life as I had before, and that, in turn, made me reckless.

I was not foolish enough to go all the way down, but paused on the landing, hidden from view, yet close enough to hear what was being said. I had not even brought a candle, but stood there silent in the freezing darkness, like a thief hiding in my own home.

Archibald had still not opened the door, though the demands for him to do so were loud in the air. He was engaged in a spirited debate with Mrs. Engel at the bottom of the stairs.

". . . they have come for her now," I heard the woman's grating voice. "There will be no escape this time!"

"Have you lost your mind, Mrs. Engel?" Archibald wanted to know. "Are you truly prepared to lose your livelihood over this nonsense?"

He did not wait for her to reply, but—from the sounds that reached me on the landing—turned the heavy iron key and yanked open the front door. The clamor outside briefly died down.

"What in God's name is this stupendous folly?" his thunderous voice demanded to know.

"We have come for the witch!" I recognized the voice of Morris, the breeder. He who had seen Owen and me by the well.

"She has eaten our children and now she has to pay!" another voice sounded.

"My wife has the choice of the finest meat that money can buy, and hardly a need to hunt for *your* scrawny pups," Archibald informed them, sounding mightily irate. "Now have the good sense to return to your beds or you will have neither work nor coin come morning!"

"But it is ungodly what she does!" I thought that the voice belonged to Mr. Hart, the father of the missing Elsie. "We cannot abide such devilry in F——."

"I decide what we can abide or not in F——," Archibald told him, in a tone that even had *me* cringing from his arrogance. "What we surely cannot abide is rousing good men from their beds to embark on fool's errands," he kept up his speech. "The judge has had his say," he added as an afterthought. "He is a man of wit and reason, and I suggest that you follow his stellar example. Only simpletons believe in witchcraft nowadays. If you cherish the work I provide for you, you'd better depart at once!"

Everything went quiet for a couple of heartbeats as the crowd outside made up their minds. I found that I was more curious than afraid, as I stood there waiting, clad only in my nightgown. What did the townspeople want most? Their revenge or their livelihood?

The answer to that question came with a mighty crash as the front door hit the wall; suddenly the shouting rose to a crescendo, as the angry men, and even some women, came pouring into the hall, blatantly ignoring Archibald's protests. My heart started pounding fast and painfully in my chest, but I did not run away—no, I did not try to escape to the cellar or lock my-self in the attic. I stood my ground, if for no other reason than to show them that I was no coward, and they could not break me. As they came thundering up the stairs, I stood firm, and did not even flinch when the first bearded face appeared within my sight. The man glared at me with bloodlust in his eyes.

"I got her!" he shouted. "I got the witch," he called to his compatriots as they came up beside him. All of them were cheering and looking at me with crazed eyes that twinkled like rodents' in the lantern lights.

From the hall, I could faintly hear my husband's feeble pro-test. "Outrageous!" he declared. "A scandal!" he shouted, but no one listened to old Archibald anymore.

"What have you done to Owen Phyne?" I cried as the first pair of filthy hands landed on my arms. "What did you do to him, you scum?"

No one cared to answer me as I thrashed and fought in their grip. More hands came to seize me, and before I knew it, I was down on the floor with my cheek pressed against the rough floor-boards. All around me, the townspeople were crying out. "Seize the witch!" urged one. "Bring her out!" demanded another.

Finally, the fear in me won the battle with my pride, and I added cries of my own to the ruckus. "I did not take them!" I cried. "You are mistaken!" But no one cared to listen. Instead, an ill-smelling burlap sack was pulled down over my head, and my hands were forced behind my back and secured with what I deemed to be twine.

"No!" I cried within my dark prison. "No!" I cried again, but there was nothing I could do as I was hoisted up in the air and carried down the stairs. No matter how much I wriggled and fought to free myself, there seemed to be ever more hands to hold me, to carry me downstairs, through the hall, and into the night.

Next, I found myself flung across a horse. The animal scent

should have been soothing to me, as I had always cared deeply for such beasts, but on this night, which I knew might be my last, the horse's warmth and familiar smell did not comfort me at all; rather I wondered if this unwitting creature was to take me to my doom. They secured me with ropes and then the horse moved. I heard other riders both before and after me, and flickering light reached me from time to time, filtered through the burlap. I heard the swishing sound of branches overhead, and smelled pine and wet soil, so I knew we were riding through the woods. A wild hope suddenly flared in me: perhaps they would take me to where Owen was. Perhaps they had kept him somewhere, sound and alive, but then the hope died, for suddenly the horse stopped, and I recognized the cool, metallic smell of the well.

Was this site, which had held such sweetness for Owen and me, really to be my grave?

I did nothing but cry as the rope that had kept me secured to the horse's back was loosened, and my slumped form was pulled down from the beast's broad back. I sobbed as my head hit the wet, hard ground and my nightgown grew wet with moisture. Around me, my captors laughed at my misery. Someone kicked soil onto my shivering form, as if I were worth nothing at all. I could hear more riders coming into the clearing; each new arrival seemed to me another death knell, as I figured they were waiting for all to arrive. Carl Morris was there, I knew, and Mr. Martin, too, and Tobias Green's father. I wondered if Mrs. Engel was among them, eager to see me defeated at last.

I knew why they had brought me there, of course. It was where Margaret's eggs had been found, and young Tobias's shoe, the last traces of the lost children. It was where I had been seen with Owen Phyne, and where the stick dolls had been found, protruding from piles of animal bones and wearing fabrics from my gowns.

Now it would see my death.

I did not even bother to struggle as I, once again, was hoisted up in the air. I was frightened, yes, but mostly I was beset by an anguish that it had all turned out so horribly wrong. Now I would die for no reason, while the one who had taken the children, be that beast or man, would walk free.

Without me ever learning what had happened to Owen Phyne.

It all seemed to me such waste.

"Throw her in!" they shouted next. "Kill the witch!"

I was crying again by then, though my tears were hidden by the burlap sack. They never even took it off, afraid, perhaps, to see my eyes as they threw me in.

For throw me in they did, accompanied by many joyous shouts and cheers. Still tied up and blindfolded, I was tossed down in the well, into the cold, black water below.

And that, dear reader, was the end of me.

The end of Ilsbeth Clark.

# Summer

# 26

*Elena Clover's journal*

*June 25*

I know that my relationship with Ilsbeth is one thing, and that Cathy's stupid, childish pranks are something else entirely, but it still feels tangled somehow. It's as if her malice has spread and tainted everything that has to do with Ilsbeth. Even Ilsbeth's voice has become quieter, though perhaps that's because I don't want to hear it so much, but push it away whenever she peeps up. What used to be like a strong and heady dream has become all gray and lifeless, and I do blame Cathy for that.

What upsets me the most is that after she got caught, she tried to pretend that it was nothing, just a silly joke between old friends, but trespassing and pouring bugs into my house and placing roadkill on my stairs is nothing to laugh about, and she has to be pretty insane to even think that. Officer Rogers told me that Cathy did it to put me off my book and leave F—, which honestly only makes me more determined to write it. I really *should* write it now, if only to prove that I'm not so easily scared, but then maybe *I am*, because just thinking of delving into Ilsbeth's story again makes me feel cold all over. The fire that I felt before has suddenly turned to ashes.

Erica only laughed when I told her what had happened. She remembers Cathy only too well from our time at the castle as children. "She has always been a little weird," she said. "Remember that time when she stole your pajamas? The blue ones Mom gave you for Christmas?"

I hadn't before, but I remembered when she said it. Cathy had taken them out of my drawer and stuffed them into her red little backpack, where I discovered them just by chance. The backpack had fallen off the bed and down on the floor, spilling its contents all over: toothbrush, T-shirts, and underwear; a red diary with a plastic lock; a porcelain doll's head; a strand of fake pearls; a grandma brooch set with yellow rhinestones; and my poor pajamas, rolled up tight.

"Yeah, I remember," I told my sister. "What does that have to do with anything?"

"Nothing much." I could almost hear her shrug through the phone. "Only that Cathy is jealous of you—always has been."

"Who can blame her? It's not like she's had it easy. I'd be jealous of me too if I were Cathy. There's always been something so *sad* about her." I knew that I was being cruel, but also just honest.

"It was good of you, though, to spend so much time with her before."

"Sure," the sarcasm cut through my voice. "If I had been a little less kind as a kid, she might not have come traipsing here now, carrying fresh roadkill."

"Maybe she's like a cat, bringing home the bacon." My sister was just reveling in the absurdity of it.

"A scary cat," I said. "She just wants to keep me away from Ilsbeth."

"She wants to steal your pajamas again."

I had to laugh at that. "Sure, but this time she's saying she had them first."

"As if we can't *all* wear the same pajamas," she replied, which I took to mean that we could *all* write books about Ilsbeth Clark.

"Some of us wear them better than others, though."

"True," Erica agreed. "And you always did have style."

I still can't bring myself to write, though, which is maddening, and makes me feel as if Cathy is sort of winning, and she doesn't deserve that after everything. I remember after the pajamas incident, Cathy cried and cried. I tried to talk to her, but it was as if she didn't hear me, she just sat there on my bed with her knees pulled up and cried into her hands. In the end, I had to bring in the grown-ups to help. Uncle John made her cocoa and everything, but none of their efforts worked. I remember Mom followed her home through the woods, and was angry with me afterward, even if it was *Cathy* who had stolen from *me*.

"Cathy isn't like Veronica back home," she scolded. "She doesn't have the same *opportunities*. You have to be patient with her, Elena, and *kind*. Not everyone is born with a gold pin in their butt." This was her spin on the silver-spoon thing.

I wonder if Mom had still been around, she would have berated me for being upset now as well, or if the dead rabbit would have offended even *her* sensibilities. I really can't tell what would've been more likely. Maybe she would have regarded the whole thing as a cry for help—*I* sure have thought about it, but I just don't think it's my job to save poor Cathy from herself.

"You just can't with people like that," Will said when I aired the thought. "Not when they become threatening." I should have expected him to take that position, as he was the one who insisted on the restraining order. Left to my own devices, I would probably just have let it go, or sent Cathy a text or something. What she did was childish and stupid, but not really dangerous. Will, however, went up in arms, and had I been a better damsel I suppose I would have found that flattering, but to be honest I found it a tad annoying. Suddenly there's paperwork and shit, and I can't help but think of poor Brian, as who wants to be "the crazy lady's kid"?

I do see where Will's coming from, though, and that rabbit was both ripe and nasty, but it's not like she planted a bomb, and I just don't think Cathy would hurt me for real. Will doesn't know her as I did.

Maybe it's just Mom's ghost haunting me, telling me to be *kind*.

All this upheaval hasn't been great for my creativity, though, and my new book seems further away than ever before. How can I think about nature and MAGIC with all this drama going on? It's not all about Cathy, either. Having a boyfriend takes its toll, and then there's some doubts I find it hard to address, as just acknowledging they're there at all makes me feel filthy somehow.

It started shortly after the rabbit incident, and was really just stray thoughts at first—*not mine,* mind you. Like when we were driving to the police station and I found my hands in my lap tying the fringes of the green shawl I'd thrown on; nine knots in every single tassel. Without knowing how I knew, I just realized that the purpose of the knots was to do Cathy harm. I was sitting there, next to Will at the wheel, and cursed a woman over and over, without even thinking about it.

Then, the next day when we were in the garden, I kept ogling the blackberry brambles for no discernable reason, before Ilsbeth's voice reached me: *Make a thorny braid and put it under her doorstep,* and suddenly I knew without a doubt that it would cause Cathy to trip and mess up the old damage in her legs. The worst part was that, instead of shying away from that thought, I started wondering if putting the braid in the trunk of her car would cause it to fly off the road. It was really disturbing, having those thoughts.

Yesterday, as I was making an omelet with mushrooms from the well and some fresh organic eggs I'd bought directly from the farmer, I came across one with a bloody yolk. At once, I had the thought that I should preserve it and plant the mess in Cathy's garden, as nothing but bitterness would grow there then—not that it would make much of a difference, mind you. I think Cathy is great at cultivating bitterness all by herself.

I don't like having these weird ideas, though. Rather than being a blessing, Ilsbeth has become more of a slithering snake, whispering all sorts of nastiness. That, in turn, makes me question all that I thought I knew, and I find myself wondering if Ilsbeth Clark really was a *good* witch, an innocent being with magic in her veins, or if she really did kill those children . . .

I know I can't really trust these thoughts either, as they could just be me making things up because the world has become a little weird and unpleasant. If I'm right in being wrong, however, I've made a horrible mistake. What if the witch I let into my heart is not at all a creature of light, but one of malice and darkness—how do I even get her out again?

Right now, I'm just ignoring her, hoping that it'll be enough to drive her off. What is absolutely for sure is that I really don't want to write about her right now, unless it's in you, trusted journal. I just can't write an ode to Ilsbeth Clark's many virtues with all this shameful *doubt* nagging deep inside me.

How did it all become so distasteful?

### July 1

You would think that after all that has happened, Cathy would keep a low profile, but no! Last night she was at it again, with jingling bells. I just don't know what to do with that woman!

Yesterday started out pretty nice. I had told Will that I needed the day to work on the book so I was on my own for some much-needed restoration. The weather was lovely as well, and I was outside for most of it, lounging under the cherry tree with a bottle of chilled wine doing nothing at all but scroll on social media and read new reviews for *Awakening* (all good!). I also sort of made a new plan for clearing out the house, and was about to actually do something about it as well, like sort through Uncle John's clothes upstairs, but somehow I ended up painting my toenails a lovely shimmering pink instead. I took a picture, of course. #seashell #nailart #metime

I'm utterly hopeless, I know. No wonder Erica says that I give her an ulcer.

Without me really noticing, the day went by, and besides a short trip inside for some leftover chicken salad, I barely moved all day, and it was, to be honest, *glorious*. I really needed that after everything, just a day alone with my thoughts and myself.

Though I'm never really alone anymore, am I? A day with "just us girls" is probably a more fitting description. Ilsbeth didn't seem to mind giving me some privacy, but stayed in my head as a gentle humming, sometimes remarking on the color of a butterfly or mourning the plum trees that no longer grow on the lawn, but otherwise keeping her peace.

It really was a lovely day.

It was just as dusk was setting in, the temperature dropping, and I was readying myself to go inside that I heard those keening sounds from the woods again, the ones I think might be foxes but which perhaps are not. I'd been hoping to hear them when Will was around to have his opinion as my local wildlife expert, but of course, they had to come when I was all alone.

They are creepy, too, and really give me the chills.

I found myself in a hurry to grab my plate and my wineglass and get my ass inside, but then, as I crossed the distance between the cherry tree and the castle, I suddenly caught sight of something lumbering toward me, just behind the tree line. Something large and white.

Yes, that's right! It was the horse again!

I had almost forgotten about it after all that had happened with Cathy and the rabbit, but obviously the horse hadn't forgotten about me, or that was my first thought anyway, as it paused just at the edge of the lawn, next to the blackberry brambles, and stared at me with its large black eyes. As before, I found it hard to move away, as if its gaze somehow froze me in place. It's a big thing with a very long mane and no bridle or anything like that.

The fox—or whatever it was—had stopped keening by then, which was a blessing, but also left the night so very quiet and somehow lonely. I only vaguely remember how my hold on the plate became slippery with perspiration and that the china fell down in the grass, unharmed. The horse stomped with its foot and took a few steps back, enough to snap me out of my trance, and it was *then* that it hit me, painfully clear and sharp as a razor blade: this was Cathy, again! The knowledge was so strong and sudden that I instantly felt ashamed for not having pieced it together before. This was the moths all over again! It was another sorry attempt to make me give up my book and leave—just another dirty trick!

"Fuck you!" I yelled at the horse, before fishing the plate up from the grass and striding back to the house. I couldn't believe that I'd let her intimidate me again, and by the time I reached the kitchen, I was fuming with anger.

I called her, of course. Maybe I shouldn't have. Will thinks I should have reached out to the police instead, but his sage advice came way too late, as my first impulse was to phone Cathy directly. *She* was even more the fool, though, because she actually answered. Not to criticize her or anything, but if someone had filed a restraining order against *me,* I would maybe not have been so eager to pick up—but she did.

I was out on the lawn again by then, because I wanted to check if I could hear her phone ringing in the woods, where she doubtlessly was, hiding with her pony. I stood beneath the canopy of the cherry three listening with all my might, but she must have had the phone on mute because I couldn't hear a thing, except for some rustling in the branches.

"What?" she barked when she picked up, sounding utterly hostile. "What do you want?"

"What do I want? What do *I* want, Cathy? Are you fucking kidding me?" I said, or something along those lines.

"What?" she barked again. "What more could you possibly want *now*? An apology, is that it? A slow crawl on my tummy to show you how remorseful I am? Haven't you done enough damage, ruining my life and reputation?"

For a moment there, I was speechless. The guile of that woman is truly spectacular. "It was *you* who put that putrid roadkill on my steps," I reminded her. "You don't get to pretend to be the victim here, Cathy!"

"Pah!" it sounded on the other end of the line. "You know as well as I do that it was a harmless prank! It didn't mean anything—"

"Everyone, including the police, strongly disagrees with you."

"Yeah? What about Ilsbeth? What does *she* say?"

I remembered the bloody egg and the blackberry braid. "She's not thrilled," I told Cathy, which only earned me a bout of bitter laughter.

"Ilsbeth was an adept hunter and wouldn't have lost it over a dead rabbit. She even skinned and butchered her prey herself. How does that fit with your little hippie narrative?"

I had of course not known that, but it sort of made sense with her hunger for meat. "That has nothing to do with anything," I said, quickly regaining my focus. "I'm calling about what happened tonight, with the horse and the screaming."

"What horse?" Cathy sounded wryly amused.

"*Your* horse, Cathy! The one you let into my garden!"

She went quiet for a moment. "I haven't let any horse into your garden," she said at last, but she sounded insecure. She had probably not expected to get caught.

"Oh, please, Cathy, just give it a rest. I know what I *saw*." Now it was my turn to sound bemused—as if *denial* could get her anywhere at this point.

"Maybe you *did* see a horse," she conceded, her voice a little brittle. "It didn't have anything to do with me, though. I'm *sure* it had nothing to do with me." But she didn't sound so sure. "I've never been taken with horses," she finished, as if that proved anything at all.

"But your sister is quite the equestrian. I'm sure she has a white one in her stables."

"I really don't know if she has. I never venture there myself. Are you sure it wasn't a bear or something? An albino deer, perhaps?" She sounded almost hopeful, and again I experienced a flicker of doubt. She really did sound very sincere, and if there's one thing I know about Cathy, it's that she folds quickly and easily under pressure—like when I confronted her with the theft of my pajamas. "You think it was me because of Owen Phyne, don't you?" Her voice had regained some of its usual brashness. "Because of that ridiculous story about him riding a white horse in the woods while playing a flute? It's just fairy tales, Elena, and I would never have chosen something so ridiculous—"

"As if a rabbit is so much better."

"Well, no, that really was just a stroke of inspiration."

"A really, really stupid idea!"

"Well, yes, I'll admit to that."

"I don't know why we're even having this conversation. *Of course* it was you who brought the horse."

"No, Elena, it wasn't."

"I'll go to the police," I said, suddenly realizing how ridiculous it was to even be arguing with her.

"Please do." She sounded cool. "If they check my phone, they'll see that I've been at home all night."

"Just leave me alone, Cathy," I warned her.

"More than happy to oblige."

She ended the conversation after that.

I don't care what she says, though—of course it was her! There's no other explanation that makes sense! Unless the horse is a runaway, of course, but it really would be too much of a coincidence if all of the stuff with Cathy happened, and then some animal who fits nicely with the lore just comes scampering through the castle woods.

The world doesn't work like that.

Had this been a year ago, I probably would have thought that the horse was some sort of message from my SOUL and not thought to link it to Cathy at all. As it is, I just think the animal is creepy and weird and hope that it'll stay away. It's as if there's something dirty about it. Something that warns you not to get too close.

Ilsbeth has been strangely silent since the horse appeared, and somehow that worries me more than anything else. Maybe Cathy's vehemence is too much to handle even for her. I tried to coax her forth again by serving up a couple of steaks, but she won't be so easily bribed. Now that she's not here, I sort of miss her and feel sorry for having had such mixed feelings and doubts. I really should nurture our relationship if there's ever to be a book.

Tomorrow, I'll call the police about the horse, and put a stop to Cathy's childish shenanigans.

She has clearly completely lost her mind!

# 27

*Transcript from the Nicksby Documents*

I cannot stand it when she is so well pleased with herself, her blue eyes sparkling with glee. How is it that she cannot fathom how the arrangement with Elena is in both our interests, that I am doing this for *her* as well as me?

"What you are doing is merely foolish theatrics," I tell her. "Nothing but a needless diversion." Inside I am fuming, as I cannot stand her meddling in my plans, and especially not for such an unworthy cause. But then she was always a loyal beast, protecting her witch even when such help was neither wanted not required. I think she might have misunderstood her bond with Catherine from the start, recognizing the taste of the child and latched on to her wretched soul without a second thought. She rarely does think things through—she *wants* and she *needs,* that is all, and one of the things she most frequently needs is to be adored by the one she is bound to serve. That, alas, is not me anymore, but the disturbed girl with the crow's nest hair.

I simply cannot make her stop nurturing that foolish notion.

"It will be just as the last time," I warn her while pouring soup into her trough. The frog's meat is uncooked and the water is rancid, but my mistress does not seem to mind. She licks the slick meat off a piece of bone and drops the latter down on the dirt floor. Behind her protrudes her mountain of "gifts"; the flame of the tallow candle glints off a piece of silver foil. Her favorite offerings are piled closest to her hooves: necklaces and china, shards of colored glass, finger rings and thimbles, a cup of tin, and a leather-bound book with a silver clasp. Much of it comes from Catherine—but not all.

"If you do not listen to me, it will happen all over again, and we will be left with nothing. Elena is the right one, I swear!" I am so desperate to make her understand that my voice is quivering as I stand there, holding the pot and the tarnished ladle. If I were still alive, I would cry. "You must give up on your quest for Catherine . . . The girl is long gone, even after all you did for her. What sort of gratitude is she showing you, leaving you here to rot on your own, after you fulfilled her every wi—"

She does not reply as such, but throws a sharp piece of bone at my forehead. Her face is wrinkled up with dismay and her black lip lifts in a snarl.

In life, I might have bled from the impact, but as things are, I barely feel it. I have had cause to be grateful for that, as my mistress does not always take care with fragile humans. She does not think twice about lashing out when annoyed, and when she was younger, even her childish playfulness could have dire consequences for soft girls and boys. In maturity, her lashes are delivered with precision and delight, and they smart much worse for it, even though my flesh is numb. It was better before, when I could believe that the hurt she inflicted was merely an accident.

I drop the pot and the ladle and sit down in my canvas chair. It creaks and moans under my weight. "Surely you don't want another one of your charges to fall down in the well," I say, keeping an eye on her hands all the while, in case I have to fend off flying frog limbs. "I'll have you know how unpleasant it is, falling into the dark water." Especially looking up and seeing your neighbors staring down at you from above.

"It will not end well," I mutter, but my mistress has lost all interest in me and my doomsaying. She thinks she has the upper hand; she thinks she is about to remove Elena from the board. It is a rejection of the girl, of course, but it is also a rejection of *me*. She has made her choice and will not have me meddling, even if *my* girl is ripe and ready, while hers is only dallying about, not even knowing *why* she does the things she does. Had there been any hope at all, she would have come to the well many moons ago, but my mistress does not see time as humans do. She thinks the continued flow of gifts is proof that their bond still stands.

I certainly know better. I went to see her myself, after her legs were ruined and she no longer came to the well. I wanted to coax her back to us, as I still had hope back then. I slipped into her as she lay in bed at her father's farm, with both legs wrapped in casts. I tried my best to speak to her, to send her dreams and messages, but she was like a blunt thing then, no longer open and free as before, but closed and bound by her misery. The dreams became nightmares and the messages twisted. She *did* come to the well again after I instilled such a longing in her heart—and one time she even brought Elena—but in the end, the only thing my visitations ever truly accomplished was to cause in her a growing obsession.

She thinks that she is *me* now, taking all my pain upon herself and spelling it out in ink, not blood—but though she believes herself to be clever, she truly does not know a thing. She does not see how it is the traces that I left behind that are playing tricks upon her mind. *She* will surely never sign her name—she barely even remembers my mistress. So yes, I am most dismayed that the beast will not welcome Elena, but keeps clinging to the hope of Catherine. Her meddling only makes everything harder to accomplish, as it turns Elena away from me, and closer to the mundane. She only thinks of her anger now and not of me at all. It truly is infuriating, but then what can I do? It is not as if I particularly enjoy my time with Elena, either. She is sulky and vain, and also a coward. Yet she *is* my girl.

I bend down to pick up the bone shard from the floor, then I throw it right back at my mistress. It bounces off her muzzle and has her howling—from surprise, not pain. The earth around us shivers when she swings her large head in my direction, her blue eyes blazing with both fury and hurt. Suddenly, I feel so tired of it all, and everything seems so hopeless.

"You gave that girl everything," I try again—one last time. "Yet where is her name written in blood? Where is the bridle and the flowers? She does not deserve a creature like you. She is obsessed with her fears and her sorrows."

My mistress enters my head then, sneaks in like an icy draft through a crack. She shows me a picture of a long gnarled hand—her own—engulfing the small and soft one of a child. Then she shows me a picture from underwater; I recognize the muddy, reedy bottom of the lake. I do not understand the latter.

"You never went swimming with Catherine," I say. "That must have been one of the other ones. Annie, perhaps, or Natasha." Though I dearly wish to, I do not remind her what happened to the woman. It makes me dizzy just to think of how many people we have tried to coax into the well, to sign their name in blood, and how often we have failed. It should have been an easy thing, but though we are strong, the living are stronger yet. Whatever connection we make with them, it is fragile and fine as spider silk. They cannot come unless they *want* to, and are sadly easily derailed. Worldly matters makes them hard to reach, and their fear is another obstacle yet. Our only hope lies with the lonely and the lost, as their minds are not as closed to us.

That, and the blood, of course. My mistress will have the right blood. I have told her many times how we cannot afford such a luxury, that we ought to take what we can get—someone yearning and ripe, like Elena—but she will not budge.

Not since she found Catherine.

When I look up from my reveries, I am startled to see the vehemence in her eyes. She has lifted her lip in a silent snarl, and her fingers have frozen around a piece of bloody meat. Her gaze meets mine with cold fire.

"Oh, you would not dare!" I say, suddenly aghast. I rise to my feet and stride toward her, stopping just as my toes touch the trough. "You would not do that—not *now*!"

My mistress only laughs at my misery, finding me so very amusing.

When will I ever learn that she has nothing but scorn and loathing left for those whom she no longer serves?

# Summer

# 28

*Elena Clover's journal*

*July 5*

Erica called last night to let me know that she and the kids are coming tomorrow and will stay over the weekend. This isn't exactly ideal. I just might have slightly exaggerated how far I've come with the packing, and Erica might have smelled a rat. I know that she worries—I wish that she wouldn't, and I know her trip to F— is just as much about checking up on me as to "enjoy a few last summer days at the castle," but what can I do?

This is Erica's house too.

I think it was me telling her about the horse that did it, to be honest. Even if Erica laughed about the rabbit, she cursed when I told her about the horse. She said that she found it "worrisome" that the restraining order didn't work, and she kind of has a point.

Though I really wish I were one of those people who, when faced with their own shortcomings, is able to laugh them off, or incorporate the flaws into a glamorous persona, I sadly have to report that I am not. Especially not when it comes to my sister. Which is why I've been running around like a maniac ever since we talked, trying—and failing—to make up for months' worth of work in one single night.

It really is stupid to react like this, as there's no way I'll be able to make much of a dent in Uncle John's piles of junk before Erica arrives, but at least it exorcises some of the guilt, and that's perhaps the point.

I'd just like to feel a little bit less of a terrible person when Erica arrives at the door.

The first thing I did was to make up the bed in Mom's old room for the kids, and the one in Erica's old room as well, so at least they'll feel welcome when they arrive. After that, I drove into town and bought ice cream and hotdogs and more lemonade to aid Erica in her quest to re-create the past. I bought chicken breast, too, and lettuce, in case she'd like to make Uncle John's chicken salad.

Ilsbeth argued all the way. *Get the roast,* she urged me as we passed through the meat section. *The veal looks red and nice.* She kept sending me pictures of what a proper family dinner ought to look like with glazed pork, sugared fruits, and tarts with golden crusts. The only thing we agreed on was the wine. I can't make her understand that in this day and time one must be rich to live simple, and that fatty foods are not in vogue. She only sneers at my smoothies and avocados, and had me retching one night as I ate some kale. *Food for cows and peasants,* she informed me as I spat acid into the porcelain bowl. *We ought to set some snares for fowl.* She doesn't object to soft fruits and berries, though, so that's where my diet is currently headed, and she didn't get any veal—I'm still the boss of us.

It was Marion at the counter again, and I asked her if anyone had mentioned my note about the horse, which still hung on the board by the entrance. She shook her head with a sad expression.

"No one seems to know it. Poor horsie," she added with a pout.

"I saw it again," I told her. "I'm really worried that it's living wild." I decided not to mention Cathy, but hoped that if Marion told enough people, the story would get back to Cathy's sister Louise. If the latter recognized the horse as hers, she might not give Cathy free rein of her stables.

"How is Brian?" I asked as I was about to leave.

"Same as ever," the girl shrugged. "His mom doesn't like *you* much, though, with the restraining order and all."

"You know about that?" I was honestly surprised.

"We all do," Marion said it as if it were nothing. "You can't keep secrets in F—."

"Oh!" I know about transparency in small communities, of course, but didn't think it encompassed police business. "How is Brian taking it?" I just couldn't help but feel sorry for him.

"Well, you know," another shrug. "He knows that his mom is *special*."

"If it's any help at all, I don't think Cathy liked me much before this happened either."

"Obviously not." The girl rolled her eyes. "She wouldn't have trespassed if she did."

With the shopping out of the way, I had no excuses left, and have since spent every waking hour trying to make sense of Uncle John's books and fishing gear. I hindsight, I think I should have chosen something bigger, more visible, to work on, like getting rid of the couch. The few measly cardboard boxes of "books to keep" don't quite reflect the hours it took to find the treasures amid the junk.

It's too late for regrets now, though. Erica will be here tomorrow.

Will came to help me last night, though I'm not sure how much of a help he really was, as he mostly seemed to distract me. I had been hoping he knew a little about fishing rods, but as it turned out, he did not. He kept googling the different models for information, which I easily could have done myself. I suppose I should be grateful that he bothered to show up. He also made sure that I paused to eat and clear my mind, and that is never wrong.

About midnight, he made an omelet and poured me a generous glass of red wine. We sat on the kitchen counter while we ate, both of us sweaty and slightly dusty, reeking of musty and old. It was the best food I've had all summer. Will had found some rolls as well and buttered them up for me while I ate. I made a video of our spread. #truelove #foodisgood #soulfood

"It's probably a relief that you'll be able to sell this place soon," he said while busying his hands with the bread and the butter. "I suppose you can't wait to be out of here, with Cathy and everything."

I really hate it when men do that: fishing for information instead of asking outright. That kind of tactic brings out the worst in me. "Yes," I answered with a bright smile. "It'll be great to leave F— behind."

"But what about your book?" He shifted on the counter; he was really far too big for it, with arms and legs hanging over the edge. "Shouldn't you be here to do research?"

He really couldn't have said anything worse; my heart started racing and a shudder ran down my spine just from the onslaught of stress. "I don't know," I said. "Maybe I'll put it on hold. There's a lot to deal with, you know."

"With the estate, you mean?" He had abandoned the rolls to scoop eggs into his maw.

"No, I mean with Cathy." No one would blame me for giving up the book after all I've been through this summer. "It's been an ordeal." I sipped my wine.

Will arched an eyebrow. "I thought that only made you more determined. That's what you said before."

"Yes, well, I suppose that's how I *ought* to feel, but I don't think I do. Not anymore." It felt like the most honest thing I'd said in weeks.

He gave me a sort of embarrassed smile. "But what about

Ilsbeth? Don't you have a *soul connection*?" He looked flustered all of a sudden. Will isn't very in tune with his SOUL.

I shook my head and drank some more wine. "I don't think she ever cared about the book."

Will didn't reply to that but only gave me a weird smile, as if he were embarrassed on my behalf. Just a few weeks ago, I would've been devastated that he responded like that, as I was so wrapped up in the idea of Ilsbeth and Owen Phyne, but I found that I didn't really care anymore.

I have been thinking lately that maybe Ilsbeth chose me because I am lonely, and I think that she might have been lonely too. This is not the sort of loneliness that a boyfriend can fix, but that other kind, the SOUL kind. I never played well with others, not really. I only became adept at pretending that I do. There's a certain power that comes with that, playing at being normal.

Cathy never learned that trick, and that's why her weirdness shows. It's embarrassing, to be honest, like a nipple showing. Still, in a strange twist of fate, I think she may actually be the person in F— who is the most like myself. Perhaps it wasn't just chance that brought us together when we were kids. Perhaps we saw something similar in each other?

In another time, in another world, I think we might even have been friends as before. Maybe we could have truly connected and left all the loneliness behind?

That will never happen now; we are far beyond that point, so instead I have Ilsbeth—dead but not gone.

Together we are less alone.

*July 11*

Erica and the kids have finally left and I'm *exhausted*! Maybe I have spent too much time alone out here, because one weekend of company and I am DONE. If I don't have to see another person again for a month, I'll be thrilled!

I argued with Erica when *she* pointed it out, of course. "Erica," I said. "I'm not alone. There's Will, and Cathy, obviously—and I'm also on first-name basis with Marion at the grocery store. Besides, I'm always online, so how can I possibly be alone?"

"That's different," she shrugged, sitting in her old place under the cherry tree, sipping raspberry lemonade through a paper straw. "I don't know about Will, but Cathy is hardly company. Besides, it's just when you've spent too much time on your own that you come up with all these crazy notions—"

"My inspired—somewhat *brilliant*—ideas," I corrected her.

"Whatever you'd like to call them." She rolled her eyes.

"It's only when I'm alone that I can hear my own head."

"It's not good to be alone so much. You should have your own family."

"Uh, no," I replied, while watching my niece and nephew play with the old croquet set on the lawn. Julia was green, Ethan blue. "That just isn't for everyone."

"What about Will, though? Do you think he'll last?"

"Oh, I don't know . . ." On the one hand, just the thought of having him always around made me feel like the walls were closing in around me, but then again, he was *Owen Phyne*—wasn't he?—so I really should want to have him with me. It was all very confusing.

"Oh, Elena," Erica sighed. "You always do this."

"Do what?"

"Well, you're reckless. You start all these relationships and then you dump the poor guy the moment it starts to get serious. Men are people too, you know. They have hearts like the rest of us." She scowled at me over the polka-dotted straw. Her hair was shorter since the last time I saw her and shaved at the neck. Just a froth of chestnut curls were left on top of her head. Both of her kids had inherited that hair, and it was a bitch to untangle after bathtime.

"I don't mean to be cruel," I muttered. "I'm just not very good at it." *It* being relationships.

"You never learned how to compromise," my little sister scolded me.

"Maybe it'll be different this time." But of course, I knew it wouldn't be. Owen Phyne or not. "There isn't a universal rule, you know. Not everyone needs to be with someone."

"No, but I think it would be good for *you*." Such a nice and unremarkable sentence, which still held so much. What she really wanted to say was that she worried for my sanity, and would rather not be the one to pick up the pieces if I one day shattered. She would never ever say that to my face, though. "How is the book coming along?"

"It's great," I lied. "Just wonderful! Ever the more reason *not* to keep people around."

Besides a few skirmishes like that, the visit was surprisingly nice. I could tell that Erica had decided to be on her very best behavior and not berate me more than absolutely necessary. It also helped that the kids were with her. It's hard to fall into a full-blown fight with an eight-year-old and a ten-year-old running around and pleading for ice cream.

The kids really loved the castle, and Julia cried a bit when Erica told her that we were going to sell it. I was right there with my niece, truth be told—this really is a lovely place, strange horses and dead rabbits aside. It seems like an idiot move to sell it, but then I need the money, so there's that. We spent most of

Saturday and some hours on Sunday packing up more of Uncle John's stuff, so the sale is definitely still happening.

Erica didn't come right out and complain about my lack of progress, but remarked, a little surly, that I should perhaps not have tried to clear out the house, get a new boyfriend, and write a book at the same time. I told her that all of it would have worked out just fine if only Cathy hadn't been harassing me.

"You can't blame everything on her," Erica said then, pausing on the cellar stairs while balancing a cardboard box of camping equipment on her thigh. Her forehead was covered in perspiration and dust, and she had donned one of Uncle John's old checkered shirts as working attire. It still reeked faintly of fish. "Cathy is clearly a very disturbed woman, but you, my friend, are talking to *ghosts*."

"What is that supposed to mean?" I huffed at the insinuation. I had reached the top of the stairs by then and dumped my own box down on the floor. It was a heavy one and I was panting slightly. My pink T-shirt was smeared with grime.

"Just that the both of you perhaps should give the past a rest."

"I am nothing like Cathy," I barked down the stairs. "Ilsbeth came to *me*, I didn't go *chasing* her."

"Didn't you, though?" Her eyebrows rose.

I slammed the door in her face, leaving her in utter darkness, and shamelessly reveled in the sound of her curses as they reached me through the wood.

Clearly, she didn't understand.

Every night during their stay, after the kids had gone to bed, Erica would plant herself by the window in the living room with Will's binoculars and a bottle of wine, keeping guard of the lawn. I was there with her, though I thought it was pointless. If Cathy was up to something, we'd know it soon enough. It's not like she's been subtle. Still, Erica insisted and so there we were, each in our ratty chair, drinking the night away, while absolutely nothing happened outside the window.

"Shouldn't you write?" Erica asked.

"I'm taking a break while you're here," I replied, while guilt made my stomach churn with unease.

Sunday afternoon, we brought the kids with us and ventured out in the woods, partially to check if the boat was still at the lake—I had told Erica it was not, but she somehow didn't believe me. Our other purpose was to show Julia and Ethan the well. Erica had found the sketches from the attic, still lying in a heap on the dining room table, and I suppose that's what inspired her.

"Natasha Witt died there, you know," she had told me while standing there on the dining room floor, with the sketches in one hand and a half-eaten sandwich in the other. "First her daughter got kidnapped or something, and then she threw herself in the well."

An ice-cold chill passed through me. "How do you know?"

"Uncle John told me." She shrugged and put the sketches down. "It's a bit eerie, don't you think? That she drew the place over and over—maybe she was fantasizing about her own death."

I *did* find it eerie. Very much so—and really not the kind of knowledge I wanted to have in my head. I tried to ask Ilsbeth about it, but she remained mum.

"Why do you want to take the kids there?" I asked Erica a little later, just as we were readying ourselves to go out. It seemed a strange choice after what she'd told me. "A suicide spot isn't exactly the perfect place for a family outing."

Erica just shrugged and set to tie her shoelaces. "Bad things have happened everywhere. It doesn't *mean* anything, and I've told the kids that you're writing a book about it, so now they're all excited. Julia thinks it's a magic well."

"Like a wishing well?"

"Just that. She also hopes there are frogs living inside it. She's had a thing for frogs lately."

"That's sweet," I muttered. "There's definitely a lot of frogs."

When we came out on the lawn, it had started to rain; a fine drizzle came from above and made everything feel instantly damp. It felt like a sign, to be honest. Perhaps we really shouldn't go there. Still, I said nothing as we started down the path that would take us first by the lake and then to the well. Instead, I tried to ignore my growing unease and focus on the kids, who seemed to love both the day and the rain, bouncing before us on the narrow path while sharing trivia and asking endless questions.

"There's a bird, Mom. Oh, it flew away!"

"Ew, something pooed over there!"

"Look at this giant puddle. Do you think I can cross it without getting wet?"

"Aunt Elena, are there bears in these woods?"

"Can we have ice cream when we get back?"

It was almost a relief when we arrived at the well, but the relief soon turned to horror, as the kids instantly ran to the well and shouted into it to check for echoes. I kept expecting the old stones to crumble under their weight and the well to eat them whole!

"Come back here!" I shouted. "Be careful! Don't lean on it like that!"

Erica didn't seem the least bit concerned but moved around at a leisurely pace, admiring the surrounding trees. "It'll hold," she said. "It's been there for hundreds of years. I don't think this is the day the well will crumble."

"But what if they fall in!" I fretted.

"My kids are smart," said Erica, but that didn't comfort me at all. Before I knew it, they were gathering pebbles and pieces of tree bark to chuck down in the well.

Overhead, the rain kept drizzling.

"Did you hear a frog?" Julia asked. Her voice was brimming with wishes and enthusiasm.

"I wonder how far down it goes?" Ethan looked down in the black hole.

"Ew, it smells bad," Julia remarked.

"I think I can see a bone down there," Ethan said.

"It's probably just a stick of some kind." Erica was utterly chill. "Bones don't float."

"It'll be dark soon," I told them, having noticed how the sky bled from pale to dark gray.

"What the fuck is that?" said my sister. All her Zen was suddenly gone. I looked over, and saw her standing ramrod straight beneath a gnarly old spruce tree.

"What is it?" I asked as I bounded over, my heart suddenly working like a piston in my chest. Whatever it was she had found I knew it had to be bad for her to curse in front of her kids.

Ethan and Julia echoed my question: "What is it, Mom? What do you see?"

"I really don't know." Erica sounded more surprised than scared, but also choked up, as if she were sick. Just when I arrived at her side, she grabbed a stick and poked at something on the ground in front of her.

I looked over her shoulder, and felt a little sick myself.

Under the tree, close to a root, was a pile of yellowing bones. There was no skull, so it was impossible to tell exactly what they were from, but they weren't small, so it had to be from something large. It was maybe the way they were placed that made them look unnerving; they seemed to be deliberately piled, as if someone had placed them there.

Erica was poking at the bones with her stick. The kids had come up behind us, and seemed to be taking the discovery in stride.

"Cool," said Ethan.

"Is it a cow?" asked Julia.

"What the fuck is *that*?" my sister cursed again as she bent down to fetch something from the ground, something small and twig-like that had fallen out of the bone pile when she poked. She held it up for me to see, looking utterly baffled.

It felt as if something sharp pierced my chest when I recognized the odd little thing for what it was: a crude doll, made from sticks, and held together with strips of maroon cloth. Pieces of bright yellow yarn were glued onto the "head" to look like hair.

"What the fuck *is* that?" This time it was me who asked before snatching the doll from Erica's loose grasp. I had just seen the silvery thing dangling from the stick doll's chest. I held the doll up, close to my face, and squinted at the glittering piece of jewelry: a small earring shaped like a flower, and set with a tiny, blue stone. "That's *mine*!" I cried out. "That's fucking mine! Mom bought that for me on Cyprus, remember?"

"Oh, shit," Erica muttered and rubbed her hands as if she'd touched something that left an itch. "Are you sure it's yours? That was years ago!"

"Yes, I'm sure! It disappeared, remember? The summer I was twelve? While we were out here . . . Mom was furious with me, but you thought that Cathy had taken it—"

"Shit!" my sister said again, a little more forcefully. She spun around on her heels and looked at her children, who were blessedly mum despite all the drama. "That's it, kids. We're going home!" There must have been something in her voice that they recognized, because neither of them objected as we started on the walk back, me still clutching the doll in my hand. My fingers felt cold and stiff around it.

"Why don't you race each other to the house," Erica prompted her children in her best fake-cheery voice. The kids—no fools—looked at her with worried eyes, but thankfully did as they were told. They might not have known exactly what had happened in the clearing, but they did know that *something* had gone down, and that it was best not to pry.

"Did you leave it out there yourself?" Erica asked as soon as the kids were around the next bend. "As some sort of weird ritual or something?"

"No! God! Erica!" I hissed at her.

"Sorry! I just had to ask." We walked in silence for a minute before she spoke again. "Are we sure it's the same earring?"

"I don't know!" How could I? "But it looks the same, doesn't it?"

"Yeah, I had the same pair, only with a red stone."

"Yes, I remember," I muttered.

"You should toss it away," Erica said. "Take off the earring, maybe, and then throw the doll away." She sounded as if she were about to gag.

"I can't do that," I said.

"Why?"

"Well, it's meant to be *me*, obviously."

She gave me a worried look. "So?"

"So I can't leave me out in the wind and rain."

"What?" She stopped abruptly and turned to look at me. "It's just a *doll*, Elena!"

"Yes, but . . ." How could I explain that since *someone*—and that would be Cathy—had made it in my likeness, I somehow didn't want anything bad to happen to it. "Maybe I'll need it as evidence," I said. "In case Cathy keeps harassing me."

Erica seemed to relax a little. "Good point," she agreed.

"You always said that it was Cathy who stole that earring." We started to walk again.

"She always stole things from you."

"Besides the pajamas, I didn't notice." I had to struggle to keep up with my sister as she strode more than she walked, agitated by the day's disgusting events.

"You always had your head in the clouds—never saw anything. What is the point of it, though? Why did she leave that doll out there?" The baffled expression was back.

"They thought Ilsbeth Clark made dolls of the kids who disappeared and left them by the well, like an offering." I had read all about it in *Strange Stories and Legends from F—.*

"You've *got* to be kidding me!"

I shook my head. "Maybe Cathy hoped that I would disappear too."

"I don't know which one of you is weirder." It was Erica's turn to shake her head.

"Well, I'm the *victim* in this! I'm not the one who's roaming the woods and planting curses!" I thought she was crazy unfair.

"You *will* take the doll to the police, won't you?"

"Of course I will." It felt filthy in my hand.

"And no excuses or delays, Elena! The police have to know about this!"

"It's only a doll—"

"It was 'only' a rabbit. The woman is clearly insane!"

I sighed. "I'll tell the police, I promise."

She nodded with satisfaction, and then she said, "She must have kept that earring all these years—what kind of a person *does* that?"

I couldn't give her an answer, so I didn't even try.

When we came back to the castle, I put the doll in the drawer of my bedside table, where it has been ever since.

## July 16

That fucking horse is back! God! I thought we were done with this crap, but there it is, stalking the lawn and looking at me with big and glossy eyes. I'm watching it from the window now with you, trusty journal, balancing on my knee, and Will's night binoculars in my hand, having discovered it about twenty minutes ago when I took out the trash.

As before, it doesn't really do much but stomp around out there and look at the house from time to time, always keeping close to the tree line. I've been scanning the woods behind it keenly, but have so far not seen a trace of Cathy. She's probably hiding behind a trunk somewhere, with a portable speaker so she can play those uncanny fox sounds that currently pollute the air. I really can't *believe* that woman!

I tried to call her, of course, but she didn't pick up—too busy with her shenanigans in the woods, I suppose. I texted her too, as soon as the monster appeared out there, but so far, I haven't gotten an answer. Will is on his way, though, so maybe we'll be able to chase them off, horse and woman both.

There's no way I'm going out there alone.

That horse is really creepy! Its coat almost seems to glow in the moonlight. It also has a most unnerving tendency to move just when I'm not watching, so when I look up, it has changed its posture, moved a little to the left, or turned its head. It doesn't seem to move at all when my eyes are on it, but is just standing out there like some alabaster statue. There's some greenery woven into its hair, and the more I look at it, the more convinced I am that Cathy has put some sort of powder on it or something that makes it appear luminescent.

Its eyes are very dark.

I'm definitely going to call Louise tomorrow, and tell her what Cathy does with her horse. It has to be hers, as nothing else makes sense! I'm also going to call Officer Rogers again, and have him look into it. Granted, he didn't seem too concerned when I called him earlier about the doll, but *this* definitely feels like a threat. Not that I can tell exactly *why*, as the animal is just standing there. Maybe it's the high-pitched sounds in the air. Maybe it's the uncanny glow. Whatever the reason, I find I am afraid, and really, really hope that Will arrives soon! If the police weren't too worried about the doll, *he* certainly was, and he couldn't *believe* that they didn't even want to see it!

"They didn't think I could remember exactly what earrings I had at twelve," I told him over breakfast the day after Erica had left. "Officer Rogers kept asking if I had a receipt."

"That's just stupid," he huffed. "It was a gift, wasn't it? Of course you'd recognize it."

"Erica is looking for hers, so we can compare them. They're pretty unusual. Mom bought them on Cyprus."

"You shouldn't have to prove anything at all," said he. "You're the victim, after all."

"It doesn't feel like that, though, not when I am talking to the police. I think they see it as some sort of childish spat."

"There's nothing childish about dead animals and voodoo dolls."

"*Poppet*," I corrected him automatically. That's what Ilsbeth called it.

"They have to look at the big picture," Will proclaimed. He had toast crumbs on his lips and waved a glass of orange juice in the air. "The doll isn't that spooky alone, perhaps, but together with the rest, there's a pattern."

"Maybe *you* ought to be a detective," I said. "Right now you're definitely of more use to me than the real ones. They say that as long I can't prove that Cathy's been here—and she *still* denies it—there's nothing they can do."

"Well, of course it's her, who else could it be?"

I shrugged and gave a heartfelt sigh. "I can't even prove that she stole the earring. It's been too many years since it happened."

"Why don't you just tell Cathy that you've given up the book?" Will reached over with the pitcher to top up my glass with more vitamin C goodness.

"Because I haven't." At least not officially. "If I say that, she wins, and I don't think that her shitty behavior should be rewarded!"

"It would give you some peace, at least, while you finish up packing." He finally brought a napkin to his lips to get rid of those annoying crumbs. A flash of pain crossed his features—he really doesn't want me to leave!

"I'm sorry, but I won't give her that satisfaction." Horse or no horse.

When I looked up again just now, the horse had come closer. I wonder if Cathy has somehow trained it to stand still when watched, or if it does it by itself as some sort of survival strategy? I really don't know much about horses. It has entered the lawn proper now, and I really do hope Will arrives soon. He should have been here already.

I'm prodding my insides for signs of Ilsbeth, but she is nowhere to be found. I wonder if she's afraid of the horse too, and if so, why that is.

I really just want this all to be over with, and I miss Uncle

John like crazy. I was *so* wrong to doubt before—we *really* have to sell the castle! We have to close the door on his ramshackle house and move on!

I really wish that I wasn't alone.

The horse is close now, almost at the window. Why does it look at me like that? The noises, too, have come even closer. It sounds like there's a fox dying on my lawn.

Is the *horse* making the sounds?

What *is* this shit?

# 29

*Transcript from the Nicksby Documents*

My mother, Anna Willows, acquired the beast for herself shortly after she arrived on these shores. She had left her own mother's house at fifteen, against the family's will, seeing no future for herself among the steep mountains and fjords. She arrived in what little she could glean for herself without her mother taking notice: a shift and a dress; a book of recipes, a pair of lace gloves, and her grandfather's collection of copper coins.

"She had a gnome living in the house," Anna told me, referring to my grandmother. "The gnome was as a watchdog, looking out for her possessions. If he ever caught a stranger inside, he would make a whistling sound, so loud that it hurt in your ears. That was why I could only take lesser things," she said, "and I had to be very careful, too. I stole the copper coins one by one and hid them in a sock."

My grandmother, Ingfrid, was very powerful, and spoke to the gods of hills and woods. She traded secrets and cures for riches, and would still a man's heart for the price of a soul. The first of these spoils, she would keep for herself, but the latter she would use to barter with her gods, who relished such things to eat. She had learned the craft from her mother, who had learned it from hers before that. Our family, my mother said, had always kept a close bond to the hidden world, and had always kept daemons about.

"She said that we came from the gods in the hills," Anna

told me. "She said we were godly bastards, but I never believed much in that."

Anna was a third daughter, however, and with two older brothers as well, very little of what Ingfrid had gained would ever fall into her hands. Her mother still wanted her to stay at home and learn the family trade, as she was gifted in that way, but it was not enough for Anna. She had wanted adventure, she told me—she had wanted to see the world. She had wanted to marry, too, but the bouquet of young men to choose from in the small place where she grew up was not very tempting at all. She therefore decided to leave her mother's house, figuring that she had enough tricks up her sleeve to make her way alone, but when she shared those plans with Ingfrid and begged for a little money to start with, the old witch said no.

"I will not pour water out of our river," she had said, meaning that she would only pay for something if she gained something in turn, if that be Anna's service, or a new girl child to be trained in the old ways. She would only offer water if it ran back into the river, and so poor Anna had to steal her grandfather's coins one by one and save up for her fare across the sea.

She was brimming with hope as she arrived on the new shore, thinking the world and its wonders ripe for her taking, but of course, she was deeply disappointed. She had never been poor before—had never known lean times. The gold from the hills had always kept her fed, and she knew nothing of how to handle hunger. Soon, all the copper coins were gone, and the shift and her maidenhead, too—not that she ever missed it. She had her tricks, but had never properly trained with her mother, so they could only pave the way, not take her as far as she needed to go. She had brought something else from home, though, which would come to serve her well: the shrewdness of her mother, and a cunning and ruthless heart.

She arrived at George Willows's farm as his housekeeper, shortly after his wife had fallen ill. Anna knew nothing of housekeeping, but had charmed her way into the house. It is easy if you know how to: just a few words written in blood on parchment and hidden upon one's body. If her aim was to marry my father from the start, or if she had a hand in his first wife's illness, I cannot say for sure. I do not find it unlikely, however. She truly was in dire need of home and hearth, having so recklessly abandoned her own, and the copper coins were gone. She was too proud to turn tail and run back.

Anna always knew how to make people love her, and never even considered, I think, how George Willows truly loved his sick wife, and that the latter would not let go of life but clung to it with all her might; quivering on the brink of death for months. Anna spent her time wisely, though: mending shirts and cooking stews, charming the young Willows boys with sweet treats and fairy tales, making shadow puppets that moved on their own.

She admitted to me once, after too much wine, that she had done her very best to help Mrs. Willows along, but that the frail and sick woman had seemed immune to her charms. "I was not strong enough then," she told me, "and the woman was too deeply loved."

Yet Anna waited and bided her time, sure in her heart that once Mrs. Willows had taken her last breath, her husband, who was a handsome man at the time, if not entirely young, would have grown used to her presence in the house, and would lift his gaze from the plate of roast to admire the shapely cook.

What she had not accounted for was a rival.

Mrs. Willows had a sister, Mary, who was a pretty, blond young widow. One day she showed up with her trunks at the Willows farm, ready to help tend her sick sister. As Anna told it, the newcomer was patient as an angel, had the sweetest voice, and the whole family instantly adored her. George Willows treated her as an equal and sought her advice in all. It quickly became clear to Anna, as she served the woman meat and puddings, that Mary had the same aim as herself, and was set on marrying George Willows. Suddenly, there were *two* women waiting for Mrs. Willows to die, two women spoiling the children, and two women fighting for the privilege of mending George Willows's socks.

One of them had to go.

Again, Anna brought out her charms and spells, trying to sow discord between Mary and George, but again, her powers failed her. She ruefully regretted not paying more attention when her mother had tried to make her learn, but by then it was too late for that. Anna needed help, and fast. She had surely not been spending a year scrubbing floors and boiling broth for a sick woman just to be thwarted so close to the end. So, gritting her teeth and swallowing her pride, she penned a letter home.

Among all the daemons Ingfrid consorted with, there was one in particular that Anna thought would be perfect for her needs. High up in the mountains above her mother's house there were lakes where these creatures roamed free. Sometimes they would appear as shining white horses grazing on the banks and on the moors, while at other times, they would appear as beautiful young men, and it was hard to resist them then. No matter what shape they chose, their goal was always the same: they had a taste for human flesh and souls, and so they wanted to lure both women and men to a watery death.

Only Anna's family knew how to capture and tame such beasts, rowing onto the lakes with fishing nets they had gotten from the hills. Once a daemon had been captured, an agreement would be proposed, as one cannot make such powerful creatures servants against their will. Nothing good ever came of such attempts, only bloodshed and mayhem.

Anna, at nineteen, had no qualms about entering such an agreement, but worried that her mother would not help her at all after she had made away with the copper coins. She was planning to use the daemon, should she be able to acquire one, to lure Mary out of the house to drown herself in the millpond. She was young enough and naïve enough to be swayed by a daemon, Anna figured.

To Anna's great delight, her mother *did* reply to her missive, and even better than the letter was the present that came with it. Packed in a wooden crate stuffed with hay was a large glass jar filled with water from the lake, and in its midst floated the daemon. It was a shifting thing in the jar: sometimes horse, sometimes human, both shapes unclear and unfinished as if the creature had been hastily made from clay. There was only one problem with it.

"It was a filly," Anna exclaimed when she told me the story, adding a bitter laugh. "What on earth would I want a mare for? I had no use for such a thing—she could not seduce Mary, and even if it *had* been a stallion, it would have been far too young to do as I wished. Mother knew she had given me the wrong sort, but she wrote so prettily in her letter of how she wanted to give me a rare gift. Only one in a thousand of such creatures are mares, so I suppose that is why I kept her after all. One must treasure what is rare, as it might become of value one day."

"Did Ingfrid know just what you wanted it for?" I asked. "She might have wanted to give you a present, to reconcile—"

"Oh, not her!" Anna huffed and rolled her eyes. "Mother never did a thing without some hidden meaning. She gave me what I wanted for sure—she was generous even, but it was not what I had asked for, and was of no use to me. She was still mad, I knew that then."

Yet Anna signed the contract and let the daemon loose in the millpond. The beast was young then but grew fast and required a lot of meat, which Anna stole from the pantry. Mary died anyway, shortly after the beast was unleashed, though she succumbed to sickness in her bed, merely a week after Mrs. Willows finally drew her last breath. It might have been something in their tea. Anna's ambition came to fruition, and she married my father before the year was out. It was a shame, though, that their first year as a wedded couple was marred by the loss of George Willows's sons, who mysteriously drowned in the millpond, but such is life, as Anna used to say. Accidents do happen.

When I left my father's house to marry Archibald Clark, Mother passed the beast on to me, thinking I might find some use of it. She had also been suffering from chest pain for some time, and was reluctant to keep it much longer, lest she should die with it in her keep. It was important not to be enthralled to daemons; she had taught me as much early on. I was young and strong, though, and none of us thought I would die so young. I had meant to keep it as a guardian, being a young woman in a strange place, but that, of course, was not what happened.

Even before death, she ruled me.

I had not had the beast for long before I realized how Mother had been too impatient, too unwilling to learn and observe, for the daemon she gave me can indeed sway a heart with a promise of love. She might never have had the appearance to seduce with a promise of lust and release, but she could surely lure with the love of a mother, or that of a sister—a kindred soul.

When the beast called Elena to the lake, I stood nearby, watching.

## 30

I had fought so hard to keep Elena safe, to keep her mind intact, but I am in the beast's service, and so her presence will render me mute, just as it will stay my power.

She will have what she wants, and that is the truth of it.

I will say that I tried the best that I could. In the days since she showed me the image of the watery grave, I made Elena turn up the music whenever the beast was keening, and had her take the medicine to help her sleep at night. I even urged her to put up some wards, though the beast only laughed at that, as she knew it would not work. When I returned from my visitations, she sat beside me in the burrow, humming, while spinning a longing for death. She lifted her black lips and smiled at me as she set her snare and prepared for the catch.

Just as my uncles once caught *her*.

It was a full moon on the night when it happened, and an uneven trail of glistening light cut the black lake in half. I knew that my mistress had left the burrow and I knew what was to come—yet I had hoped, I suppose, that she would change her mind, even if she never had before.

Elena was crying when she arrived at the water's edge, lying on my mistress's broad back and clutching at the braided mane. Her painted nails gleamed in the light from the moon, as my mistress's coat shone in the dusky night. Elena did not even try to escape anymore, she had sensed in my mistress a promise of love, of care and of joy eternal, for such is the power of her song. At first, it sounds like a painful keening, but then, as you listen, the tune turns sweet with longing. If you are unlucky enough, it slithers into your mind. Elena was not taken by force, but had climbed onto the beast's back willingly.

I stood there, under a weeping willow, as my mistress's hooves touched the water's edge, and there was not a sound but Elena's soft crying. There she went—my hope—my girl, into the cold of the lake. Further and further out they went; deeper and deeper in. My mistress moved at a leisurely pace, knowing only too well that she had won our battle. As soon as Elena was fully submerged, my mistress would break the spell of her song and strangle the woman with her bare hands, for no other reason than to feel her squirm, to see the terror in her eyes when she learned she had been played.

As the water closed over Elena's head, I could not help but remember them all, the ones who came before, the other wild hopes that had burst like bubbles.

Karen Smythe was a maid at Nicksby and she came to the well to drop flowers into it, remembering me, as it was, as she had been in my embroidery circle as a girl. My mistress was willing to capture Karen and take her in my stead, but the woman did not have the constitution of a witch; she believed herself to be consorting with the devil, and opted for death instead.

The next one was my mistress's pick, and for once, it was a man. He was a poor farmer named Russel Abrahams who was quite enamored with the beast, even though she looks fearsome. He kept coming to the well with gifts for her, just trinkets and such that he gleaned from his neighbors: a cup made from tin and a box of nails, a bottle with a silver stopper. Treasured goods for a poor farmer. Meat, though, he did not bring, thinking it too precious, and that was the end of him.

The next year, there was a spinster called Mariette Spoon, who tasted foul, according to my mistress. She prefers blood that is strong and rich, and laced with something of the gods from the hills, which is rare around here.

Ella Nivens, mother of five, did not have the right blood either, but like Elena, she was touched in the mind, and prone to speaking with the unseen. I chose that woman, and advocated fiercely on her behalf, though my mistress was reluctant. Our argument concluded when Ella started fretting about the safety of her children should she enter such an unholy covenant. I deemed Ella a lost cause, and let my mistress do as she pleased.

Next, there was another man, a woodchopper named Stevens who fell under my mistress's sway for a while, and then a young woman, Esther Fredrick, who also had an ill-fated change of heart. Then Natasha, of course. Natasha Witt. The wife of Michael Witt, who built the new house on the Nicksby ruins. I first came to know her after Lena, her daughter, disappeared on a stroll with her nanny in the woods. It was my mistress who had taken her, of course, taken her and eaten her up, bones and gristle and all. The young mother often went searching for her missing child, and the sounds of her crying and heartbreak filled the clearing for days. Mayhap that was why I went to her and lodged myself inside her, wanting to ease her horrible pain.

Natasha tasted right, according to the beast. Her blood smelled of the hills and was sweet on her tongue. I had hope then, and it seemed the woman was ripe for the taking—eager as a pup to have her pain taken away. It all fell apart when she found a silver button in the well, and figured out that it was my mistress who had taken little Lena.

Mrs. Witt ended up floating in the well.

I lost hope after that, and my spirit diminished. I barely even noticed the heartbroken who flocked to the well and threw themselves in. Some of them ended up in the trough at my mistress's feet. I barely even gave it a thought when the beast went hunting, and did not pay attention to whatever schemes she spun, not before Catherine—and then, Elena.

I had thought that there was hope after all.

So I will admit to being disappointed when my mistress brought Elena to the lake. I had so dearly been hoping that this time it would work. Elena had seemed so perfect in every way: struggling and lost—bitterly lonely, and with a penchant for enchantment and dreams.

Now she was nothing but waterlogged flesh that would slowly rot and be gone.

"Don't you see that it is the both of us you hurt?" I said when we had both arrived back at the burrow. "She would have come to you! I am sure of it!" I held the skull of a trout in my hand and slammed it against the table as I spoke. The fragile thing fell apart from the impact and was nothing by the time I was done. It reminded me of Elena, that fish: battered until she gave in.

My mistress only shook her head and reminded me in her wordless way that Elena had not much liked my company anymore—she had often refused to listen, or pretended not to sense my presence—so what was it to me if the girl lived?

I only snorted at all that. "It is you who have set her against me," I said. "You and that fool you so adore." Before their meddling, Elena had been as soft and pliable as clay. It was only the fear they had stirred up in her that had made her harder for me to possess. "I don't see why she had to die," I said next. "Surely you could have just chased her from Nicksby."

I knew it was in vain, though. The girls—and boys—we courted always died in the end, if it was the beast's intention or not. It seemed to be imprinted in the daemon's nature.

She will always destroy.

We learned that lesson early on, Owen Phyne and I. The beast was young then, as they do not age as we do but slowly over the years, and whenever there is a new contract, they receive a burst of vitality and revert to a younger self.

She was also hungry, and though Owen and I did what we could to sate her, giving her as much as half a bull at a time, she would still smell the people who came to the Nicksby well and emerge from its depths to feed or to play, leaving bloody wreckage in her wake.

Yet we tried.

Owen found that she was soothed by music, and so he would play his flute for her. I thought that she was like any other child, and would gift her toys to play with. She liked all that glittered or shone, and so I gave her mirrors and silver teacups. She enjoyed being groomed, and so I spent many an hour combing through her mane and braiding it with flowers and leaves. Owen thought she needed a friend, and so he brought a young foal from market, but our ferocious beast just ate it up.

Owen was still mesmerized by her, even if our efforts were in vain. Ever since I told him of my secret daemon, he never ceased to wonder what it would take to tame her power and put her under our sway. Unlike me, who came to see her as a danger, Owen, like Anna, saw a weapon—something that could be trained and put to use.

His skull in the corner tells me he was wrong, and that I, in the end, was right. It certainly gives me no pleasure, though. I would rather have been wrong and had Owen by my side. I wonder just why she killed him, as she *did* seem to care for him before. Perhaps it is customary among her kin for a daughter to kill her father as she comes of age—or mayhap she was merely hungry.

We shall never know.

But now she has killed Elena, and I am once again trapped

in this dark, dank hole with my scourge—my mistress—and no closer to respite. The beast is aging, that is true, but I do not know how long she will live, or if her death will even make a difference. If my worst nightmares are to come true, my mistress will die, but *I* will still be here, trapped in the well forever—and even more alone than before.

I would like to say that the latter does not bother me, as the beast is surely poor company, but I have come to appreciate even meagre comforts. At least her ugly and pale visage is better than looking myself in the eyes, though one might argue that those two are one and the same. The beast is I, and I am the beast now, or so I have come to believe.

Perhaps I am finally losing my mind.

I do not know how it works, though, this bond between us— this tether of blood—and that is why I am in such a rush to escape this place before she succumbs to old age. I know that the words on the parchment mean nothing to her, that they are for humans alone. It is the intent that matters, and the taste of the witch—the offering of the blood itself. She is as a duckling just hatched from the shell, latching on to taste and scent. Following blindly and loving fiercely, until death, at last, makes a servant of the mistress.

We so easily sign away our fate when we are young and foolish and untried. Not even once did I think to ask just *what* it entailed, this "servitude beyond the natural life."

Perhaps I do deserve my fate for unleashing the beast upon this town. She has done much damage over the years. Yet I cannot quite fathom why she would not even try to love Elena. Surely my mistress must be sick of me by now, with my constant complaints and my surly disposition. Even *I* am sick of me at times.

"You should not have done it," I tell my mistress every day. "Elena could have been the right one."

Then every day she shakes her head, in denial of my wisdom, I always thought, but tonight she gives me something more: an image in my head of a young girl in a nightgown littered with moons and stars, limping toward our clearing. Her dark hair is braided, and in her hand is a gift for the well, wrapped up in a plastic bag.

"Catherine?" I scoff. "Catherine is not the right one—"

She interrupts me with a flare of annoyance that begins at my toes and ends at my crown. She tells me that I do not understand.

"What is it, then?" I ask. "Why are you showing me this?"

In my head, the girl is coming closer; her little face is scrunched up with intent. Her hand is in the plastic bag, pulling up a twisted thing, holding it up in the light of the moon.

Finally, I get my mistress's meaning.

"You did not desire to kill her," I say, and for once, I am astonished—and afraid. "It was another's will at play."

# Fall

## 31

*An open letter to the people of F—, continued*

For the longest time I had been hoping that I wouldn't have to talk about it, at least not here, in my open letter to the people of F—, but as the rumor mill keeps churning and people's treatment of me deteriorates, I feel that I have to address it after all.

I'm of course speaking of what happened on the night Elena died.

My lawyer will likely flog me for this candidness, and my son might not come around for pasta again for a while, but I'm up against a wall here, and don't know what else to do.

Some of you may find such a statement utterly melodramatic, and even doubt that the pressure I'm under is anywhere near as severe as I describe, but to you I just want to say: you don't even know the half of it!

As late as yesterday, I had an email titled "You Are the ReAL Witch in the Well!" sent to me from a Gmail account: a.person .of.F—@gmail.com. In the body of the email, this person went on to tell me that they knew very well that I had killed Elena, and that they would gleefully pop the champagne when I went to prison. If I somehow failed to be convicted, this person would see to that I got my punishment anyway. I got the distinct impression that they'd prefer the latter option.

If you read this, a.person.of.F—, know that I have forwarded your email to the police.

Needless to say, this was not the first email I have received since the law's beady eyes fell upon my person. There's something new almost every day, a text message or suchlike designed to scare me. I suspect I have the plumber to "thank" for much of this animosity—he never much liked me, that one, and after Elena died, his hostility has been boundless. I know he spends a lot of time talking about me in town, and you—you fools—you gobble it up, every single lie he spews, as if sleeping with Elena has somehow given him a claim to the truth. I used to think that my worst tormentor was gone when Jeremy James disappeared from this town, but now I realize there are many among you who are just as bad as he was.

Especially after I decided to publish *Ilsbeth in the Twilight*, people have been ugly toward me. Perhaps I should have waited longer. Elena had barely been gone for a month, and with me being in the crosshairs for her alleged murder, I should maybe have considered the appropriateness of publishing what was essentially at the core of our disagreement, but I didn't think of it like that then. I just wanted to have the book out in the world before all the unpleasantness that was sure to follow with the trial and everything. I admit that I also wanted to have the book out there before some other dilettante with a pen came along and decided to pick up Elena's "mission." I could see it all so clearly in my mind, the horrible and crude headlines: *Elena's Voice Is Not Dead!—Young Author to Finish Deceased Influencer's Magnificent Opus!* I figured that Elena's death would attract such individuals like carrion flies. What better way is there to mint a career than to take a fresh and bloody kill and serve it up as an act of righteous sacrifice? People do like that sort of thing, and so I simply decided to stake my claim on Ilsbeth's story before something of the sort could happen. The manuscript was finished, after all, so all I had to do was to send it to the printer. I had saved up money for the first run already, and I thought—in my sad delusion—that you lot would *appreciate* the book being out, so you could see for yourselves what our spat had been about. I thought you *wanted* to read about Ilsbeth.

It turned out I was wrong.

Can you imagine my surprise and heartbreak when I, after years of painstakingly unearthing this grim chapter in our town's history and painting the truth on paper with words, was *not* showered in praise, as I might have expected, but was met with words like "tasteless," "macabre," and "ghoulish"? Can you even fathom what it felt like when the *F— Daily* refused to write as much as a word about the book, and the historical society suddenly barred my access to the archives? I gave everything for the opportunity to contribute something of value to this town, and all you gave me in return was a cold shoulder and words of disdain. Just like your ancestors condemned Ilsbeth Clark to her fate, you have already judged me and declared me guilty!

You all ought to think on that for a minute. Yes, even you, a.person.of.F—.

It's with all this in mind that I have decided to tell you what happened on the night Elena died. It is not like you deserve it, but I will give you the truth anyway, so perhaps all this nonsense will come to an end, and *Ilsbeth in the Twilight* will be cherished rather than scorned.

On the night that it happened, on August 7, I admit that I was in the woods by the castle. It was fairly dark, so I wore a headlight of excellent making that lit up the woods around me sufficiently. I was, as always, alone.

As I was trekking along the forest path that runs by the lake, I became aware of a tree log or some such that was floating in the water close to the shore. At first, I thought little of it, but seeing that it was just where John Clover used to keep his boat, I became curious. I hadn't seen the old rowboat there in a while and wondered if Elena had found it stored somewhere and had decided to use it, but then the "log" seemed much too small, and so I wondered if said boat had sunk while tethered. My next thought, as I came closer, was that Elena had bought a canoe or something, a smaller boat in which to venture onto the lake.

It wasn't until the dark water lapped at my shoes that I recognized that the "log" wore clothing, and that freshly dyed blond hair was drifting on the black water's surface. She was lying face-down, wearing nothing but a pink nightgown. I recognized her at once, because who else could it be? Who else would be in that part of the woods, late at night, but her?

I cannot adequately explain my next action—it clearly wasn't sane—but instead of wading out there to bring her body to shore, I found myself a good long stick on the forest floor to poke her with. I think I was hoping that she would respond, turn over in the water and laugh at me, or something along those lines. I suppose I assumed that it was a joke—a payback for filling her house with moths.

Elena remained still, though.

Not even then did I have enough clarity of mind to bring her onto dry land, something that would haunt me later, when the police asked me why not. I was shivering by then; I felt cold to the bone. My fingers when I found my phone in my pocket were numb enough that I struggled to make the call. I don't remember what I said to the responder, only her voice: high-pitched and energetic. I suppose it had been an otherwise quiet night and she was more than ready for some excitement. She was still on the line when I found a fallen tree log and sat down. She asked me all sorts of questions while I waited: Had I touched the body? Had I brought her up? How far was she from shore? I don't think I answered any of them. I only remember the harrowing dark—and thinking that, now that Elena was gone, I was truly, utterly alone.

The plastic bag in my hand made crinkly sounds by my feet.

Out in the water, Elena's head softly touched the grassy shore, as if she wanted climb out of there and live again.

It seemed like it was hours before anyone came.

Officer Rogers was there with another officer I had never seen before, a woman called Lana Hart. There were paramedics as well, two of them with a stretcher, though after the first few minutes, no one was in a hurry anymore. It was plain to see that Elena was dead.

When they had brought her onto dry land and turned her over, I could see that her face was all white, and that her lips were the color of blueberries. Something glinted at her earlobe, a faceted stone in an earring, perhaps. Her wet arms fell to the filthy ground and were crowded with debris when the paramedic folded them onto her chest. I saw pieces of tree bark and dead leaves. Flecks of green moss and black dirt.

When they had carried her away on the stretcher, the police officers both turned to me. "How did you know it was her?" they asked. "How come you didn't try to save her?"

I answered as well as I could, but the questions just wouldn't stop.

"Why are you here in the first place?" they asked.

"Where were you headed when you found her?"

"Why are you carrying that meat around?"

Why did they need to know, I thought, and simply refused to answer. What did it matter, anyway? Elena was dead and gone.

I also knew then, as well as I do now, that some things I do are just hard for others to understand. How could I explain that I was going out there to hold a vigil by the well, to focus my mind and strengthen my intent? To others, I assume it must seem fairly insane to go out there in the middle of the night, but I have done it many times before, ever since I was little, and the meat, well, it wasn't much, just a couple of raw cutlets in a bag. I didn't mean to do anything wrong with them. I wasn't setting fox snares, as some of you have suggested—whatever would I do with a fox? I was just going to slip them into the well, and that, too, I've done many times before. It is just a part of my ritual—a silly writer's quirk.

One has to pay some to get some. That's just the way it works.

It was only later, at the police station, that they asked me, "Why did she have all those bruises on her neck?"

I clearly couldn't answer that question.

# 32

*Transcript from the Nicksby Documents*

I cannot find it in my heart to ignore my disappointment. Not this time. Seducing Elena was both challenging and tiresome, and then for Catherine to just come and topple the tower I had so carefully built . . . I do not believe I can stand for it.

I do not like the sway that girl has over my mistress either; the cloying sort of sentiment that fills her empty chest whenever the girl is mentioned. The beast has shed tears many a time while lamenting the girl's reluctance to commit. Now that very girl has sent Elena to her grave and rendered my weeks of hard labor useless.

I miss being out in the world as well. With Elena gone, there is no one there for me to inhabit, and so I am locked inside the burrow again, cooking frogs and squirrels for my mistress. When I was young and still lived at my father's farm, Gertie, who worked in the kitchen, would often tell us fairy tales when we ate our bread at night. Sometimes she would tell of young girls enslaved and forced to work for a wicked old hag, usually in the woods or some such, and the girl would live there in torment until some event involving a prince, a spell, or a special skill suddenly came to her aid.

Now I have come to understand that those fairy tales were not lies, but stories of young and gifted girls like myself, who had been tricked to sign their name in blood and been imprisoned with a daemon. Mayhap that is why I have worked so hard to free myself—to break the spell—because the stories had led me to believe that there was a way out. If only you found the magic word, did the right deed, or outsmarted the daemon, freedom could be yours once more.

I no longer believe that is the case. Elena was not my first bid for freedom, so perhaps I was foolish to believe that this attempt would end any differently. I cannot blame myself for nurturing such hopes, though, because if I cannot have *that,* I have nothing but the burrow and my mistress and myself. It is not much of an existence, and I have Catherine to thank for my continued misery.

I suppose that is why I am doing it, making one last attempt to be free. Although I am loath to let my mistress have her way after all that has passed, those very events might have opened the simpering girl's mind, and made her susceptible at last. It would surely be a fitting end to her—and a fitting *revenge* for Elena—if Catherine ended up rotting in here. I travel through the ether and find her in her bed; several crumpled-up tissues litter the ivory nightstand beside her, among books with colorful covers showing ladies in garments like the ones I used to own and letters embossed in gold. Her glasses are neatly folded up, a glass of water half-consumed. Her phone is charging silently in the night. The woman herself is propped up on large pillows with frilly casings. She is breathing slow and deep in her sleep.

I slip inside. I am inside.

I look at her dreams: her son is there, a young man with worried eyes; and her former husband, too. She misses them both, I can tell. In the dream, the three of them are celebrating Christmas, but there are no presents for Catherine under the sprawling, glittering tree. She is disappointed, but she also feels like she deserves it for being a poor mother and a difficult wife. "Not all women are meant for such things," I tell her, as it seems pointless to me to grieve one's nature.

"The turkey is too dry," she replies, "and I forgot the salt for the table."

Her son, suddenly a curly-haired toddler, is racing around in the living room on a tricycle; the vehicle is shiny and new. "Be careful, Brian!" Catherine's heart steps up its pace. "Be careful!" She rushes after the gleeful toddler, terrified that he should hit his head, but her mother-in-law's pearls are weights around her neck that make it increasingly hard to move.

It is a tiresome and confusing dream and I do not care to dwell in it any longer.

"Elena," I whisper, and the scenery changes. Now we are down by the lake. Elena is there as well, as a young girl with very blue fingernails, sitting in a rowboat. Catherine is calling for her to take the boat to shore, but Elena just sticks out her tongue at her and keeps rowing to the other side.

"I didn't take your pajamas!" Catherine cries, though we all three know it to be a lie. She *did* take the pajamas—and then she took more.

"Come back to me!" Catherine calls, but Elena is out of her reach.

"You should not have done it if you miss her so," I say. That is nothing but common sense. "There is someone, though, who could make all this pain go away," I say next. "All you need to do is go to the well and offer up a bleeding vein."

She sees me for the first time this night; her eyes widen as they turn on me and her lips mouths my name. "This is all because of *you*," she says. "None of it would have happened if weren't for you!"

"My mistress will take good care of you," I say, not deigning to correct her. "You will be safe once you give yourself to her; no one can harm you anymore, not the man and not the boy—"

"Stay away from Brian!" Her face becomes a mask of fear

and revulsion. I notice how she is still wearing her Christmas attire, a burgundy dress of a soft material, and those pearls, of course, still heavy around her neck. I, too, am fashionably clad in my riding cape of yore. It is Catherine who has dressed me thus; she has done this for a very long time, dressed me like a doll in this or that while committing her tale to paper. In her dream, my skin is smooth and my hair is thick; all signs of death have fled.

"No one will harm the boy," I assure her, "lest you should one day want to hurt him."

"Oh, no," she burst out, shaking her head. "I've done enough harm already!"

"Your husband, though, 'the butcher's boy'—or his new bride? You have already found out how to do it, and I applaud you for that feat. The beast is at your beck and call—"

"What beast?" she hisses, her face twisting up. "There is no *beast,* Ilsbeth. That's just a superstition." Yet I can feel her fear like a tangible thing, slithering and cold.

This will not be easy.

"You know her," I whisper. "You have always known her— she has been waiting for you for so long." I conjure the beast from her memories; ones she would rather not recall, and have hidden so deep that they are barely there—I know my mistress, though. I could sense her anywhere. It does not take much for *me* to make her come cantering out of the woods; a specter made from half-forgotten memories and dreams.

She stops when she sees Catherine and makes a loud keening noise. Before our eyes, her horse-form recedes and only the crone remains, taller than she truly is and with a mouth crowded with sharp teeth. Black blood trickles from her lips to her neck and flows across her naked breasts; her hips are clad in folds of skin and membrane.

Catherine turns to flee.

"No!" I call to her. "No! She is here for you—to serve you!"

The woman does not heed me, though, and scampers through the undergrowth. As she runs, she changes, and is no longer an adult in a Christmas dress but a girl in celestial night-gown. The beast, following a well-known script, starts chasing the child through the woods.

I groan to myself, then I follow as a wind. Catherine's fear is everywhere, frenzied and confused; it changes the land-scape around us to a maze of tangled branches and thorns, impossible to escape. When she finally stops in a clearing, I descend before my mistress arrives, and try to reason with her one last time.

"She means you no harm—you know this!" I plead, impatient for sure, but soothing, too, I hope. "She only ever wanted to be your friend." I smile, but for some reason that only makes her more afraid. She is standing before me as a shivering thing, cold and frightened in the dusky woods. "If only you would give her some blood," I plead. "Write your name, easy as that!" I snap my fingers in the air, and that is when I see it: my hands are not my own anymore, but the gnarled claws of the beast. I look down, and see hooves where I should have riding boots. She has made me into my mistress.

I give up then. Leave. Nothing has changed from before, and Catherine will never sign her name in blood. She is much too confused—and too frightened.

When I open my eyes back in the burrow, I am angry and impatient. I had not truly thought that anything new would come of this, my last attempt, and yet I must still have hoped. I do not much like to be thwarted, though, and certainly not by someone like *her* who does not even appreciate the power that she has been given. No, instead she clings to the image of *me*, and sees in me a sister of the soul, while cowering in fear of the one who found her blood so sweet that no other witch will do.

It was never *I* who was Catherine's sister.

Her true sister is restless. She is pacing the burrow with long strides so her hides are shaking between her legs. She tosses her mane and makes impatient noises. From time to time, she will lose control of her form and her face will elongate and bristle with fur. Her eyes bleed from blue to black, and then back to blue again.

I think that she will run tonight.

She does not often hunt anymore—not in the way she did before. She much prefers to sit in the burrow and sing her songs, spin her nets, and have the prey come tumbling down the well. The hunt for Elena must have inspired her—awakened some bloodlust long dormant. She wants to run and tear and render, games I thought she had left in her youth. It was such a shame with the children she murdered. At the time, it nearly broke me apart. Owen and I found excuses for it: the beast had just been playing, we said. She was merely too wild, or too strong, for her own good. She had only wanted to befriend the children, sensing in them an equal youth. In the years that have passed since my death, I have come to believe otherwise. I think that she cannot be anything but what she is, and if the flesh is tender on her tongue, she will have it. Having long been deprived of my beef, I cannot truly fault her for it either.

"Sit yourself down," I still say to her. "You are not a young filly anymore, and ought to save your weary bones." Why I show such care for her well-being, I rightly cannot say. Perhaps it is merely habit. The sorry truth is that she is the closest I ever came to having a child of my own. "If you are hungry, there are frogs," I say. "Or you could find yourself another fool to call."

Calling takes time, though, and patience. Time she did not have with Elena. The very fact that she climbed the slippery walls of the well should have told me right away that she was doing someone else's bidding. Old women do not go trotting through the woods, but sit quietly in their lairs and wait for the prey to fall in.

The beast neighs at me and tosses her head; her eyes are mostly black.

"Polish your silver," I tell her impatiently. "I am sure you have a few tuna cans that dearly crave your attention."

She hits me with the back of her hand. The blow is hard, but I can barely feel it—such is the plight and the blessing of the dead. I laugh at her rather than complain.

"I will have you know that you are not the only one to yearn for murder!" I take these very pages and wave them in her face. They are very precious to me, the only pages left from my satchel on the day I went down the well. They are brittle and yellow and have numbers from Nicksby scribbled on the backside: *Four cows and a calf, three pigs for slaughter, another barrel of wheat is missing from the barn* . . . I had just inspected the farm when they came for me and chased me into the woods. I rode as hard as I could for the well, thinking I could somehow convince the beast to help me, but they had anticipated my route and set a snare for my horse, making it buckle and fall. Next, they were on me like a swarm of gnats. Now, the few musty pages I have left from that day are to become my weapon—my very own spell to weave. For what little power that is left in me, this I can surely do.

I mean to avenge Elena, and punish the culprit who ended my scheme. If I cannot make her come to the well, another revenge must be sought.

What else is there but to cry and wail, or be ground down to nothing by the power of my misery? Vengeance can be a most potent elixir—a strong and rejuvenating force.

Surely it is something to hold on to. Mayhap it is even better than hope.

# 33

*An open letter to the people of F——, continued*

My lawyer, Nora Green, did not much like my last installment in this series of letters, and told me so, plainly, on the phone last night. She thinks I'm harming my own defense by being so candid with you—but how can the truth ever hurt me?

Perhaps I'm overly naïve to think this way, but much like Ilsbeth Clark, I have a deeply ingrained belief in my fellow man that will not so easily be extinguished. Despite an abundance of evidence to the contrary, I firmly believe that common sense will yet prevail and I'll be victorious in the end. I believe that if I give you the facts, you will puzzle the truth together yourselves.

Sadly, my lawyer does *not* have the same confidence in you. She says that it will greatly compromise the case if I keep talking about it in public, and claims that even *one* wrong word that somehow differs from my official statement to the police may have grave consequences for me in court. That doesn't make much sense to me, because you never use the *exact* same words when telling a story, but that doesn't make the meat of it any less true, and *if* we are to be perfectly honest, the jury in the courtroom is one thing, but the real judge and jury in this town is *you*. Judging by what happened to Ilsbeth, it doesn't matter at all if I'm acquitted by the *real* jury, for it is you, the good people of F——, who will decide if I even have a future here. So excuse me, Nora Green, but I do believe it is important to tell my story to the citizens of F——.

I'm sure you all agree.

Another person who is not so thrilled about me spilling the beans online is Erica Clover. She came to my house today and caused quite a ruckus on my porch. She had her whole family with her; they were waiting in the car. I could see the curly heads of her offspring in the backseat, and her goateed husband, Joe, in the front seat, watching us with Argus eyes. The engine was running, which I took as good sign, as I supposed it meant that she wouldn't stay for long. It's not very good for the climate, though, an engine running like that.

Naturally, I was cautious as I stepped out on the porch. I somehow didn't think that Elena's sister would break bread with me anytime soon.

"It's probably not a good idea for you to be here," I said, and wrapped my torso in a green cardigan to hide the mess underneath. I hadn't been sleeping well, and neither had I felt inclined to do much laundry. My hair had been piled high on the top of my head, but half of it had already fallen out of the tie and fallen down around my face in greasy tendrils. I had also stepped on my glasses, so they sat a little askew on my nose. "I'm sure the police have warned you not to come and see me," I continued while taking in her pale face and the purple crescent moons beneath her eyes. I clearly wasn't the only one who had been having trouble sleeping.

"I don't fucking care what they say," she hissed, and bit her lip so hard that it looked painful. The Clover sisters were always so vulgar, cussing and swearing all over the place. "I had to see you, you know? I had to see you, just so—" She paused to draw a deep breath, and her gaze dropped to the tips of my bare toes. "Just to remind myself that you're an actual woman of flesh and blood and not some *gorgon* from a fairy tale—"

"Of course I'm real." I was also very puzzled. "Is that all you came for? To see that I'm real?"

Her eyes were wet with tears when she looked back up at me. "How could you do it, Cathy? How could you do that to Elena?"

"I didn't," I shook my head with confusion. What a ridiculous thing to ask. "That's what the trial is about, remember? Whether or not I did—"

"Oh, don't you berate me, you fucking troll!" Her pale pallor was quickly turning pink, then red. "You have been bothering her all summer, turning the castle into a house of terror! We all know about the moths and the rabbit—and the doll, too. I was there when Elena found it, you know. Out there by the well. That ugly little thing! Is that what you were arguing about on the night she died?"

"What doll?" I didn't quite follow.

"The one with the earring you stole from Elena! The one from Cyprus, with the blue stone!" She was babbling as well as shouting at this point and didn't make much sense. "I saw it, you know, that disgusting doll! We all knew that you stole from her—you always had sticky fingers—but to hold on to those earrings for . . . how long? How many years? If you wanted to scare her, congratulations! She felt sick after we found the doll! *Sick!*"

I did my very best to appease her, but it was hard, as she was so upset. "Well, I can assure you I know nothing about any doll—"

"Oh, *please!*" she interrupted me. "You don't know anything about those earrings, either, I suppose, but I'm here to let you know that I've turned in my own identical pair to the police today, so we can prove that the one on the doll was Elena's." She looked most haughty in that moment; her chin was up and her nostrils flared.

"Well," I murmured, "there's a far cry from it being Elena's trinket to proving that *I* had anything to do with it all."

"Oh, *please!*" she cried again, and rolled her eyes. "Who

else could it have been, Cathy? You always took her stuff: her pajamas and her notebook and the purple glitter pen . . . It was always you!"

I thought that accusation was highly unfair, but seeing that Erica was in such a state, and had just lost her sister, I decided to give her a pass. "I know how hard it can be—"

"No, you don't! You don't know shit, Cathy!" she all but bellowed the words in my face. "I have no idea how you pulled it off, the doll and the white horse and everything, and I honestly *don't care.* I just want to let you know that I won't rest before you are held to account!"

"The horse was just a misunderstanding," I hastened to say. "We cleared that up, Elena and I."

"Not according to Elena." Erica was panting before me; her hands were clenched into fists by her sides; the knuckles had turned all white. "She said that you kept harassing her, setting that animal loose on her lawn. She was going to talk to your sister about it."

"Who? Louise?"

She rolled her eyes again. "Who else? Do you have another sister with stables?"

It was my turn to roll my eyes. "Look, unless you think a dead rabbit or a bunch of twigs somehow became sentient and strangled Elena, I clearly had nothing to do with her death!"

"So it's just a coincidence that you had been after her all summer?" She gave a hard and joyless laugh.

"Must be," I shrugged. "How could a woman my size even strangle Elena and drag her to the lake? It doesn't make much sense, does it?"

"The police say you drugged her," she countered.

"But they didn't find any traces in her blood," I snapped back.

"Not everything leaves a trace," she retorted, "and you're quite the woodland witch, aren't you?"

"No," I replied curtly. "That would be Elena."

"Don't you *dare* speak her name!" Suddenly she was all fury again. Behind her back, I could see that her husband had opened the car door and was ready to come to her rescue if need be. He wore a pained expression. "Will has told me all about you. How you taunted her . . . How *scared* she was, even more so than she ever showed me—and all over a *book,* Cathy? What the hell is wrong with you? A fucking stupid *book*!"

"It didn't seem so stupid at the time." Not to any of us, I reckon.

"What harm would it do if you *both* wrote about Lisbeth Clark? It's not like she'll complain!"

"*Ilsbeth,*" I corrected her. "Her name is *Ilsbeth* Clark."

"Ilsbeth, Lisbeth—what the fuck does it matter?"

Less and less, to be honest, but that is not what I said. "I didn't kill Elena, not over a book or anything else. I also didn't let a horse loose on her lawn."

Her face became a vivid scarlet again, and her nostrils flared like little wings. "Oh, Cathy, if you would only admit to *something,* but it's just lies with you—always has been! You won't admit to shit before you're caught with a jar of moths in your hand, or pajamas in your backpack. This time you won't be able to *weasel* your way out of trouble, though . . . I'll see you behind bars if it's the very last thing I do!"

With that searing remark, she finally took her leave. Her fists were still clenched and chalky white when she made her way toward the car, where her kids watched her come with large and frightened eyes.

Just as she reached the car door, she looked back at me and

said, "You should at least have had the good taste not to describe her body online." Which I suppose was valid criticism, coming from Elena's sister. I hadn't really considered that she would go and read it, and was sorry to learn that she had.

As you can see from this exchange today, we have now entered the phase of this witch hunt where things like "reason" and "proof" mean nothing. Erica Clover and Will Morris are at the forefront of this campaign against me, and they will not put down their pitchforks before there is blood. They won't rest in their righteousness before my head is firmly set on a pike.

The irony that this exact type of situation was the reason why I wanted to write *Ilsbeth in the Twilight* in the first place does not escape me—it might even feel like this whole scenario was somehow unavoidable. Clearly, we have learned nothing since 1862. You all want a convenient scapegoat, and here I am—the village witch, ready for the stake.

It really doesn't matter if I truly killed Elena.

I really hope Nora Green is as good as she says, as this is bound to get messy.

# 34

I went back to the well today. I hadn't been there since Elena died, and have to admit that I was dreading it. Although the well has always been a comfort to me and a part of my routine—a place to escape to as a crippled child—the memory of Elena's waterlogged body had warded me off, as I really didn't want to go by the lake.

Yes, I can hear you all scoffing now, and mumbling something about a guilty conscience, but I *assure you,* that's not it. It's just not a pleasant thing to think of: Elena lying there all blue on the ground. We used to swim in that lake—we used to row there—it was where our friendship was forged, and now it has become a place of dread.

I suppose it was the visit from Erica that first ignited a longing in me. It was hard seeing Elena's sister so wretched—and so *angry.* It was the last thing I needed, truth be told, with everything else being so difficult. You really won't leave me in peace, not even for a day. If I ever find out who you are, a.person.of.F—, you have a libel suit coming your way.

Then it was my visit to the archives. Last night, after many emails and messages left on his phone, Mr. James of the historical society finally got back to me. I suppose they have come to realize that they can't just bar me from the library cellar like that, not when I still have my tea mugs down there and a brand-new kettle that I paid for with my own money. The society really didn't have any legal right to keep me from my things, and since I am the only one who has been working down in the archives over the last few years, no one else knew just what was mine—thus, they let me in to gather up my belongings.

Oh, it was a bittersweet feeling, walking down those stairs again. They are brown and worn and reek of dust, but to me they hold the sweet nostalgia of love, discovery, and dedication. Never mind that the moment was soured somewhat, not only by the knowledge that *they did not really want me there,* but also by the added humiliation that Nina Starling, the society's eager secretary, had to let me in, as my key card has been wiped.

The woman seemed angry and restless around me; she probably thinks I've caused the society's reputation irreparable harm—or perhaps she is one of the trolls online, convinced that I throttled Elena. If so, it must have been quite the eventful afternoon for her, aiding a bloodthirsty murderer. Perhaps that was why she kept clutching at her purple plastic pearls; she wanted to protect her tender neck. Whatever the reason, her badly painted red lips did not smile as she swept the card and sent me into the dungeon. Her happy red curls did not bounce even once. The lines in her face only deepened when she frowned, eager to usher me down, then away.

I don't think anyone had been there since I left the archives for the last time, shortly after Elena died, and just weeks before I published *Ilsbeth in the Twilight.* It still looked and smelled exactly the same: my desk was there among the walnut shelves, heaped with my notes and research materials. Even an empty tea mug was there, sporting a green ring at the bottom. I had not even taken the time to rinse out my cup before I left, so sure was I that I would return, that the archives were my domain.

I had brought a canvas bag with me to gather up my stuff, and as I unzipped it, my heart was heavy and my eyes welled up with tears. I just couldn't believe that it had come to such ugliness! I couldn't believe that you would *do* that to me, even if I've had ample evidence. I only ever wanted to do some good for this town—for Ilsbeth's reputation—and thought that I had been poorly repaid for my considerable efforts.

And the well was always where I went as a child if things were bad at home, or if I needed a safe place to cry my little heart out, lamenting the state of my legs and such. It felt as if I were with a kindred spirit there, as if a cloak of understanding were wrapped around me. I could give in to whatever was troubling me and be comforted and reassured. For some reason, by the well, I felt loved.

I think it was that feeling of love and acceptance I sought when I started out today. It was hard, though, to see the castle's ugly green façade, and its windows like black eyes staring at me as I passed it by, and later the tattered remains of police tape hanging from the bushes by the lake like dirty garlands. It made everything that had happened feel all too real.

In my hand was a plastic bag containing some meatballs and a steak. I had debated for some time whether I was even going to bring any meat, seeing how it got me trouble on the night Elena died, but then I thought that I would not give in to people's ideas and perceptions. If I want to bring meat to the well, it's surely my right, and no one can tell me differently. It is *my* meat, *I* paid for it, so what I choose to do with it is my business and no one else's—and a visit to the well just wouldn't feel complete without it. It's a compulsion, I know, and probably not a very healthy one, but who does it harm if I chuck some pieces of meat down there? It's not like anyone drinks the water. As far as I recall, it's toxic now, and the lake water too. It has become polluted over the years, though no one knows exactly how.

It bothered me, too, to think of the fact that Elena and Erica had been there, snooping around. It had bothered me all summer that Elena frequently went there. I cringed every time she dropped a picture from the clearing online. The well was always too bright in Elena's photos; the contrast and warmth turned up to the max. It lost all of its melancholy atmosphere then; the sweet sadness that always lingered there was erased by the bright colors and artificial sunshine.

It wasn't my well at all.

I think I wanted to go there just to make sure that the well was still there and still the same, that the comfort it brought me made it all worthwhile: the research and the writing, the argument with Elena, and all the unpleasantness that has followed. I suppose, to me, it's sacred somehow, like a shrine for the lost and misunderstood, and perhaps that's why I bring the meat. Some people honor their gods with incense or carefully prepared meals; some offer money or liquor; but for me it has always been meat, and a shiny trinket from time to time.

I think that I honor myself, by honoring the well.

I was relieved to find that, at least on the surface, the clearing and the well looked the same—like themselves. I cried, to be honest, from the sheer joy of being back there again after weeks apart. I still sniffled when I slipped the beef and the meatballs down in the darkness and seated myself on the same jutting rock I had been sitting on ever since I was a little girl. I remember how I would sometimes squint into the dark woods behind the well, and imagine that I saw a cabin there, a small hut of sorts.

When I had been sitting there for a while, contemplating my own misfortune, I became aware of something shiny jutting out of the pile of animal bones that has accumulated by the well. As a girl, I thought that those bones were what the well had spit out after I had fed it, but later examinations have revealed that they come from forest animals: deer and rabbits, squirrels and frogs. What I saw today, though, was not bone.

Upon further inspection, I saw that the shining thing was a lidded glass jar gleaming in the sun. When I pulled it out of the bone pile, I caught sight of a handwritten label that said *Strawberry Jam* in faded letters. There was something else inside it, though, and my heart started racing as soon as I saw it. My many hours in the archives have made me extremely familiar with the sight of old paper, and so I figured at once that what I was looking at was just that: a wad of papers, tightly rolled up and pushed into the glass jar. Like a bloodhound with a scent, I just couldn't contain myself; I undid the lid at once and pulled the brittle papers out of the jar, then I unrolled them with shivering hands. It felt like they were for me—as if they were a gift from the well, although I know that sounds just silly.

My heart started racing when I saw the slanted writing, curling across the page in brown ink: *The burrow is not a place of beauty: the walls are damp, slick, and black,* it said. *Fungus grows between the rocks. It reeks in here from rot and tallow candles, and no matter what we feed the hearth it smokes but gives off no warmth, only another foul odor. The clothes on my back are falling apart, ruined by water and time. I wear my mother's woolen shawl about my shoulders, but it gives no warmth either, as it will not dry . . .*

What is this peculiar thing I have found? Can the papers be genuinely old? They seem that way, but if so, they are in remarkably good condition. Someone must have put them there for me to find—I can see no other explanation. But who would know that I would go there today when I didn't even know it myself?

For the first time since I finished *Ilsbeth in the Twilight,* I can feel the old excitement—the hunger for discovery—course through my veins! I am very excited, as I think I glimpsed the word "Nicksby" written on one of the sheets. I'm worried about damaging the pages, though, and won't look at them again without proper equipment, mainly a pair of white cotton gloves and a magnifying glass to help me make out the words.

I only hope that this is a *real* thing, and not some prank one of you made up.

Time will tell, I suppose.

# 35

My sister Louise came here with groceries earlier, as I can no longer go to the store myself. She must have felt the barb of your tongues as well, as I could tell from the logos emblazoned on the bags that she'd driven for nearly an hour to get my soup cans, cookies, and tea. She honestly looked quite the wreck as she scrambled in through my door, holding the bags in the crooks of her arms before slamming them down on the kitchen counter. All out of breath, she sank down in a chair and dragged a hand through her graying hair. She had kept her old blue coat on; it is made of wool, so its appearance means that it's getting cold. Fall has come with blazing colors, painting my garden in shades of fire.

"I had to wade through *trash* to get to the porch," my sister huffed. "*Trash!* My god, don't they have anything better to do with their time?" She was of course referring to the mess you have made in my driveway by turning the trashcans over. "And the graffiti on the wall . . . Cathy, you simply cannot live like this—it's dangerous! There's just no telling how far they'll go!"

I suppose you have all seen it by now, the ugly black letters on the side of my house. Though I can't complain about the spelling, I will note that the hand holding the paint can must have been a smidge unsteady, as there is hardly a straight line to be seen. Not in WITCH, not in KILLER, and absolutely not in BURN IN HELL.

Unlike my sister, I'm not surprised in the slightest by what you people do. I have always known that there was rot in your midst, just waiting to fester and bloom. Though the childhood bullying ceased somewhat after Jeremy James disappeared, I have still felt it, always, lingering in your whispered words and your disapproving looks. This town is a simmering pit of hate, and I bet it feels good to finally let it all out, to take your resentment and disappointment in life and just pour it into a "righteous" cause. Yes, that's who you are: simple, stupid people. That's what the lesson of my book was all about! I wanted to show you a pattern, but I suppose it is too late now to guide you to the light.

You have already violated my property, and I, for one, know the past well enough to know what happens next.

My sister was less prepared than I was to see this ugly side of her fellow townspeople. "How can they do this?" she asked the air. "Have you spoken to the police?" That question was for me.

I nodded my head as I put on the kettle, but I couldn't find it in me to join in her rage. "Yes, but there's no use. The police don't like me much either."

"Well, you're not convicted yet," she huffed, as if *that* means anything at all.

"Maybe I can padlock the trash cans," I mused.

"Maybe you should stop posting things online," said she. "My God, they all think you're insane, with those weird dreams and the stealing . . . I really had no idea that it was *you* who took off with all the silver. Mom always thought it was Dad, you know. You should have said something back then."

"And get punished all over again? No, thank you. The car crash was quite enough." I slipped tea bags into bright yellow mugs and watched my sister's face as the realization slowly spread on her features.

"Oh, you mean—because they argued about that before . . . That had nothing to do with *you,* Cathy, you know that, right? We didn't wreck the car because you had stolen things. That was just bad luck and coincidence."

"Maybe," I admitted, "but as a child I thought it was about me. *I* was the one who got the worst damage, after all."

"Yeah, but *I* broke my arm, Mom got a concussion, and Christine was pretty beat up too, and none of us ever stole anything." She took the scalding-hot mug when I offered it to her. "Didn't you think of that?"

"Your injuries seemed so small compared to mine," I tried to explain. "It did feel like I was the *real* target." I added a slight smile, just to let her know that I wasn't as convinced about this anymore. "I thought I didn't have to come clean about the pilfering because the punishment had already been doled out." Which sadly didn't keep me from continuing my cycle of theft and disposal. As soon as I was out of the sickbed, I was at it again. It was a disgrace, really. "Our stuff is probably still in the well."

"All ruined now for sure," Louise mused. "It really is a shame, though. Some of the pieces of jewelry were gifts." I don't think she said it to make me feel bad, she was just stating a fact. "You shouldn't have taken the horse out without asking me, though."

"What horse?" I had been so absorbed by thoughts of the past that at first I didn't get her meaning.

She gave me a pointed look as I sat down in the chair opposite her. "A *white* horse on the castle's lawn? It had to be Mira. There's no other white horse in F—."

"It wasn't Mira, Louise. I never even went near your horse."

"She is old, you know, and doesn't walk well. You really shouldn't have taken her that far from the stable." A frown had appeared on her forehead.

"I never *did*." I shrugged, but realized as soon as I said it just how futile my denial was. "I'm sure Mira is a great horse, but she never went on a midnight stroll with me. You are the horse enthusiast, not I."

"Oh, you can handle them well enough." I'm sure she meant that as a compliment. "I don't like my girl being a part of your scheme, but then you probably knew that already, when you didn't ask."

At this point, I could have continued denying the allegations, but I really didn't see the point. It was perfectly reasonable for my sister to assume that the horse Elena claimed to have seen was her own trusted mare, white as a sheet. I had always liked Mira just because of that, she reminded me of the ghost stories surrounding Ilsbeth Clark, and maybe of the horse lady, too, even if I didn't realize that at the time.

"You took those earrings, didn't you?" Louise asked me next. "The ones that Erica said they had found?" This is the curse of my candidness—everyone suddenly knows all my business.

"I took a lot of things back then," I said. The time for denial was gone there as well. "I probably took Elena's earrings."

"To throw them in the well? Oh, God, *Cathy* . . ." Her dry hand came to cover mine on the table. "How lonely you must have been to act in that way." She sighed deeply and sipped her tea: jasmine and orange blossom. "And none of us even *knew*. I guess we were too wrapped up in all that was going on, with Dad and the gambling and the drinking and—"

"Please," I said. "Can we not do this?"

"But you *never* want to talk about it." She slowly retracted her hand.

"What is there to talk about?" said I.

We both knew only too well that we hadn't had a very happy childhood.

# 36

Since I cannot go out—or at least not venture where there are people—I have stumbled upon a delay in examining the documents I found in the woods. I have ordered several pairs of gloves and a large magnifying glass that can be screwed onto the table, but they will take a while to get here, so in the meantime, I'm just ogling the tight scroll whenever I pass by the glass jar, while butterflies dance a wild rumba in my belly. It's the only thing that brings me any joy right now.

Joy and anticipation.

I obviously don't know what they are yet, but the little glimpse I got left me hopeful enough that I just call them "the Nicksby Documents" in my head. I know I have expressed that my time with the Ilsbeth Clark story is over, but you cannot just shed a lifelong obsession. I don't think there'll *ever* be a day when I don't perk up at the sound of Ilsbeth Clark's name.

What am I hoping to find? I don't know! Something to shed a light, perhaps, or a new, hitherto unexplored angle to the story. A precious and rare knowledge that no one else has but me.

I'm also fully expecting to be disappointed. Though it *looks* genuine, I don't put anything past Will Morris and his posse of trolls. I wouldn't be surprised at all if I, on page three, suddenly find the words DIE BITCH, or something else like it. But if it *is* a hoax, they've put a lot of thought and energy into it, and that, at least, is admirable. I've always applauded thoroughness, no matter the cause or mission.

No matter their origin, I won't ruin them by being impatient, though. I'll wait like a good girl until I can examine them properly. There's some sweet anticipation there, as if I'm a child yearning for Christmas. In the meantime, I try my very best to focus on the upcoming trial, though the closer it gets, the more unreal it feels—as if it has nothing to do with me.

I know that it has, though. Of course I do.

Today, it was Nora Green who graced my kitchen table with her slick and efficient presence. I haven't had as many callers in years—I wish I had known before that all it took to have people come knocking on my door was to be suspected of murder.

Nora was a fickle guest, though. She sat there all frosty and gray-clad, wanting coffee rather than tea, and promptly refused my offer of wine, suggesting, even, that I might do well to cut back myself.

Brian was with us too, but that was just a coincidence. He just came by to see if I was still alive. My boy looks pale around the cheeks and seems a bit subdued. I think it's been very hard on him having a mother accused of murder. He offered to clean up the driveway, but I told him there was no point. You would only think of something else—maybe something *worse*—to leave there instead of the trash. This morning I found a dead deer on the patio, doubtlessly a wink at the rabbit I left at the castle. What goes around comes around, I suppose. I wheelbarrowed it behind the rose bushes to rot, since I cannot easily maneuver it to the well. Frost will set in soon enough and mask the stench of decay.

I served my son tea and cookies, and made some black brew for Ms. Green. For myself, I only poured the wine. I don't much care what my lawyer says.

"I'm not sure what you're aiming for here. An insanity plea, is that it?" Nora's cool gaze measured me as she frowned. "These *stories* you leave on the internet, they don't do you any good, Catherine. All they do is confuse people." She said nothing I haven't heard before.

"I'm only telling the truth," I replied—again. "How can the truth ever hurt me?"

"Well, as we talked about before, you'd better save your testimony for the stand. All it does now is to rile people up, and I'm seriously concerned for your safety."

"You should listen to her, Mom," Brian piped up. He had crumbs on his chin, as if he were still a little boy. "They're all just waiting for the next 'open letter' to drop, so they can rip it apart. They don't *want* to hear about your innocence. They just think it's bullshit." He glanced up at me from under his curly fringe. He really should have had a haircut.

"If it's an insanity plea you're after, it'll take a little more than some childhood fantasies to get that," Nora Green informed me. "As far as I know, you've never been treated for any *serious* psychological problems in the past?" Her voice went up at the end, turning the words into a question.

I shook my head in reply. "I'm not insane," I said. "I'm not after anything."

"I'm really glad to hear that," said Nora, "but this posting online must stop."

"It really, really must," Brian nodded with a grave expression on his young face. He, poor thing, looked utterly pained.

"Now, I do have some *good* news for a change." Nora's lips, immaculately painted in a deep shade of red, split in a blazingly white smile. "The police called me a few days ago to let me know that they have found Elena Clover's journal hidden in a crevice in a cherry tree." She shook her head, as if to wrap her mind around the unlikely occurrence. "Apparently, the tree was about to fall down, so Erica Clover went at it with an axe."

"How can this be good news?" I asked. "It's probably just scribblings of how much she hated me." In my chest, my heart had started racing.

"Well, there's that"—Nora nodded her blond head—"and that's why they're using it as evidence, which is why they sent me a copy, and I must say there were some interesting things in there . . ."

"Like?" I prompted, feeling reluctantly hopeful but also somewhat anxious.

"Like the fact that she was planning to break up with Will Morris." She gave me a telling look. "They really should have looked at *him* in the first place. It's always the boyfriend, isn't it?"

"He's the one who's talking shit about Mom all the time." Brian nodded eagerly. A little light had suddenly come into his eyes, and a rosy pallor had chased the paleness. My son was sensing hope again. "Every time someone online tries to defend her, he's there at once, telling everybody how scared Elena was."

"That's just the thing," said Nora Green. "According to her journal, she wasn't really that scared. Mostly annoyed, really. She didn't think you would really hurt her." Her gaze met mine across the table. "It makes more sense, doesn't it, that a big, strong man did this to Elena than a scrawny middle-aged woman like yourself. Even the jury will see that, or at least there will be ample cause for doubt."

"He always made it seem like they were perfectly happy," I mused, thinking of his interview with the *F— Daily,* and his public Facebook posts sporting pictures of him and Elena sharing delicious meals and basking in the sun. "He made it sound like they were ready to get married."

"Well, Elena was ready to leave him behind, and he might not have liked that much." Nora was still smiling, and her eyes had narrowed to slits. She looked like a cat who had spotted a mouse. "She stopped writing in the journal a few weeks before she died. Perhaps that was when things got bad."

"Do you really think you can do it?" Brian asked her. "Do you really think you can get Mom off?"

"I think our chances have dramatically increased," said Nora. "Men kill women all the time, and jurors know that. It was just a lucky break for him that you were already fighting with her," she said to me. "If not, the police would have looked at him first."

"It was lucky with the journal, too," said Brian. "Why would she hide it in a cherry tree?"

"Because she was afraid," said Nora. "Because she wanted the truth to be known."

In my inner eye, I saw it so clearly: Elena running across the dusky lawn with her precious journal in hand and slipping it into the hole in the old cherry tree, before sprinting for the woods with Will the plumber hot on her heels.

Yes, that was certainly a plausible scenario.

"Have the police talked to him yet?" my son wanted to know.

Nora shrugged. "I don't know. I have certainly told them that I expect them to."

"I never liked him," I mused. "He is just too pretty," I stated, which makes me no better than you, I reckon: *She is just too strange.*

"Now that we have something real to move forward with, I really urge you to stop posting fantastic stories," Nora Green said next. "The F— police called me yesterday to convey their concern for your safety, one that I wholeheartedly share, so no more posting online." Clearly, I didn't heed that though, because here I am again. Posting. Online. I think this has become an obsession of mine, my very own way of squirreling away the truth in the belly of a cherry tree.

I only ever wanted it to be known.

# 37

It didn't take more than a few minutes after I had posted the last installment before Bobby was on the phone. I didn't want to talk to him, of course, I was halfway through my nighttime ritual already; the chamomile tea was ready, and I was looking forward to reading a few chapters of a book, but he's paying Nora Green's fees and so I felt like I had to.

"Have you utterly lost your mind?" he raged. "Nora just called me and threatened to quit! How can you even think that it's a good idea to post confidential information like that online? That journal is your weapon, Cathy! It's what's going to get you out of this mess! I don't even know what to say, Cat! I *just* don't know what to say!"

"I think you've found quite a few words already," I informed him. "*Loud* ones, even."

"Please don't do this, Cathy." Suddenly he was pleading, and his voice had grown thick too, as if he were at the cusp of tears. "Don't make a joke out of this! It's a serious situation, you know that—and you're not *handling* it well . . ."

"I'll see a shrink if you want me to," I said to appease him, while carrying the teacup to my bed.

"That's not the point, Cathy!" He was raging again. "I think you maybe sometimes forget that there are actual people reading your ramblings, and they're not all your friends—"

"Oh, I know *that*," I chuckled.

"But outright accusing Will Morris like that—"

"I did not," I cut him off as I climbed in under the duvet. "I just thought it was important for people to know that there might be another explanation than me strangling Elena for a slight over a book—"

"Well, if you had ever bothered to read your comments you would know that's not how people see it. They think that you're accusing him, Cathy, and that is a dangerous position for you, because what do you think Will Morris will do?"

"Continue his crusade against me for sure." I couldn't help but chuckle again. I put the phone on speaker while picking up my book and settling in.

"Do you even remember him from school?" Bobby asked. "He always got into trouble. He had a *horrific* temper."

"I can't say I remember him much." Though I *did* try to. It was just that I had taken a couple of sleeping pills and so it was hard to focus. "All the more reason, don't you think, that people should look to him and not to me."

Bobby groaned. "I just don't get why you're baiting the bear! What if he really killed Elena—and what if he comes after *you* next?"

"Then he would be a very foolish man," I noted. "Who is he going to blame for Elena if I'm dead?"

"Well, maybe he *is* that foolish," said my ex-husband. "Maybe he'll be creative."

That was a very silly suggestion and I couldn't help but laugh out loud. "Will Morris doesn't really strike me as the type to be very creative," I said between bouts of chuckles.

Bobby didn't share my amusement. "That might be, but he is pissed off and maybe dangerous, and you have just accused him of murder."

"*I* didn't," I clarified. "Nora Green did, somewhat."

I shouldn't have mentioned the lawyer, though, because then he went off again. "How *could* you?" he raged. "How stupid is it possible to be? Did you *ever* stop to think about Brian?"

That last question shut me up, because no, I hadn't, and I should have. I know that.

"I only want people to know the truth," I said at last.

"You have a . . . a *compulsion*," he hissed. "A *sickness*!"

"You don't have to help me anymore," I told him, and hated how my voice sounded brittle and small.

Bobby gave a deep sigh. "I'm not helping *you,* I'm helping my son."

"Is Nora Green still my lawyer?"

"For now," he said, after a while. "But you can't keep sharing that kind of information—"

"I won't," I said, and I'll try not to, but it doesn't feel right to leave something out when I've sworn to tell the truth.

Bobby gave a sad and tired laugh. "The worst part is that he could very well *be* the killer, and Nora might very well use that angle in the defense, so you can't exactly backpedal, either."

"Well, they're already accusing *me,* even if I had nothing to do with it, so why shouldn't I be allowed to make a few accusations of my own?" It only seemed fair when I thought about it. I picked up the lavender-scented hand cream from my nightstand and set to moisturizing my hands.

"Just be careful," Bobby sighed again. "Will Morris could be dangerous, and you're a single woman living alone—"

"Hah!" I sat up with such force that both cream and book flew down to the floor. "Thank you pointing *that* out, mister! Whose fault is that, exactly?"

"Cathy . . ." he started, but I ended the call.

I didn't need his gloating in my bedroom.

# 38

I suppose this should be a time of hope and rejoicing for me. As Nora Green said, we have something *real* to use at last. Something that can put all suspicions to rest and exonerate me forever. *If* she stays on as my lawyer, that is.

Nora, if you read this, I really hope you do.

But I just can't seem to be happy. There's too much nagging *doubt*!

When I first started this series of letters—this *confession,* of sorts—all I could think of was to free myself of your horrid suspicion. I wanted the world to know that I *did not kill Elena Clover.* Much has happened since then, though, and while it sickens me to the bone, my statement has gone through a metamorphosis and become more of a question.

*Did* I kill Elena Clover?

I don't think that I did—and surely not with my own two hands. I never meant for it to happen, but could I still have caused her death?

My head is spinning with the possibility—it *reels* at the impossibility—and yet, perhaps I did?

It was just a game. Nothing but a lonely child's feeble attempt to gain some semblance of control. I never thought that it *meant* anything. I never thought that it was real—even if I wished that it were—even if I *wanted* it to be, when I was a child.

The first time I brought a doll to the well, I was nine, and I had just come back from the hospital. I was back in school then, as they said it would be good for me, but I was a broken thing, scrambling along on my crutches. That's when Jeremy James saw a window of opportunity. From my first day back, he was after me, trying to trip me up. As my legs were far from healed at that point, and had metal spikes poking out everywhere, falling was simply not an option, and I spent an enormous amount of time and energy just trying to avoid that wicked boy. Why I did not ask my teachers for help, I don't know, but I wasn't a very trusting child. Perhaps I thought they couldn't help me. Perhaps I thought I had to handle it on my own.

I often felt like that when I was young.

Jeremy had a toxic tongue as well. Whenever he saw me, he would rile up our classmates and engage them in feisty name-calling. "Crab" was one thing they called me, due to me moving so slowly, and with the crutches as extra "legs."

"Here comes the crab! Hurry up, crab! Hurry up!" he used to shout.

Another favorite of Jeremy's was "spinning-top," as I quite often lost my balance while trying to maneuver across the pot-holed tarmac in the playground. This frequently caused some ungraceful moments with the crutches flying everywhere, while I—terrified and out of breath—scrambled to regain my footing.

One day, I stole a T-shirt out of Jeremy's gym bag. It was a reeking thing, clearly not washed. I remember it was yellow with horizontal green stripes. The red gym bag was hanging from a hook in the hallway and had his name displayed on the side, written in black marker. It's pure foolishness leaving something of one's own in a public space. If you ask me, it's only looking for trouble, so I didn't feel overly concerned with the theft as I hastily pushed the T-shirt into my own bag, and left it there—reeking—all day.

When I got home, I brought it out, and took it with me into the woods, to the well. I didn't know much about Ilsbeth Clark at that point, so I hadn't heard about the dolls that were found by the well, but I suppose it's the simplest form of sympathetic magic, one that even a child can deduce. Perhaps I was working on pure instinct—a subconscious impulse passed down through the ages—when I picked up the sticks and set to tying them together with pieces of twine. I had brought out scissors, too, and cut into the stinking T-shirt to give my doll a dress of sorts. When I was satisfied with my handiwork, I left the ugly thing on the pile of animal bones by the well, while wishing Jeremy the worst that my little heart could muster.

Not a week later, Jeremy was gone. They searched for him everywhere, in the woods and beyond. They never did find him, though, and soon most people simply thought a stranger in a car had kidnapped him. They often thought that back then. I suppose such roaming child-nappers had taken the place of the bears of yore.

I didn't really think his disappearance had anything to do with me, but I *liked* thinking that it had. I enjoyed the idea of having that kind of power, so when the next obstacle arose, which was a frequent and unpleasant head-butting with a hospital nurse, Mary Frit, who wanted me to walk without aid before I was ready, I was quick in stealing a pair of sunglasses and a handkerchief from her purse. Mary drowned herself in the well a month later. Apparently, she had been depressed for a while.

Then there was Flora, a girl I had the great misfortune of knowing as a child. We were often set to play together because she was our closest neighbor under the age of twelve. Flora was two years younger than I was and not very kind. After the car accident, she often ran away with my crutches and left me stranded where I was. She even sniggered about it later when the adults berated her for her pranks. In addition, she had picked up the names I had gotten at school, and called me both "crab" and "spinning-top."

I quickly decided that Flora had to go, and fashioned a doll out of a pair of pink mittens that she had carelessly left at my house. Imagine my delight *and* horror then, when Flora disappeared within a month! Again, the hounds were out sniffing through the woods. Again, the police came in their vehicles and parked in our yard to access the path.

Again, not a trace could be found.

With all of this floating in my past, it was perhaps not so strange that when things came to a head with Elena, I regressed to my earliest mode of defense. I fashioned a doll and gave her a dress made from one of Elena's old scarves—and the earring, of course, hidden for years at the bottom of my jewelry box. Not because I thought that something would come of it—honestly!—but only because it gave me a feeble, yet worthwhile, sense of control. It had been years then since the last time I went to the well with a doll, and I had left all my childish notions behind, but with the restraining order and all, it felt like the very last card up my sleeve.

My very final trick to pull.

If nothing else, I figured, it would make *me* feel better, as if I had done *something* with a situation that had turned so very uncomfortable. At that point I had of course learned about the dolls in the Ilsbeth Clark case, crafted in a similar fashion, but opted to think it was a mere coincidence—nothing but a quirk of the universe.

I certainly didn't think it would work!

It really is disconcerting that these thoughts are upon me— haunting me—just when we have a found a silver lining. Perhaps it has something to do with how that silver has become a little tarnished?

Late last night, just before I was about to go to bed, Nora Green called me. I had already taken my medication by then, so I was a little sluggish when I answered the phone. Nora didn't seem to notice, though.

"When did you handle Elena's journal?" she asked, without even giving me a proper greeting. I had been prepared for a scolding like the one Bobby had given me the night before, but this seemed to be about something else.

"When did I what?" I mumbled.

"Well, they have dusted it for fingerprints, and yours are all over the thing."

I didn't quite know how to reply to that, so at first I opted to say nothing. Though even through the lovely haze of my medication, I could still feel some stress coming on.

"Please, Catherine," Nora sighed. "Please tell me it wasn't you who left it in the cherry tree."

My mind at that point went through several different options, but in the end decided—as I always do—on telling the truth, and nothing but.

"It—it was just lying there," I stuttered—because of the pills and not guilty conscience. I'd only done what I did to help, after all. "It didn't seem right to just leave it there, on the ground by the lake. I knew the police would come trampling all over, and maybe even step on it, or it would fall into the lake."

Nora Green gave a deep sigh. "Why didn't you turn it in?"

"Well, I meant to, but they were asking me all these questions, and it made me nervous . . . I thought it would seem odd that I had Elena's journal."

"So instead you put it in the cherry tree?" Her voice was very dry.

"We always put secrets there as kids," I defended my action. "It seemed appropriate to leave it there, since it was Elena's secrets," my voice petered out.

"Did you *read* the journal, Catherine?" Nora gave another sigh, just to tell me how disappointed she was.

"Just briefly," I blurted out. "I just . . . flipped through the pages." My cheeks reddened with shame. "I just wanted to know what she said about me."

"Oh, Catherine." I could all but see her scowling at me. "This journal was our best defense, and now I'm not sure how things will play out. I don't know how it might hurt us that it's been in your possession."

"I didn't change anything," I defended myself the best that I could.

"Well, there are pages ripped out, and who's to say it wasn't you who removed them?"

"Well, yes, I suppose that'll be hard."

"This *does* paint you in a peculiar light."

"I know," I said, feeling utterly defeated.

"Oh, well." Nora Green pulled herself up by the bootstraps. "We'll just have to work with what we have, and hope that the dice fall in our favor."

"Sure," I replied, relieved that at least she hadn't quit—yet.

"Don't you *dare* post about this online." Her voice was very serious. "You shouldn't breathe another *word* about the journal—and especially not about Mr. Morris. Don't forget that the man might very well be a killer."

I know she is right—I do! And yet, here I am. I suppose I just don't want anyone but me to tell my story, ugly though it might be.

I don't want to become another Ilsbeth Clark.

# 39

This morning I woke up to several text messages from my son.

> Don't go online Mom!
> I mean it! Seriously! Don't go online!!!!
> Stay away from Facebook!!!!!!

Of course, I promptly went online, and was able to see for myself the ire that my last installment had caused. I think that I should clarify that I didn't really think that something bad would happen to Jeremy and Flora, I just hoped that it would. This does *not* make me a child killer. The only thing I did was to put some dolls out in the woods, and no court of law is going to sentence me for that—besides, I was only a child myself.

I'd also like to point out that "witchcraft" is not considered to be real, so you'd be hard pressed to justify hanging me from a tree or burning me in my own house. In my humble experience, none of you are geniuses, so chances are you would likely be found out, and though a lot of things have remained the same since Ilsbeth's time, it's harder to keep things contained these days. The local law enforcement is no exception; they can't turn a blind eye in quite the same way as before, so I'm pretty sure a vigilante attack would end badly for all involved.

That's not to say that I don't sympathize with your sentiment: *of course* it's wrong to kill children—but as far as we know, Jeremy disappeared in a van, and Flora was taken by her father—there's no *proof* that those dolls had anything to with it. The same thing goes for Elena. Yes, I made that doll, yes, I put it out by the well, but that's not to say that I killed her. If—contrary to all reason—

something *did* happen because of my artistic creations, I definitely didn't mean for it to, so I can hardly be held responsible. To the best of my knowledge, "accidental manslaughter by witchcraft" is not a thing.

Please, do try not to lose your heads!

In addition to my son's dire warnings, I also received several text messages from Nora Green today:

> Maybe it's time to think about protection? Do you even have a home security system?
>
> Maybe you should go away for a while? To your sister's perhaps?
>
> Maybe you should get some rest? I know of several great facilities. I really think you should talk to professionals.
>
> Don't think of it as a defeat, you would be doing it to help yourself! Plus, you would be safe there.

She tried to call as well, and Bobby called me too, but I didn't answer. I texted back to Nora that I'd take her suggestions under consideration, but truth be told, I'm too tired to think. I did answer the phone when Louise called. I suppose it's because she is my big sister, and it would somehow feel wrong to slight her.

"Have you talked to your son today?" she said before even greeting me.

"No," I replied, as I had evaded his calls, too. I just couldn't think of what to say to even begin to justify the strain I had put on him. I had brought the phone with me into the bathroom, as there are no windows there, and was sitting down on the rim of the bathtub with my teacup balancing on the broad, old-fashioned metal faucet. The scent of black tea and spices was strong in the air.

"Well, he called *me*"—Louise sounded upset—"and he was very worried. Apparently half the town is calling for your blood! What did you do that for, Cathy? What on earth was the *point*? They're riled up enough as it is after Elena—why did you have to tell them about your stupid dolls?"

"It just . . . came to me," I tried to explain. "I felt like I had to write it down, to make sense of it—"

"Then keep a journal, for God's sake! You don't have to paste it all over the internet!"

"Good advice, but too late."

Louise sighed, "I know, but I'm really worried, Cathy! People are seriously angry after that last story—some of them actually think you're a *witch,* and scared people do stupid shit!"

"Don't I know it," I muttered.

"Maybe you and I should go away for a few days? Not far, just a trip, to get some perspective and *think*. We could bring Brian as well."

"That's very tempting," I said, and I meant it too. I really don't have a strong desire to stay in F—.

"Great!" She sounded pleased—and relieved. "I'll book something nice."

"Great," I parroted, but I didn't feel the relief. No matter where I went, Elena would be just as dead.

"Keep the doors locked and put the police on speed dial," she warned me before ending the call. "Try to keep your mind occupied—and *don't go online*!"

Yet here I am, again.

There must be something wrong with me, I realize as much. I don't know why I keep expecting you to be reasonable and smart about this. If anything, Ilsbeth's story should have served as a dire warning, but somehow I still keep putting my fate in your hands.

Maybe I just want you to prove me wrong, to be better than I think you are.

I know that it might very well come back to savagely bite me in the ass.

I *have* something to occupy my time, though, something that I know is bound to be a pleasure, no matter its contents: the jar on my dining table. The Nicksby Documents.

My gloves are finally here, and the magnifying glass as well. *That* is something you have not as of yet been able quench: my joy of discovery, my inquiring nature. Tonight, I will get out a bottle of wine, close all the curtains, and open the jar.

Then, behind locked doors, I'll finally learn its secrets.

# 40

This is *not* my truth!

I am looking at the pages, those ugly, brittle pages, water-stained and reeking of rot, and feel nothing but disgust! I should burn them, probably. Rip them up and throw them away! I am crying as I write these words—I'm sure you are thrilled to hear *that*—but the turmoil in me, the sickness, it—

People of F—, I have no words.

This, too, I'm sure will amuse you.

To think that I spent a small fortune on a magnifying glass—that I waited *for days* so I could wear the right gloves—that I treated this abomination as if it were made of the finest spun glass, painstakingly transcribing every word. I feel stupid now. Duped.

I suppose you must be laughing now, just reveling in my pain.

Oh, how dearly I hope it is you who have played a nasty trick on me. For a moment there, I actually thought that it was so. I just couldn't see any other explanation for this *vile* story—this twisted imagination! No other explanation but that it is true.

Yes, I'm frightened, for if these pages truly are genuine, I have been wrong all along. More than fear, though, it's disappointment that I feel. I am crushed, people of F—. Crushed and broken. I have staked my fate and reputation on something that is not what it seemed at all. The most important story was not what I thought, and here I am—the fool—having gilded a piece of shit in my writing, and made a martyr out of a monster.

Please, tell me that you made it up! Please, tell me that it was you! I will gladly be your villain, if only you restore my belief in Ilsbeth and her legacy—my destiny, as it is. For if I'm *not* to write about Ilsbeth and defend her name, who am I, in all this?

I wish I had never read the Nicksby Documents. I wish I had never laid my eyes upon them. God, how I wish that I had never heard of Ilsbeth Clark—or that my parents had indeed gotten that divorce so my mother could have taken me away from F—.

Yet here I am, finished and empty.

Throughout all the harassment of the last few months, it was always *she* who pulled me through. The idea of Ilsbeth, my sister in spirit, who had also suffered horribly at your hands, was what made me get up in the morning and shuffle into the kitchen for tea. It was the thought of *her* that made me sharpen my pen and fight so hard to redeem myself. Now all of that is lost to me. In place of something pure and righteous, there's just wickedness and rot.

My last cherished thing has fallen.

If it *is* you that's behind the documents—and you really have gone through all the fuss of making something that looks so authentic—I applaud you for being so thorough, for reading my open letters carefully enough that you could convince me. But I fear you too, for with an imagination like that, there really is no telling *what* you can do. Not that it matters much anymore. There's nothing else you can take from me, now that I have lost what I loved the most. If anything, I just beg you to tell me it was you—to put me out of my misery—I will gladly admit to murder, if only I can learn the truth!

But then, there's a voice in me that tells me that it *wasn't* you, as the Nicksby Documents know too much; they have such a knowledge of everything . . .

And so I went to the well.

I did.

I fed the beast within.

I remember the horse lady more clearly now, with every passing hour. I remember the bristle of fur on her skin, the faceted eyes, and the feeling of her tongue on my skin. I remember the neediness of her, the feeling that she wanted something from me.

I remember the smell of her too: rank water and raw meat.

I remember Ilsbeth, her voice in my head as I lay in bed at the farm with my legs in casts: *Come in, come in, come in . . .*

Your ancestors always did say she was a witch, so I suppose I'm the idiot for having believed any differently. Elena, too, was right, and even that doesn't annoy me, it only grieves me, for she too was led to believe that Ilsbeth was something else. We were used, both of us, chewed up and spit out. Dancing like puppets on hellish strings.

My life's work has been in vain.

As I'm sitting here typing on the couch in the living room, I hear noises outside the walls. Not the keening of a fox, like the ones that plagued Elena, but scratching noises, as if something is out there, trying to get inside. As if someone is dragging a rake across the boards. There is a clamor, too, which sounds like wood on wood—and voices whispering; more than one? I tell myself that it's only the wind—but there is no wind tonight.

The pages of the Nicksby Documents are spread out on the table in the dining room. I can barely stomach looking at them. I wonder if it's their author who's visiting me tonight.

If so, I ought to give the pages back, as *I* for sure don't want them. If what they're telling me is true, I *did* kill Elena, and other people, too, and I don't think I can live with that knowledge.

Yes, I should give them back—every single scrap of paper. It is the only fitting ending to this drama. As soon as I have finished this last letter to you, the people of F—, I'll gather up the Nicksby Documents, and then I'll meet their maker.

What will I find when I open the front door? A furious witch with vengeance on her mind; or you, Will Morris, brandishing some crude tool, like a hammer or an axe? Will it be the lot of you, coming for me as you came for *her*?

I don't think I'll survive the night.

# Catherine Evans Dead in Witch's Well

*Identity revealed!*

The F— police confirmed late last night that the woman found dead in the witch's well earlier this week was Catherine Evans, an employee of the F— primary school.

Besides her work at the school administration, Catherine Evans had taken a great interest in the town's history, particularly in regards to the well where she drowned, and had recently published a book about Ilsbeth Clark, who also drowned in the well, in 1862. Furthermore, Mrs. Evans was a suspect in the ongoing investigation into the death of Elena Clover, who was found in the lake earlier this year.

Officer Rogers at the F— Police Department says that it is too early to tell if the allegation and the planned trial had something to do with Mrs. Evans's death, but cites that it is likely, as the death has been ruled a suicide.

Mrs. Evans's sister, Louise Mills, says that her sister had been depressed following the serious charge.

—I do not believe she would hurt Elena. I will *never* believe that she would hurt Elena, but it was hard on her that so many people believed that she did it. She was always very sensitive like that.

Mrs. Evans's employer, Principal Myers, says that she is "torn up" about the news of Catherine Evans's death.

—It is always a terrible shock when someone chooses to end their own life. Tonight, we have lost not only a knowledgeable and dependable co-worker, but also an unusual human being with several good qualities. The school will not be the same without her.

Principal Myers would not comment on the criminal charges against Mrs. Evans, but the deceased's lawyer, Nora Green, had the following to say:

—Catherine's great cause in life was to stand up against unjust persecution and heresy. That was why she wrote her novel, but in the light of what has happened, it seems like the gossipmongers got to her after all. I have every confidence that we would have won the trial, but now we will never know. I hope the citizens of F— will take a good long look in the mirror tonight and examine their conscience keenly, as I find it very unlikely that Catherine would have ended her own life without some external provocation.

Catherine Evans is survived by her former husband, her teenage son, and her sisters.

# 41

*Transcript from the Nicksby Documents*

At least she did not eat them.

Not that it would have made much of a difference to *me* if she had. It would have sated her hunger for a while, and that I suppose would have been *something*. There is nothing quite as bitter as an effort with no reward. Had my mistress had her hearty fill, at least I might have known some peace. Instead, she is keening under the moon, and cries fat droplets of salt down in the dirt. I have no comfort to offer. She surely had none for *me* when *my* girl died.

The beast's song this time is nothing compared to the ruckus she made when *I* died. For many nights, she cantered through the apple orchard at Nicksby, where my body was laid out in the parlor, and sang for joy. So happy was she that my natural life had come to an end and she would have her servant at last.

I, newly hatched wraith that I was, was drawn out of the house to meet her there, under branches heavy with cherries, and it was then that I fully realized what those droplets of blood for ink truly signified. She meant to have me make good on my promise.

Her loneliness had come to an end.

Catherine and Elena are no longer in this world, and so they both escaped my fate. I am nothing but bitter for it. Surely it is time now for my loneliness to end, even if there is nothing but oblivion before me. I had harbored such hopes this time, that my servitude would be concluded, but there seems to be no escape from this sordid tale. No word, no magic skill, no riddle to set me free.

Sometimes I wish that the beast had just eaten me.

I think of all the hours Owen and I spent trying to sate her when she was young, and we both had strong, beating hearts in our chests. I remember the poppets she made from sticks and fabric scraps that I brought from Nicksby. I thought it was a sweet thing then, how she would sit by the well for hours, making little friends for herself. Only later did I realize how those tiny effigies *summoned* the children to the well—to *her*. Her youthful innocence was always tainted, laced with something dark and self-serving.

I do applaud Catherine, though, for making poppets of her own.

Had I known in my time that the beast could be commanded thus—used like a dog to hunt down a target—I surely would have made some poppets, too, starting with one in Archibald's likeness, and continuing with half the citizens of F——. But it was Catherine who found that out, so that wan, sappy girl must have been cleverer than I ever gave her credit for. Perhaps the beast taught her herself, or maybe it was my sister's blood in her, guiding her small hands just right.

The admiration does not make me regret what happened, however. An eye for an eye and a tooth for a tooth. The beast took mine and I took hers.

Elena floated up in the lake, and Catherine went down in the well.

In the burrow, our time together continues—endlessly. I braid her mane and cook her meals; I spear the frogs and skin the deer. My mistress is meek and then she is wild. Her nature is as ever befuddling to me, but there is nothing human about it. I do think she would have been happier somewhere else, surrounded by others of her kind. Mayhap that is where it all went wrong: she was never truly meant to serve us.

I blame Mother and her family for that.

I do mourn Elena, I do—or rather, the hope she inspired, just as I suppose my mistress still grieves the promise she tasted in Catherine. We are wretched beings, the two of us, unable to escape each other. I cannot tell anymore just how many times we have tried.

Time moves in peculiar fashion for us, but it *does* move, and her bones are not getting any younger—and so I fret! What will become of me once she is gone? Will I sit here alone in this burrow forever? When these dark thoughts are upon me, I take heart in the one thing that has proven to be sure.

There will always be others.

They come to the well whether we want them to or not, pulled by the power of our misery. Like calls to like, and there will always be the lonely ones who see in me—in *us*—a most enchanting reflection.

Maybe the next one will sign.

# Winter

From: Brian Evans <brevan@xxxxx.com>
Date: Tue, Jan 11 at 6:02 PM
Subject: Mom's papers
To: Harold James <harold.james@xxx.com>
Hello Mr. James,

I did what we agreed to on the phone and went through Mom's desk, but I couldn't find the Nicksby Documents anywhere. I know you'll be disappointed to hear this, as you and your friends at the historical society were doubtlessly eager to read them, but if she ever had them, she must have hidden them somewhere safe, and I can't think of where that might be.

I did find something on her computer, though, and have attached it here. It looks like it's a transcript of sorts? From the Nicksby Documents? To tell you the truth, it looks more to me as if Mom were writing another novel or something, just making things up.

It's a pretty chilling read, if you know what happened later. Especially the last part made me feel a little sick. It's been hard, you know, with all that's happened. I showed it to my dad, and he said it was a symptom of her illness, or a way to make sense of what happened over the summer. Maybe she was trying to make a forgery, he said, to save herself. If so, it was a shitty attempt (sorry about the language), because the story is super wild.

Whatever she was thinking, she sure wasn't in a good place when she wrote it, so I hope you take that into consideration when you read. I probably shouldn't send it your way at all, but then maybe you'll see something I don't. Something about the *real* Nicksby Documents, maybe.

If they even exist.

I hope you won't share it with anyone else, though. It's bad enough what they say about Mom as it is.

I also found some pages from what I think is Elena Clover's journal. I should probably give them to the police? I don't think I can do that, though. After everything that happened, just seeing Officer Rogers in town makes me feel sick to my stomach. I'm dropping them off for you at the library instead, so you can decide what to do with them. Having them in the house makes me feel weird.

Please let me know if you find out anything!

Best Regards,
Brian Evans

## ACKNOWLEDGMENTS

This book started as a series of fragments and images in my head and would very likely have remained just that if it hadn't been for the following people:

My amazing agent, Brianne Johnson, I am forever grateful for your wisdom, skill, and support. I would also like to thank the rest of the team at HG Literary for taking such good care of my books.

To my editor, Miriam Weinberg, and everyone at Tor who has helped make this book a reality. I am immensely impressed by how you make my story shine. I'm equally grateful to my UK editor, Simon Taylor, and the rest of the team at Transworld; you truly make my books into something special.

To Liv Lingborn, for endless support and fruitful discussions. You really are the best!

I'd also like to acknowledge the countless women back in the day who were suspected of witchcraft just for being quarrelsome and unpleasant. They might not have been perfect victims, but they were definitely an inspiration for this book. I'd also like to thank the "difficult women" in my own life, past and present; this book wouldn't have been the same without you.

A little gratitude also goes out to my old colleagues at Ki Magickal Shop some twenty-odd years ago, who taught me a lot about belief and the winding roads it may take. It truly was the experience of a lifetime.

Finally, to my son, Jonah, and my kitten, Tussa, for calling me back to the world and keeping my sanity intact while I worked.